His wife was pregnant.
It could not be his child.

He put his hand out on the wall to steady himself.

She had cuckolded him. She had given herself to another man and now bore proof of her sin. Humiliation and dishonor would once more be his and his family's to bear because of her. Everything within him screamed for vengeance.

Unanswered questions burned through his mind. Then the plan behind this struck him. Queen Eleanor had definitely plotted this. Her words on their wedding night came back to him. *There will be no repudiation of this marriage by either of you.*

But Emalie. What had been her part in this? Who had she lain with? Whose baby did she carry now?

He almost laughed at the irony. He had sold his soul to regain his honor and now stood to lose it anyway, once the truth was known....

Praise for new Harlequin Historical author Terri Brisbin

"A lavish historical romance in the grand tradition
from a wonderful talent."
—*New York Times* bestselling author Bertrice Small
on *Once Forbidden*

"A welcome new voice in romance…
you won't want to miss."
—*USA TODAY* bestselling author Susan Wiggs

"Terri Brisbin writes with her own unique,
sweet, lyrical style."
—*Romantic Times*

"…lush narrative, crisp dialogue and powerful
descriptions. Medieval Scotland comes to life
under the skillful storytelling of Terri Brisbin."
—*Rendezvous* on *A Love through Time*

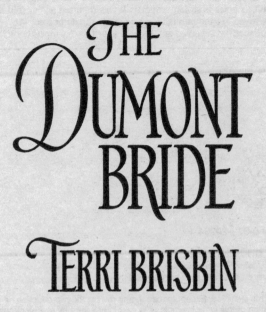

THE DUMONT BRIDE

TERRI BRISBIN

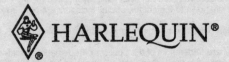

HARLEQUIN®

TORONTO • NEW YORK • LONDON
AMSTERDAM • PARIS • SYDNEY • HAMBURG
STOCKHOLM • ATHENS • TOKYO • MILAN • MADRID
PRAGUE • WARSAW • BUDAPEST • AUCKLAND

ISBN 0-373-29234-1

THE DUMONT BRIDE

Please address questions and book requests to:
Harlequin Reader Service
U.S.: 3010 Walden Ave., P.O. Box 1325, Buffalo, NY 14269
Canadian: P.O. Box 609, Fort Erie, Ont. L2A 5X3

This book is for Walt and Rose—
the real Sir Walter and Lady Rosalie—for the years of
friendship and support and more things forgotten than
I can remember now! Hey, it's almost like a ride....

ACKNOWLEDGMENT

The idea for this story came to me while listening to the
music and words of "My Own Prison" by Scott Stapp
and Creed. My thanks for their inspiration!

Chapter One

Greystone Castle
Lincolnshire, England
May 1194

Eleanor Plantagenet, Queen of England, by the wrath of God, watched as pride and anger stiffened the spine of her young ward. Although she wanted to scream out her own anger and cry tears of sorrow for the way she suspected this child had been ill-used, she did not have the luxury of either. Only action on her part would save the kingdom and possibly this girl's life, as well. Since it was her son's actions that had caused the damage, and since it would be that same son who would continue his pursuit until his desires were satisfied, only she could step in and circumvent his plans.

"So, Emalie," she said, "I will ask you only once more. Give me the name of the man who has dishonored you."

"I know not of what you speak, Your Grace." The girl would not meet her gaze.

"I am not a fool and do not expect to be treated as

one by you!'' Eleanor snapped, trying to break
Emalie's calm demeanor to get to the truth. Other than
a slight trembling of her clasped hands, there was no
change in her expression or in her willingness to answer.

As Eleanor walked closer to the girl and prepared to
ask another question, a commotion began outside the
door of the solar. Rising voices and scuffling feet soon
gave way to the door being thrown open as her private
bodyguards made a valiant attempt to keep her son
from the room. At her signal, their efforts ceased and
the soldiers instead took up places on either side of the
open door.

"Madam," John said, with an arrogant nod of his
head as he sauntered to where she stood. "You are
looking well this fine day." John tilted his head down
and touched a cool kiss to her cheek. She fought the
urge to shiver at the dangerous, slippery tone of his
voice and look in his eyes. 'Twas at times like these
she wondered how she had ever birthed and raised a
viper like this.

"I gave orders not to be disturbed. Those orders
were intended to give us some measure of privacy for
our discussion." She rose to her full height and faced
him with her truth. "Those orders were to keep you
out until I bade you enter."

"Ah," he said, reaching out to Emalie and grasping
her hand. "The ever-fair Lady Emalie Montgomerie…" John leaned over and pressed his lips to the
girl's knuckles. He purposely allowed Eleanor a
glimpse of his tongue touching the top of Emalie's
hand. Not quite as practiced at ignoring her son's vile
habits as she herself was, Emalie recoiled from his
grasp and tucked her hands tightly at her side. The girl

turned an even paler shade of white as John smiled his oily, toothy smile—one that did nothing to hide his intentions. "With one so lovely awaiting me within, not even two full companies of your bodyguards could keep me from this room, Mother."

Eleanor wondered if the girl knew she was moving herself ever so slightly in Eleanor's direction, as if claiming protection from John. John clearly noticed, for he stepped quickly into Emalie's path.

"John! Enough of this. Stop toying with the girl and tell me your reasons for interrupting my discussions." Eleanor made her way over to one of the two tall straight-backed chairs near the windows. With a wave of her hand, she directed Emalie to the other one and watched in sympathy as the girl sank into it. She was clearly an amateur in the ways of conniving men.

"I am here on behalf of my friend, William De-Severin," John began. He, too, walked to the window and looked out it, affecting his favorite disinterested expression. Nothing good could come from this situation. Nothing.

"And what has that man to do with Lady Emalie?"

"He has come to regret his overzealous behavior toward you, dearest Emalie," he said, glancing first at Eleanor and then turning his attention away from her and toward his true target, "and wishes to come forward and save you from disgrace."

"Your Grace, I am not in need of being saved from any dishonor," Emalie answered in a soft voice.

"Nonsense, lady, all in the castle and village know of what I speak."

Eleanor could not let this go any further—she must take control before all was lost.

"I, too, have found no reason for Sir William to save Emalie," she boldly claimed.

"Mother, as I told you in my message that summoned you here, William has confessed to carnal knowledge of the countess and is now willing to marry her to prevent her dishonor."

"And I repeat, I have found no reason for that marriage to go forth."

"Her servants know—"

"The lady's servants have sworn on their immortal souls that she is an innocent."

"They are lying then, for I—"

"You, John? Had you something to do with trying to dishonor the Countess of Harbridge? 'Tis bolder a move than I thought possible for even you. And brave, considering the love and esteem that your brother had for her father before his untimely passing." Eleanor met her son's gaze and read the truth there. Emalie had been his goal, William his puppet, and the girl's disgrace the tool to bring her into his power.

She took a moment and looked over at Emalie. The girl's shallow breaths and pasty complexion told her Emalie was nigh to fainting. And Eleanor's stomach churned at the realization of John's intentions.

"I have spoken to every person in this place whose name you presented to me and not one, not a single one, has said anything but the most glowing of words about their mistress. Not her personal servants nor the whores in the village. To a person they have denied your allegations, leaving me no choice but to refuse William permission to seek her hand in marriage."

"Madam, I think you should consider this carefully," John said softly, his voice more menacing than when he lost control and shouted his anger to the world.

"Richard is king once more and he will not permit this undisguised grab for control. Now, I think that you and yours should turn your ravenous gazes elsewhere, for we are done here."

With an angry wave of her hand, Eleanor called to her guards. "Escort the lady to her chamber and let no one delay you." Eleanor nodded to Emalie to follow the guards. The girl stood and made a wobbly curtsy before turning to leave. Then stiffening her back once more, Emalie left the chamber as the Countess of Harbridge and not the terrified girl of a few moments before.

John watched with obvious lust as Emalie walked past him and out of the solar. This was not over yet. And, as if to confirm her own worst fears, he voiced it for her.

"I am not pleased by your interference, madam, not pleased at all."

"Pleased or not, I am here at your request. And I will stay until I am sure of Emalie's safety."

"Or until something requires your attention elsewhere." John walked to her side and leaned close once more to kiss her cheek. He did not step away but whispered his warning in her ear instead. "Take your concerns back to Richard and leave England to me, old woman."

Eleanor sat completely still until the viper had left the room and the guards had closed the door behind them. And then, for the first time in a very long time, Eleanor, Queen of England, allowed every one of her seventy-two years to press down momentarily on her shoulders. And that great weight took her breath away as she sought a way out of this dilemma.

Chapter Two

Anjou Province, France
June 1194

Christian Dumont gnashed his teeth, hoping to block out the noises of the scurrying rats on the dank floor of his cell. In his months of imprisonment, he had become quite proficient at ignoring the sounds of rodents, screaming men and even the emanations of his own empty stomach. But the ever-weakening coughs of his younger brother Geoffrey he could not ignore.

He rushed to Geoff's side and helped him sit up as the coughs wracked the boy's body, a body which grew thinner and more fragile with each passing day. Patting his brother on his back seemed to help the spasms pass more quickly though the bouts came closer and closer together. Christian watched as Geoff's entire body shuddered and then slowly the boy began to breathe without struggle.

"'Tis over, Chris. I am fine now," his brother whispered, pushing him away.

Christian walked to the small pail that held their remaining water and dipped a battered cup to the bottom. 'Twould not last them much longer. He held out the cup, recognizing his brother's humiliation in the slump of his frail shoulders as he accepted the cup.

"Is there more?" Geoff asked, not meeting his eyes.

"Aye. We will have water to drink for at least another day or two." Christian knew the boy did not have the strength to walk to see the pail himself, so he felt comfortable in his lie. Why should Geoff worry when it would do nothing more than weaken him further? Christian pulled the boy's blanket higher around his shoulders and helped him lean back once more.

Their coins had run out almost a sennight before and he knew there would be no more assistance from any of the guards. They were helpful only as long as the gold appeared in their palms, and the Dumonts' supply of that was gone. During their time in this godforsaken place, Christian had sold all of his possessions, save their father's signet ring, to keep food and water in good supply for his brother.

Turning away from Geoff, he touched the ring now hanging on a piece of twine around his neck. 'Twas all they had left of their father…their heritage…their wealth. Christian laughed roughly at how far the old and mighty Dumont family had fallen. And all due to his father's reckless and dangerous efforts to back the wrong man.

Richard, *Coeur de Lion,* thankfully looked the other way when he inherited the throne from his father, ignoring most of the nobles who had supported Henry's battle against his sons and wife. A king could be magnanimous in victory. But the king felt differently now that he had been released from his own imprisonment and was faced with the machinations of his brother.

Years of John Lackland's tightening control over the Plantagenet holdings in England and the loss of many on the continent had changed the face of his kingdom and Richard was determined to clean house. And the House of Dumont was one of his first targets.

Christian ran his hands over his face and sighed, careful not to let his brother see the signs of despair on his own face. He was out of ideas. They were out of money. And soon, if nothing changed, they would be out of time.

The loud yell of the guard's voice woke him the following morning. Leaning over his brother, he watched the slow rise and fall of Geoff's chest as the boy still slept on the low bench. Christian stood and stretched, trying to loosen muscles long unexercised. At the call of his name, he turned and faced the soldier making his way down the low corridor of cells.

"Aye, you, Dumont. You are to come with us." The guard was joined by two more soldiers, while another stood nearer to the dungeon's door.

Christian smiled at the thought of them needing four to take his one. In better days, mayhap, but certainly not now. The toll of not enough food, not enough rest and not enough practice was a stiff one. He looked over at Geoffrey and wondered if they were both called.

"Nay, not the whelp," the guard answered before he could ask. "Only the elder son of the traitor is called now."

Christian grimaced at the insulting reminder of his new position. A traitor. His father had dishonored all who bore the Dumont name before and after him by his treasonous acts. As one of the men took his arm to pull him along, he shook off the hand that grabbed him.

It was replaced by two more that pulled him even more strongly and swiftly out of the cell and along the corridor.

The group moved quietly through the damp lower floor of the castle, then up two flights of steps to the main floor. Prisoners called out words of encouragement and words of insult as he passed them. Christian fought to keep up with the pace. He did not want to be dragged to his fate. He would face whatever awaited him like a man, like the warrior he had trained to be. He would uphold the shattered honor of his family in spite of his father's failings.

The bright sunlight, pouring into the hall through high windows of glass, tortured his eyes. The darkness of the dungeon left him unready to face the full power of daylight. He tried to raise his hand to shield his eyes, but the guards would not let go of his arms. They moved farther into the cavernous room, the clip-clopping of their boots on the stone floor echoing ahead and behind them.

They came to a stop before the dais at the front of the room and tossed him to the ground. Unable to regain his balance, he sprawled on the cold stone floor for a moment, dazed and out of breath. A few muted snickers and whispers wafted through the room. Although he could not see clearly yet, he looked from side to side, searching for those who spoke. Pushing his matted hair from his eyes and rubbing them to clear them, Christian climbed shakily to his feet.

A heavy hand on his shoulder forced him to his knees. Christian looked up on the dais and saw the reason he knelt—he was in the presence of the king. Lowering his eyes, he swallowed and prepared to face his judgment. As the eldest son, he could accept death, not without question, but he would not lose control. His only thought was to somehow save Geoff from that same fate.

"Ah, the Count of Langier, though not of late it appears."

The king began to laugh at his own wit and the others joined him. Christian looked at those surrounding Richard and recognized no one—no one who could speak a word or two of support in his cause.

"Rise, Dumont, I would look on your face as you speak."

Christian struggled to his feet and tugged on the frayed edge of his sleeve. Standing in the presence of the king, who was splendidly attired, he felt ashamed of his appearance for the first time in his life. Magnificent fabrics and decorations had never mattered to him before, but his months of imprisonment had turned his mind to the simple things he never paid attention to in the past. He even dreamed of things such as clean, well-fitted clothes, food and water and fresh air and the sun's light.

He faced the king and then realized that Richard and the others were eating at the high table. The aromas of well-cooked beef and hot bread and cheeses surrounded him and his mouth watered. Without thought, he licked his dry lips with his parched tongue and inhaled once more the luxurious smells.

"Come, Dumont, join us at table. I am certain that the fare below is not quite up to the Count of Langier's high expectations."

Although he knew Richard mocked him, the thought of hot food, freshly made and free of crawling vermin, was too much for him to resist. His feet moved forward to where the king pointed and he dropped onto the bench. Although his seat was at the far end of the table, several of those seated nearest to him slid away, wrinkling their noses and grimacing at his appearance. Only the king's presence and invitation kept them from bolting completely.

A servant filled his cup with wine, placed a trencher of food before him and stepped away quickly, another sign of his putrid condition. Christian did not care—the food before him was the first like it in over two months and he would not be driven off by their sensitive noses. Startled by a young boy's sudden appearance at his side, he sat dumbfounded until the boy lifted the laver of water closer to him.

Table manners were not required in the dungeon and he'd grown out of practice with even the simplest. After a hesitation, he dipped his hands into the scented water and took the drying cloth from the page. Humiliated even more by the filth he left behind in the bowl and on the towel, Christian turned his attention back to the food in front of him. Before a morsel passed his lips, he looked once more at his clothes for a way to wrap some of this food and take it back to Geoff. A chunk of bread and cheese would go quite far in their present situation, especially if he ate now and then did not need to share in what he took back with him.

Desperation filled him and his hands shook as he reached for the bread. Tearing off a piece, he lifted it to his mouth. Closing his eyes he savored the crisp crust and soft, chewy inside of the loaf. Too long, much too long since food of this quality had passed his lips.

"I have only seen such reverence for a piece of bread when it is consecrated in Communion. What do you think, Ely?" Richard's mocking continued from his place at the center of the table.

The Bishop of Ely, Richard's embattled chancellor, murmured words Christian could not and did not want to hear in response and the others laughed out their agreement. Refusing to look into their jeering faces, he swallowed the bread and reached for his cup. The bread sat as a lump in his throat and would not move. Only a mouthful of the wine helped it pass.

The pain in his gut was not only from his long hunger, but also from the realization that just a few short months ago, he would have gleefully participated in this game. And he would not have felt a moment of shame or compunction in taking part in shaming someone less in the royal favor. Many lessons had been brought home to him during his imprisonment and none of them had been easy to learn.

His hands shook less as he reached for another piece of bread. He chewed slowly, both to enjoy the taste and feel of the food and to keep his stomach from clenching while eating too fast. He fought a battle within himself not to grab and shovel the food into his mouth as he wanted and needed to do. Knowing that acting as the disgusting prisoner he now was would simply give those around him more to mock, he held himself under an iron band of willpower and forced his hand to take but one piece at a time. He would show them the dignity of the Dumonts of Langier.

A few minutes later, Richard signaled the end of the meal and, with a wave of his hand, dismissed their company from the table. Panicking, since he'd been unable to hide and save any of it for Geoffrey, Christian searched his shirt for a pocket or someplace that would hold a hidden cache of bread and cheese.

"Guillaume? Since the count was so lately called to

table, make certain that his plate is delivered to his cell.''

The man standing at Richard's elbow nodded and stepped toward him. Lifting the trencher from the table, the servant piled the small loaves of bread and cheese on top.

''And Guillaume? Make certain that it is delivered there immediately and as it is.''

Richard mocked even in his generosity. Christian would get on his knees and kiss Richard's hands and feet if that was what it took to get this food to Geoffrey. The servant covered the food with a large linen napkin and carried it from the room. In another moment, he was alone with the king. Now he would discover the reason for this summons, and he knew that generosity had nothing to do with it.

Richard stood and walked to the end of the table where he still sat. Christian started to rise, but Richard motioned with his hand for him to stay seated. He did so. Feeling a growing sense of dread, he reached for his cup of wine and drank it down in several mouthfuls. He sat in shocked silence as Richard lifted a pitcher and refilled his drink and then sat down on a bench next to the one where he sat.

''Your father is dead and your lands and fortune are in my control,'' Richard began. ''Only you and your brother remain, and it will take only a lack of action on my part to see to the end of the Dumont family forever.''

Christian could do nothing but nod in agreement at the king's words. He knew how precarious his and Geoff's situation was; this was simply a reminder from Richard about who held the power.

"I find that I am in need of a service that you are suited to provide."

"A service, sire?" Christian fought to stifle even the smallest of hopes at Richard's words.

"Aye, my mother has asked that I send you to her in England so that you may prove yourself free of the taint of your father's sins."

"England? Is there no way for me to prove my loyalty to you here or at Chateau d'Azure?" Christian ached to return to his family's lands, to the place of his birth.

"Do not worry, your lands have been cared for during your imprisonment, unlike some others." The reference to John's raping of Richard's English estates was not lost on him.

"What must I do in England?" Christian wanted to get this out into the open—discover why Richard seemed willing to let him live and what task he faced.

"My mother asks only that I send you and, in her own inimitable fashion, has declined to give me an explanation." Richard chuckled as he spoke. "I learned long ago that my mother explains herself to no man unless she chooses to. My father complained of this fault of hers many, many times."

Richard stood, walked down from the dais and crossed to a door on one side of the hall. He motioned someone inside, and a priest carrying a thick pile of parchments followed him back to the table. The cleric spread out the documents into several small piles. Once he was done his organizing, he sat with his hands folded before him and waited on Richard. Christian waited as well.

"Here is the deed for your properties in Poitou and an accounting of your wealth. And this," Richard said, lifting another scroll and holding it before Christian, "is my decree reestablishing the title of Count of Langier and bequeathing it to you and your heirs. All here, all ready to be signed by me, if you agree to perform any service which my mother requests of you once you arrive in England."

Christian could not make the words come from his mouth. Everything within him that desired, nay craved, a restoration of his name, his wealth, his properties, his honor, fought to scream the words of agreement. But a small part of his being held back.

"And the task which I must carry out?"

Richard's hand slammed down on the table and parchments flew in all directions. The priest simply blinked several times as though familiar with these outbursts from the king.

"I offer you all you hold dear and you dare to question my orders to you? I could throw you in that dungeon and no one would ever hear the name of Dumont again. Is that what you wish? To die the son of a traitor? The *sons* of a traitor?"

Christian swallowed deeply, trying to lessen the terror that gripped him as the king reminded him quite clearly of the results if he refused to perform this unnamed service for the king. Rising, he bowed his head to Richard.

"Nay, sire."

"Then give the word and I will set all of this in motion—your estates back in your control, your name cleared of any taint of treason and your brother freed from his prison."

Christian hesitated for only a moment longer before giving the king what he wanted. He'd only dreamed that this would happen. He'd prayed continuously for a way out of this terrible turn of events facing him and Geoff and now the king presented him with exactly that. He must not lose this opportunity to regain his very honor.

"I am your man, sire." Christian knelt down before Richard and offered his hands in homage to the king.

Richard took Christian's hands in his and then lay one hand on Christian's head. "Then you are now once again the Count of Langier and my liegeman. The estates and wealth of the family Dumont are now restored to you, but will be held in trust by the Crown's chancellor until your service is completed."

Christian raised his head to look at Richard. His but not his? Richard was not finished yet.

"You have one week until you must leave for England—use it well. You may take your brother back to Chateau d'Azure and then be at my disposal here on Tuesday next."

Christian rose and stepped back from the king. He was saved! His brother would live! And his honor would once more be restored. And all in exchange for some task for Queen Eleanor.

Some task for the queen. Another wave of foreboding passed through him. What if the price was too high? What if he could not complete this mystery task? Nay, he could not fail…he could not afford to fail…the family Dumont, all past and future bearers of the title of Langier and most of all his brother, were depending on him.

Richard then leaned over the documents and scrawled his signature on the many sheets. Christian added his own, as directed by the priest. After giving more instructions to the priest and nodding to Christian, the king walked down the steps and through the hall. Just as he reached the doorway, he turned back.

"Langier." Richard used his newly restored title to address him now. "Report to me when you discover my brother's involvement in all of this. I smell his foul odor even from across the Channel and in spite of his claims of innocence."

Christian nodded to Richard, agreeing to this additional term.

"Directly to me and to no one else."

The king left without hearing his response, leaving him in astonished confusion.

Chapter Three

Sunlight streamed into the large room through the glass windows her father had commissioned years before, to please her mother. Emalie shifted on the cushion beneath her, trying in vain to get comfortable. Leaning back and away from the loom, she looked at the others in the room. Every one of them was more than content to sit and weave or embroider or sew until the light was no longer useful. Not her, though. She had not spent this much time in the solar in the few years since her mother's death.

Unable to remain still, and eager to feel the summer breezes flow over her face, Emalie gathered her skirts and stood, easing the bench away from the wooden frame so she could step back. The room grew quiet as her actions were noticed.

"Milady? Is there something you require?" her maid asked, putting down the embroidery frame and rising to attend her.

"Nay, Alyce. You may continue here. I am just anxious for a breath of air. I shall return anon."

She expected that none of her household would question her leaving, but she was unprepared for Lady

Helene's challenging frown. The lady was one of the queen's retinue and had spent most of the past week trailing behind her and reporting, Emalie knew, directly back to Eleanor. Every move she made and every person she spoke with was the subject of scrutiny. And it grated on her that, after months of being in charge of her father's estate, she was now relegated to the role of hostess only.

Eleanor had banished John and his minions after the near-debacle the day she had arrived, and placed her own people in key positions both in the keep and throughout the demesne. Emalie now spent her days in the solar sewing and weaving, or in the chapel praying. Eleanor's feelings on the power and importance of prayer in a young woman's life were made clear on her second day at Greystone. A new priest arrived and proceeded to offer the Mass that morning and on every one since then and Eleanor insisted on Emalie's attendance.

A new captain of the guards worked in tandem with her own captain, a new cook fought to wrest control of the kitchens from her own and even some of her personal servants had been replaced. Eleanor was nothing if not thorough in her attempts to get to the truth. Where John had been devious and dangerous, Eleanor was simply persistent and irresistible.

Emalie ignored both Lady Helene's glare and her attempts to follow her out of the room. With a nod to her maid, Emalie walked quickly from the solar, down a corridor to the stairway that led to the highest floor in the corner tower. Not slowing for a moment, she pushed against the door and was soon on the walkway that surrounded the keep. The wind, wild and warming in June's strengthening sun, tore through her hair and against her clothes. Shaking her head, she closed her eyes and let the power of the breeze calm her ragged nerves.

Leaning against the crenellated stone wall, Emalie fought back the tears that had threatened for weeks. Her life was now completely out of her control. Oh, she knew that as a woman she had little control to begin with, but her father had encouraged her to believe she was in charge. And now, rightly or wrongly, she longed for the days when only the Montgomeries had ruled Greystone, the days when her parents had lived and loved, the days when she had dreamed of a husband to love and protect her.

Well, her dreams were shattered now and her life was no longer her own thanks to the insatiable hunger of John Lackland and his cronies. Although she had managed to circumvent his latest ploy, she knew it was just a matter of time before her property fell to him as so many others had. In spite of Richard's return from captivity, John still moved to claim England as his own fiefdom and she knew that Greystone was an attractive target for his greed.

His attraction to her, however, had been a surprise. 'Twas at times such as these that she truly missed her mother's guidance and presence. She knew the ways of men and women. One could not be raised in the close company of a castle and village and not witness the physical realities. She may have been a foolish optimist, but she was not stupid.

She knew also that Eleanor was looking for a husband for her. It would be the only way to keep John at bay and keep William from making another attempt to "persuade" her into a union with him. Tears filled her eyes as bits of a conversation drifted back from her memory. Turning away from the wind, Emalie pushed her long, streaming hair out of her face and tucked it back once more into the mesh coif meant to contain it.

Wishing that the past would return would not make it so. Wishing for a future of her choice would not make it so. Her only choice was to face whatever would come her way and to face it with the dignity and honor that her parents had instilled in her from her childhood.

Gathering her skirts, Emalie prepared to return to the solar. Her few minutes alone outside, enjoying the freedom of the wind high above the keep, had accomplished exactly what she had hoped for and she would enter the women's enclave with a renewed sense of calm and control. Although not ready to face her fate, she was ready to face Lady Helene's displeasure at her escape.

The door opened as she grasped the handle and the force threw her off balance and against the wall. She was just catching the breath that was squeezed from her when the perpetrator stood before her.

"Milady!" Sir Walter, the captain of the troop of soldiers who guarded Greystone, grabbed her and pulled her toward him. "I beg your pardon, lady, I saw you not behind the door."

Emalie rubbed her injured elbow as the man she still trusted with her life aided her in standing once more. "I am fine, Sir Walter. Truly. Were you looking for me or just making your rounds?"

A red flush crept up the big man's neck and face, making his ruddy appearance even more red. He reached up and ran a beefy hand through his thick russet hair before stammering out a reply.

"Her Grace requests your presence below, lady." He would not meet her gaze.

"'Tis I who must beg your pardon, Sir Walter," she said, placing her hand on his arm. "You should be in charge here and not relegated to delivering messages. Your service has been too valued here at Greystone for you to be treated in this manner."

Emalie was embarrassed that she could not promise to restore her loyal captain to his place of honor and responsibility within the hierarchy of Greystone. Until the matter of her marriage was settled by the queen, Emalie had no say in the decisions about the running of her own estate. She sighed and turned away from her man. And she would have even less power once the matter of her marriage was settled. Now it was her turn not to meet his gaze.

"Will you accompany me or do you have other duties?"

"I would be honored to give you escort to the solar." He held out his arm and she placed hers on top. Turning, he held the door open wider and guided her to the stairs. They were silent until they stood just outside the solar and still far enough from the queen's guards not to be heard.

"Remember, lady, I promised your father that your safety would be my duty. I will always be here for you should the need arise." His voice became gruff and her own throat clogged with unshed tears at his loyalty.

"I will remember that above all else, Sir Walter."

"Lady, we all know—" he began.

"Then let us not speak of it any further," she interrupted. She would not, could not, speak of what had happened.

The queen's guard turned to open the door to the

solar and Walter bowed to her and stepped away. Into the lion's den, she walked, without the one protector she trusted. The one who had been sent away the night that…

Taking a deep breath and pulling her pride around her once more, Emalie walked in to face the queen. Surprised to find Eleanor alone, Emalie closed the door behind and approached her godmother.

"If my memory serves me well, you will find him quite fair of face and his build is that of a practiced warrior. His family has held Chateau d'Azure in Poitou for generations," Eleanor began. The queen stood by the window, staring out and not looking at her as she spoke. Her words were confusing to Emalie. The queen spoke of someone unknown to her, but the tone loosed tiny shivers of foreboding that crept down Emalie's spine.

"Of whom do you speak, Your Grace?" She heard the tremble in her own voice as the words passed her lips.

"Christian Dumont, the Count of Langier. The son of one of my dearest cousins. And your betrothed husband."

Emalie could not take a breath. Fire burned within her eyes and throat and chest as the queen's words sank into her mind. She had thought herself safe. She that thought John's departure placed her back in control of Greystone. She had thought she was safe from marriage.

Betrothed to Christian Dumont? How could this be? Eleanor had said not one word of her plans and Emalie had had no warning of this turn of events before the queen's softly spoken declaration.

"Your Grace, I do not wish to marry. As I told your

son, there is no reason for it.'' Emalie forced herself to maintain control as she tried to talk her way out of this predicament.

''Emalie, please come and sit with me here. We have matters to discuss.''

Eleanor seated herself in one of the high-backed chairs and waited. Unable to postpone the inevitable, Emalie followed the order and sat next to the queen. When she had gathered her calm once more, she looked at Eleanor.

''I have been married to two kings and birthed at least one more,'' Eleanor began. The queen's gaze rested on her squarely, and Emalie fought to return it in just the same direct manner. ''I have plotted and planned and held a kingdom together these last years. I know my sons and all that they are capable of. One thing I am not is ignorant of the ways of men of power.''

The tone of Eleanor's voice struck a warning note to Emalie and she waited for the coming truth.

''I have ways of finding information and determining the truth in situations that my sons can not even begin to imagine, and I think you already know what I have discovered here in Greystone Castle.''

Emalie searched for something to say, some way to divert the queen from this course. She had no chance.

''William DeSeverin has indeed had carnal knowledge of you, as my son planned. Your virginity and your honor are lost.''

Emalie could feel the blood rush away from her face. Her hands trembled and her stomach clenched in reaction to the words of her damnation. So her secret was hers no longer. Emalie wondered who could have been the weak link in her household. 'Twas of no matter now.

"Only marriage can save you, Emalie. And a marriage done quickly and quietly may be the only way to save your name and your life." When Emalie would have argued, Eleanor delivered the telling blow. "And your people."

Emalie closed her eyes in defeat. She and her father had planned carefully to protect their people from John's rapacious greed, during the time when Richard was away on Crusade, then held for ransom. Their efforts saw their people healthy and hearty where other keeps were decimated. And when the death of her mother had caused her father to lose his dedication, Emalie had carried on their efforts.

In return, her people would protect her. John had been unsuccessful at breaching their defense of her. Her servants and villagers had steadfastly backed her word in the matter of William DeSeverin. And at great risk to themselves, if they all failed in this plan to prevent John's machinations to gain control over Greystone and its lady.

"How did you discover the truth?" Emalie asked, no longer even attempting to deny Eleanor's words.

Eleanor waved her hand and Emalie knew she was not to learn the queen's methods. "How is not important, my dear. Know you that I have, and that I now know the true danger you are in by remaining here. DeSeverin has made another attempt to meet with you, has he not? And with this attractive holding taunting John to commit further sins to gain control of it, it is only a matter of time before he, *they,* act once more."

"And you propose that I marry this Christian Dumont?" Emalie whispered, unable to deny William's failed try at another *visit*. She thought she'd been successful in hiding that from the queen. Apparently not.

Eleanor straightened in her chair, her face taking on a regal countenance once more. "I do not propose this. As an emissary of the king, I am in a position to order it."

Eleanor reached to a nearby table and lifted several parchments. As she held them out to Emalie, Emalie could see her gaze soften. Emalie's hand shook even more as she took hold of the papers that would change her life. Although she possessed the skills, it was the tears in her eyes that prevented her from reading the finely scrolled Latin writing before her. Blinking to clear them away did not work. A moment later, a handkerchief was pushed into her grasp.

"The Count of Langier is renowned for his prowess on the battlefield and in the tournaments. His blood is as noble as your own and he carries several minor titles as well. He comes to you without the need for funds as some husbands would, Countess."

Eleanor's words caused more questions to form in her thoughts. Something was missing, something about this prospective, nay, ordered, betrothed of hers.

"I hear these many good things you say about the count, Your Grace. I can also hear in your words and phrasing that there is more you do not say. Pray, continue and tell me the rest of it so there would be no surprises."

Emalie dabbed her eyes once more and tucked the linen square into the cuff of her sleeve. She wondered what would make this supposedly excellent specimen of Pontevin manhood drag himself across the Channel and lower himself to marry an Englishwoman, even a noble one with a rich estate to offer. She had met others from the French provinces of the Plantagenets and had recognized the inherent snobbery and arrogance they harbored when comparing themselves to the Plantagenet's English kingdom.

Eleanor did not answer, but instead rose from her chair and walked slowly across the solar toward the door. Emalie rose, as well, for one could not remain seated when a queen did not. She clasped her hands, trying to stop their trembling and took several deep breaths, trying to stop the panic that threatened to overpower her.

Stopping a pace before reaching the door, Eleanor turned back to face her. Her godmother smiled at her, and a genuine expression of concern filled her face as she finally responded to Emalie's question.

"No, I think not. We all have our own secrets that we bring to a marriage. He has his," Eleanor said quietly. "And you have yours. It will be up to both of you to come to some accommodations within your marriage."

Eleanor tugged on the knob and pulled the door open. She raised her voice so that all those waiting in the hall could hear her words.

"Emalie, the Count of Langier arrives at Greystone this day. The betrothal agreement has already been signed by the king—since you are his ward—and the count."

Emalie heard the gasps of her servants and household even where she stood inside the solar. She could only imagine their confusion. Alyce appeared in the doorway, concern etched clearly on her face.

"The wedding will be celebrated on the morrow. Even now, the good father makes his preparations in the chapel."

The murmuring in the great hall increased and Emalie understood her people knew not whether to applaud this latest event or protest it. Her Montgomerie pride asserted itself once more and she felt the shield of her parents' love surround her. She was the Countess of Harbridge and would demonstrate just what that meant. Knowing that her actions could be seen and would be reported back to all in Greystone, Emalie approached the queen and knelt before her with her head bowed.

"I thank you, Your Grace, for being so concerned for the welfare of Greystone and all its people." Lifting her face to Eleanor, she noticed the twinkle in the queen's eyes. Eleanor saw the move for exactly what it was—a political way of insuring her people's compliance and cooperation. And most importantly, their acceptance. "I will make preparations now for a feast to celebrate the count's arrival in Greystone and our betrothal this evening."

Rising gracefully and steadily from her knees, Emalie followed the queen into the great hall and finally saw the expressions of her people. Disbelief, confusion, anger, acceptance. She was certain that they mirrored her own feelings, though she had not the luxury of exposing hers to them. Eleanor called out to her own ladies and walked off with them on some task, leaving Emalie standing alone.

She did not have time to stand around wondering and worrying about her impending marriage. There was much to do before her betrothed husband arrived and the rituals began.

"Come, Alyce," she called out to her servant. "The

Count of Langier will see Greystone at its best.'' She smiled as she realized her thoughts included her people, her keep and village and herself when she spoke of Greystone.

Could it be Lady Ayla? She...Doubtful, at least to his
mind...in this earthen hovel impossible to tell her mother's
her own—our villains—hot to care while, she spoke of
the villain...

Chapter Four

Although he tried to fight it, a wave of admiration passed over him at his first sighting of Greystone Castle and village. Mayhap 'twas that its size dwarfed his own estate. Mayhap it was that the layout of the village and surrounding farmlands gave the entire estate a look of well-managed care. Whatever the cause, Christian found himself impressed with the demesne that lay before him, even if it was in the middle of dismal England.

Touching his heels to his horse's sides, he moved forward with his escort toward Greystone and his yet unknown task for the king. He knew that one of the men accompanying him carried messages to Queen Eleanor, but that messenger did not or could not speak of his instructions. The few times Christian had attempted to discern more information from the man, the only response he'd gained was a few grunts and nods.

Christian felt a knot begin to form in the pit of his belly as each minute brought them closer and closer to his fate. What if he discovered he could not carry out what the king demanded of him? What if it was something that would endanger his soul? Or something that would make his honor suffer even more than it already had? His mount noticed the tension in his body and soon danced nervously beneath him. Releasing his tight hold on the reins, he quickly brought the horse back under his control.

How he yearned for his own mount. Though, in his still-weakened condition, he knew he would never be able to keep his massive destrier from overpowering him. He would wait at Greystone as the king had *suggested* and leave his horses at Chateau d'Azure. But once this onerous assignment was completed, he would return to his family's estate and train once more with his magnificent bloods. And he would oversee Geoff's recovery.

Of course that all depended on him surviving whatever it was that lay ahead. The ignorance of his impending future weighed heavily on his shoulders. If it were just him, he could face this unknown much easier than he did, knowing that Geoff's fate was entangled with his own. What would become of Geoff if Christian failed?

His escort moved forward down the rough road leading to the main entrance in the castle wall. 'Twould seem that his future was moving quickly toward him. Taking a deep breath, Christian urged his mount to keep up with the rest of the riders. Wrapping the pride of generations of Dumonts before him around his shoulders as a shield, he rode to meet his fate head-on.

His unease grew as they were permitted entry without challenge. Men-at-arms patrolled along a walkway that surrounded the entire castle. The gate, open as most were during the day, was closely monitored by both the men above and several guards standing on either side. It was obvious that they were expected, even welcome. Had he been summoned to take over protection of this estate? Mayhap it and its people faced threats from outside and Richard believed him capable of defending keep and village?

But what of the owners? How could a demesne of this size and apparent prosperity not be protected? Christian felt the tension grow once more in his arms and shoulders as they passed en masse by the startled inhabitants. Men and women stopped and stared as they rode on to the steps leading to the keep itself. Finally, and not a moment too soon to his way of thinking, the group reached its destination and drew to a halt. Christian dismounted in one motion and nodded as a boy came forward to take his mount. Any hesitation on his part about the boy's ability to handle a horse so much bigger than he was disappeared as he observed the skill and caring with which the boy led the horse away to the stables.

Brushing off the dust of the morning's travel, Christian waited for someone from within to greet them. He did not wait long before the doors at the top of the steps opened and a huge man approached them. Nodding at them, he paused until the royal messenger stepped forward and announced himself as such. After conversing in hushed tones, the messenger climbed the steps and entered the building. Then the man addressed the rest of the group, in heavily accented English.

"I am Walter, lately captain of the guards here at Greystone. I bid you welcome in the name of the Countess of Harbridge and in the name of Eleanor, Queen of England, who is also in residence here. Come this way, so that you may refresh yourselves from your journey."

The big soldier stepped aside and motioned for the group to follow him. Only the promise of some decent wine and shelter from the gray English weather enticed Christian to enter in haste. At least if Eleanor were here, some tasty food and drink were probabilities as well. The queen did not suffer herself to travel without the comforts to which she was accustomed.

Entering the great hall, Christian inspected the room and its inhabitants. The people were all busy, cleaning the floors, replacing the rushes, rehanging huge tapestries on the wall behind the raised dais. All he saw reinforced his notion of the prosperity of the estate and the good handling of its resources. A short, thin man separated himself from a small group talking among themselves and approached their burly escort.

"Sir Walter, please allow me to escort our guests to table."

The captain's relieved expression told Christian more than words could of his discomfort at this task. Nodding brusquely, he stepped aside and waved them on to follow this newcomer.

"I am Fitzhugh, the steward. Allow me to see you settled with food and drink to refresh yourselves. Right this way." The steward led them up the steps to the large table and guided them to seats. Fitzhugh called out to servants and, within a few moments, platters of bread and cheeses and cold meats were placed before them. Pitchers of ale and wine along with goblets were placed on the table. Serving women circled them, offering more food and drink, until there was a full trencher and cup before each man.

Christian lifted the cup to his lips and drank deeply of the wine. As the drink washed away the dust in his mouth, Christian was overcome with a wave of homesickness for his own demesne and his own vintage of wine. Chateau d'Azure was known far and wide for its excellent quality of grapes and the wine they produced. He craved a bottle of his own even as he swallowed once and again of this local brew.

"Milord, is something wrong with the wine?"

Christian was pleased in one way that Fitzhugh had been so observant—it spoke well of his abilities. However, he knew that his own foul mood and the tension spiraling even tighter within his gut were not the steward's problems.

"The wine is acceptable," he answered, drinking down the last mouthful in his cup and placing it back on the table. "I fear that I am simply weary from our journey."

"Since neither the queen nor the countess will be able to greet you at this time, I have been instructed to show you to your rooms so that you can refresh yourselves before meeting them at supper this eve. Once you finish eating, of course." Fitzhugh smiled as he spoke. He was much younger than Christian had first thought.

Christian wanted to argue about not seeing Eleanor immediately, but his bone-deep fatigue got the better of him. After tearing off some bread, he chewed it slowly as he cut a wedge of cheese. He continued methodically eating everything before him and did not pause until all the others at table had finished. He recognized this as a sad remnant of his recent brush with starvation, however, even knowing this did not stop Christian from eating as much as he could at each meal. Only his willpower and the thought of the possible humiliation at being discovered kept him from taking food from the table and hiding it within his tunic and in his pockets.

When all the others had stopped eating and emptied their goblets, Christian brushed the crumbs from his hands and dried his mouth. Rising and following the steward through the hall to a staircase, he looked around and took in as much about his surroundings as he could. A tickle of unease moved down his spine and he searched for the source. He felt as though he was being watched, not as a welcomed visitor but as a potential enemy. No one met his gaze and all appeared too busy to be studying him with the intensity that he felt.

At the back of the great hall, they were separated and Fitzhugh motioned that he should follow. Soon they alone climbed up three flights of steps and arrived on the top floor of the keep. The steward startled him by leading him to another stairway and up to an even higher floor in one of the corner towers of the keep. His confusion turned to amazement as Fitzhugh opened the door to what could only be the lord's chamber.

"There must be some mistake?" he started. "These are the lord's chambers and obviously meant for someone else."

"No, milord. The queen was quite clear in her instructions. She instructed that you should have these rooms."

Fitzhugh allowed him to proceed into the room where he was greeted by a small army of servants awaiting his arrival. The room was sumptuously furnished with tapestries on the walls and several thick rugs spread around the room. In spite of it being summer, a fire burned brightly in the hearth, taking the chill from the room. A large metal tub, larger than most he had seen or been in, sat before the fire, its contents releasing wafts of steam into the room.

A young maid rushed forward and placed a cup in his hands. Another busied herself opening his meager baggage, which had been delivered in advance of his arrival. An older, stouter woman stood waiting next to the tub. Fitzhugh cleared his throat and all of the servants stopped their activities and looked to him for direction.

"Let us give the count some measure of privacy for his bath. You can finish your work later." And with a wave of his hand and a flurry of movement to the door, Fitzhugh and the servants were gone. Except for one.

Christian drank the wine without tasting it, for the appeal of the bath held his attention. He walked across the large room and sat on a chair to remove his leather bindings and shoes.

"Would you prefer me to leave, milord, or give you some assistance in your bath?" The voice did not match the woman, for it was softer and lighter than he expected for one of her large size. In a way, it held a resemblance to his own mother's voice with its melodic soft tones.

"Your name?"

"Alyce, milord," she answered, dipping into a slight curtsy and bowing her head.

"You would help me by setting out all I need within reach of the tub and then you may go."

Christian could not bear the thought of someone, even a servant, witnessing what months of imprisonment had wrought on his body. His gaunt appearance was one thing he could not hide, but the sores and scabs were his own private hell.

"Very well, milord." Alyce moved with an efficiency that once more surprised him and in a few moments had arranged the bowl of soap, the linens and extra buckets of hot and cold water exactly as he had requested. She walked toward him and stopped with her arms outstretched. "If you will give me your clothes, I will have them washed for you, milord."

Christian thought to refuse but changed his mind. His baggage was light, for he had brought few clothes with him. Cleaning these would be necessary. He nodded and turned his back to strip out of them. When he glanced in her direction, Alyce was standing near him, but her gaze was trained on the door across the room.

Feeling some comfort in her impersonal manner, he quickly removed his belt, tunic and undershirt. He rolled his stockings down and peeled them off his sweaty feet. Grimacing at the stench permeating them, he rolled them into a ball and held them out to Alyce. She took them without comment or glance and walked away from him toward the door. Still not moving from the chair, he waited for her to leave so he could enter the blessed bath in front of him.

"Milord?" she called from the door.

"Oui?" He answered in his native tongue without thought. "Yes?" he repeated to her in hers.

"Milady has an ointment that could help your injuries."

Shame poured over him as he realized she'd seen his body after all. Did she know how he had come by these *injuries?* He prayed not; he prayed the queen had not shared his disgrace, his dishonor with all involved in this endeavor. A lump blocked his ability to answer her offer, although any medicament that could take away the pain and itching from his sores would be welcome.

"I will return anon with it and you may try it if you

wish." Alyce did not wait for his response. He wondered if she could tell he could not answer even if he wanted to. He cleared his throat several times until he could speak.

"Alyce?"

"Aye, milord," she answered without turning to him.

"Leave the door ajar."

"Milord?" This time she began to turn and then stopped herself.

"I want the door left open."

"Aye, milord," she said on a sigh, as though familiar with the strange requests of nobility.

Alyce left the room and positioned the door so that it was open. Christian could breathe more easily now. Closed spaces and rooms without windows left him breathless and nervous. Rising from the chair, he walked to the tub and tested the water with his fingers. Stepping carefully over the side of the tub, he allowed his legs to become accustomed to the heat. As it permeated his muscles, he sat and then slid even lower until he was covered up to his neck.

He dipped below the water and wet his hair. Scooping out some of the soft soap in the bowl, he lathered and scrubbed his head until it tingled from his efforts. It would take more than a few baths to remove the squalor and filth of months without them, or at least the feel of those months and that filth. After his hair was soaped and rinsed several times, he settled back in the still-steaming water to relax his tense muscles.

Christian pulled a towel into the water and over his body to keep the warmth close to him. His thoughts drifted and soon he could feel sleep overtake him.

* * *

"What do you mean he asked for the door to remain open?"

"'Tis just as I said, milady. When I was leaving the room, he called out to me and told me to leave the door ajar."

Emalie believed her maid, she just did not understand the request. Only the lord's and lady's chambers gave any measure of true privacy and that was due to the stout doors at their entrances. To leave the door open was to invite intrusion…or to simply invite.

"Was he in his bath when you left?" Emalie demanded. At Alyce's nod, she added, "And was he alone?"

"Aye, milady. Fitzhugh knows Lyssa and her tricks. He ordered her out before the lord undressed."

Was he leaving the door open so the maid could return to him? Was he taking his pleasure with the servants in her keep even before it was his? 'Twas a fine way for the new lord of Greystone to begin.

"I will take the ointment to him." Emalie decided to look into this herself. If her new husband was going to make shaming her a regular occurrence, she would know it now.

"But, milady, I told him I would bring it. Mayhap you should wait until this evening to meet him, as the queen suggested?" Alyce frowned at Emalie's attempts to take the pottery jar from her grasp. Emalie stopped trying and held her hand out for Alyce to relinquish the jar. With a sigh, her maid finally did. Emalie picked up one more bottle, gathered her skirts and left her workroom, heading to the lord's chamber. Alyce's huffing and puffing followed close behind. Stopping in front of the room, Emalie leaned closer and peeked in.

"Go quietly, milady."

Now it was her turn to frown. "What do you mean, Alyce?"

"Poor lad, looked nigh to fainting from exhaustion, he did."

"Poor lad? That poor lad is *le Comte de Langier*," Emalie whispered in her best French accent, "one of Poitou's finest, fair of face, and warrior extraordinaire, according to the queen."

"He looked like a man worn down by life to me," Alyce answered with a snort. "Step lightly and do not disturb him if he rests."

Emalie gaped openly at her maid. Alyce's softness toward this man was frightening to her. If Alyce backed him, who would stand by her side? Deciding it was time to meet this poor lad, Emalie pushed the door open a bit more and stepped into the room. The humid air swirled around her as she approached the hearth and tub. The man in the tub did not move as she walked closer.

His head lay turned to one side and he snored lightly. She smiled as she thought of how innocent her father had appeared in sleep. Now, as she looked at Dumont, no frowns marred his strong brow and face. His hair looked to be a dark brown, but the wetness made it difficult to tell. Her gaze moved down his face and neck to his shoulders and chest. The rest of him was covered by a length of linen.

She could see some of his bones lying just below his skin. He was either very thin or had been ill and lost much of his body's weight. Was this what Alyce meant? Her trained eye noticed several lesions on his arms and chest, some unhealed sores of long standing. She suspected that he suffered with many more on places she could not see. This was truly a puzzle.

Debating whether or not to let him know of her presence, Emalie decided to let him sleep on. She placed the jar of ointment on the floor next to the tub where he would find it. Then she quietly opened the bottle she carried and poured a small amount into the bathwater. Reaching down, she swirled the water with her fingertips to mix the healing potion into his bath. Careful not to touch him, she stepped back and walked toward the door.

Once in the hall, she pulled the door closed and then adjusted it as Alyce had left it. Tonight. Tonight she would have her answers when she and the count met officially.

Strangely, as she left the chamber, only one question filled her thoughts. She wondered what he would look and sound like once awake. Too wrapped up in her own thoughts, she hadn't seen his eyes open and his gaze follow her steps.

An angel from heaven? Had he finally died and this angel was there to escort him to his judgment?

As he opened his eyes, he saw her standing over him, her gowns and long, honey-brown hair flowing around her. The flames in the hearth outlined her womanly form before him. Her face glowed with the golden fire tones and not even the frown she wore could mar the smooth inclines of her nose, the gentle arching of her brows or the fullness of her mouth. He saw her hand reach out to the water and he closed his eyes and waited, nay hungered, for her healing touch.

When it did not come, he fought with his last ounce of strength to open his eyes. She was gone. Then he saw her moving toward the door, silently gliding away from him. His strength, sapped by both his own exhaustion and the heat of the water surrounding him, deserted him completely and all he could do was close his eyes once more and surrender. And his dreams were filled with visions of his caring angel.

Chapter Five

The knock on the chamber door roused Christian from his brief rest. Still exhausted from many days of hard riding and traveling, he slid down from the raised bed, tugged on a robe and stumbled to the door. Although the door was ajar, the visitor did not presume to enter the room.

"Milord?" a man asked. "Are you within?"

Christian reached the door and pulled it open wider until the full bulk of the captain of the guard was revealed to him.

"Forgive me for disturbing your rest, milord. Her Grace asks that you join her in the solar as soon as you are ready."

"I will be there anon, Sir Walter." Christian looked back around the chamber he'd been assigned and spotted clothing laid out and ready for him. The servants were efficient and quiet, for no movements within his room had disturbed his sleep.

"Should I send an escort to guide you there?" Christian watched the large man shift from foot to foot, obviously uncomfortable with this messenger duty.

"No need. I am certain that I can find my way there."

After a few mumbled words, Walter backed away, bowing as he left. After pushing the door closed a bit, Christian dressed quickly. Recognizing that his haste was partly nervousness and partly anticipation, he slowed his actions and straightened his clothing as best he could. Tightening the belt around his waist, he grimaced at his loss of girth. He was thinner now than when he had first earned his spurs at ten-and-six. Soon, after fussing with his appearance more than most women would have, he was ready for his meeting with Queen Eleanor and as ready to meet his fate as he could be.

Retracing his steps the way he and the steward had come, Christian found himself standing within the great hall. More of the servants' efficient work was on display there—clean, well-set tables, fresh rushes on the floor, an orderly pattern to those working to prepare the room and the meal. Excitement filled the very air surrounding him and he knew from the covert glances and whispered words, and from the feeling deep in his gut, that he was the center of what was to come.

Looking around the perimeter of the room, he sought the location of the solar. A young woman approached him, curtsying before him.

"Milord? Are you in need of help?" Her eyes met his but once before she lowered her glance to the floor.

"Oui," he answered. Her gaze met his and then she dropped her head once more. Damn, but he needed to remember to speak in their tongue. He expected the English nobles to speak in French, but the servants and villeins would converse only in their harsh guttural language. "Yes," he repeated, "show me to the solar."

She curtsied once more and took a few backward steps before turning and walking in front of him. Her hips swayed in the suggestive motion that proclaimed her an available wench as she made her way through the great hall. From the peeking glances and smiles she offered over her shoulder, he understood the invitation she gave. Smiling grimly, he shook his head at the irony of this situation. On another day, his body would have reacted by this point, stirring his interest and firing his desires. On another day, in another lifetime, he would have accepted her welcoming actions and met her later for a pleasant rendezvous. However, his current physical condition and the unknown fate that stood before him kept him from responding.

Soon they approached a door set back in a stone alcove. From the two heavily armed guards next to the doorway, he knew the queen was within. The servant turned to him once more and curtsied. This time she blatantly met his gaze and smiled seductively, making her offer clear to even a blind man. Not willing to completely refuse the girl, he asked her name. 'Twould be better to have it if needed later than have to stumble through descriptions to locate her.

"Lyssa, milord. Call on me if you have need," she answered in a quiet whisper. From the snickers of the guards, she obviously had helped many of the men in the keep with their needs.

"Return to your duties anon. I will summon you if I have need." Christian waved her off and turned to the door. He knocked and waited for an invitation to enter. Hearing her voice through the door, he took a deep breath, turned the knob and prepared to face the queen.

Christian was not deceived by the old woman before

him. Although in her eighth decade of life and with an
appearance that matched her age, Eleanor was not
someone to underestimate. For more than half a cen-
tury, she had moved through their world much in the
same manner as a man and gathered power and riches,
even husbands, to herself as she did. This woman had
done the unthinkable and accompanied her first husband on a holy crusade. He moved toward her and
stopped, kneeling before her.

"Your Grace," he said, taking and kissing her hand.
He waited for her signal to rise and, when given, he
looked into her face and smiled. "You look well."

"Ah, Christian. It is as though I were looking into
your dear mother's eyes. I miss her. I miss the wise
counsel and the humor that saw me through many low
spots in my life."

His mother was a safe subject since her passing was
unrelated to his father's treachery. And she had spent
many years as the confidante of the queen.

"And I know that she valued the time she served
you, Your Grace."

Eleanor dropped her hand and sat down once more
in the chair behind her. 'Twas then he noticed the other
woman in the room. Assuming it was one of the
queen's attendants, he continued his conversation with
Eleanor.

"The king has called on me to serve you in some
way, Your Grace. He did not disclose the details to me,
only said that I was to carry out your wishes. Can you
enlighten me about these duties?"

A soft snicker pulled his attention from the queen to
her attendant once more. Passing his gaze over her
from head to toe, he glared at her discourtesy. He was,
after all, now restored to his name, his estates, his

honor, and as a count he deserved a certain level of respect from even those who served the queen.

"Richard and I," Eleanor began, "wish to protect this demesne since it belonged to a dear and loyal friend of our family. His untimely death has left it in a precarious situation and a temptation to those who would steal all it has to offer. Richard wishes that you serve as its protector and as the husband of the Countess of Harbridge."

He shook his head and blinked at her pronouncement. Protector and husband? Husband?

"But Your Grace, I am betrothed to—"

She cut off his words with a wave of her hand. "Necessarily ended months ago. You are free, in the eyes of the Church, to wed as Richard desires. And you have pledged your loyalty to him?"

He had agreed and signed his deal with the devil. And here was the cost of it. This seemed too good to be true. What hardship was there in marrying an heiress and taking control of her estate? It was his destiny as a nobleman and eldest son to do just that. Although he had thought to marry the daughter of the neighboring count, this prosperous land would be a fine replacement for that one. And there was still Geoffrey. He could marry that French heiress and add it to their family's properties.

"I have pledged to Richard, as you know."

"Then you will wed the countess in the morning."

"Will I meet her prior to the wedding? Do we not have to go through a betrothal ceremony?" This was happening too quickly. And where was the countess? Did she know of these arrangements? Ah, *certainement*. The preparations in the hall bespoke of ceremonies and celebrations.

''The betrothal was carried out before you left Anjou. Your signature is on the necessary papers.'' Eleanor pointed to a table nearby and the parchments on it. He could see both his signature and the one scrawled by the king. He smiled and nodded. Check and mate. He was now firmly entrenched in whatever games the Plantagenets were playing. ''However, so that no question can arise, the agreements will be read tonight before all.''

''And the banns?'' No one could wed without the announcement of the impending nuptials being made for three consecutive Sundays.

''Waived,'' Eleanor said, ''by Ely.''

Deeper and deeper he could feel himself being pulled into this. And the icy tremors moving up his spine told him that there was more, much more, to this than he was being told. Why was the countess unmarried? If of marriageable age, her father should have made arrangements long ago. An untimely death? Obviously, a lack of forethought and planning, as well, if his daughter was unmarried and his property unprotected.

''’Twould seem that you have taken care of all that needs arranging, Your Grace. You have my thanks.'' He bowed slightly to her. ''And the countess? How does she stand on this matter?''

''She will behave as an honorable woman does—she will make her vows to you and then carry out the duties of a wife and, God willing, a mother. Believe you me, she understands her place in this completely. You will be formally presented to each other at dinner. If you are ready, you may escort me there now.''

He heard the way she accented the word ''honorable'' in her description of his betrothed. Mayhap because his own honor had been lately restored, he was simply sensitive to it. Or was this some information about the countess? But then honor was the basis for all relationships—marriage as well as fealty and even war. Without his honor, a nobleman had nothing. Knowing this introspection would come to nothing, he looked at Eleanor.

"Of course, Your Grace," he answered, hearing the command instead of the request. Holding out his arm to Eleanor, he then walked with her out of the solar. She hesitated for a moment at the doorway.

"Join me anon in the hall, my dear," she said in a soft voice to the woman who remained standing at the queen's chair. They did not wait for a response, for one did not refuse the queen.

He was arrogant. He was arrogant and pompous and rude. He had not even asked who she was as she stood by the queen's side. Emalie stomped around the chair and plopped down onto its cushioned seat.

What had she missed? Arrogant, pompous, rude and...ah! Overbearing and Angevin. No, he was not from Anjou, but from the queen's own province of Aquitaine. She lifted the cup left behind by Eleanor and swallowed the few mouthfuls of wine left in it. Letting out the breath she held, she admitted the word that she withheld.

Husband. He was her husband. Even now before the nuptial ceremony, she was bound to him by church and law by the betrothal papers on the table. Richard, as king and as holder of her wardship, had given her person and her lands into the control of this arrogant, pompous, rude, overbearing *Comte de Langier*. And what had Eleanor told her? They would have to both make some accommodations in their marriage.

Her unasked question had been answered and that surprised her. He was fair of face as the queen had said. His hair was a lighter brown than she thought when she'd seen him in his bath, and his eyes were the green of spring grasses. And his voice...well, that poured over her like melted treacle, rich and warm. In fact, she had focused on the sound of his voice rather than the obnoxious things he was saying when he spoke to Eleanor.

Christian Dumont had faced some physical trials of late though. His clothing was too big for the form he had now. He had lost weight recently and gained the sores she'd seen on him in his bath. Had he been held prisoner with Richard on the Continent? Was she, was Greystone and the title of Harbridge, his reward for loyal service to the king? If he came as the Count of Langier, what were his lands in Aquitaine like? And who was his family?

Emalie shook her head and realized with a start that she had been sitting here contemplating her betrothed husband and his circumstances for far too long. She stood and made certain that her hair was firmly secured underneath her coif. She would go to him as the Countess Harbridge, as her father's daughter, not the maid he thought she was.

As she pulled the door open once more, another memory came to her. Christian Dumont, Count of Langier and soon of Harbridge, had been afraid of the news that Eleanor gave him. Fear had been her first impression as he entered the room and greeted the queen. He looked like a man facing death. Even when given the news of his betrothal, the fear did not leave him.

He was a puzzle, one that she would have plenty of time to solve. She knew only that Richard had sent him at Eleanor's request to prevent the destruction of her estates and her people. If he did that, she would be forever grateful. She could be content in a marriage if he took care of her people.

Christian Dumont was also a prig. Emalie seethed in humiliation and anger at his latest actions. Her introduction by the queen was met with bold laughter from him. If she were fair, she would admit that his laughter made her stomach quiver in a way she'd not felt before. Right now, she did not feel like being fair.

Dinner had been accomplished with some speed and then the betrothal agreement, with its long recitation of properties and titles, tributes and fees, knights and villeins, had been announced in a droning voice by one of Eleanor's clerks. Emalie had learned that the count was possessed of a rather large amount of property outside Poitiers as well as a few minor estates and manors in Anjou and Normandy. His titles were older than hers, but she was richer than he. Her dower property was established and would be passed to any daughter if she outlived him and would be repossessed by him if she predeceased him.

It had gone on and on and then came the moment when she had turned over her chatelaine's keys to him as a symbol of his new position as head of the household and her new lord. Langier had thanked her in heavily accented English and then attached the keys to his own belt. Even the increased murmurings of her people had not alerted him to the insult he gave her. Instead of returning them to her and, in so doing, confirming her position within their household, he kept them—a clear sign of mistrust, with all of Greystone watching.

Emalie felt the heat rise in her cheeks and the sting of tears in her eyes. Did he know her truth or did he simply think her not capable of carrying out the duties she relished? Did he suspect her of mishandling the estate? She bowed and took her seat once more, fighting the urge to scream at him or to cry out in front of everyone. Not certain which would be worse, she simply fixed her gaze on the table in front of her and fought to control herself.

This was not something she had considered would happen. Her father had intended that she should be in charge of Greystone and its people. He had told her many times that she was as capable as a son in understanding the intricacies of running a demesne the size of theirs. She thought that her husband would at least give her a chance to prove her worth and her abilities.

"I am not unfamiliar with what you are feeling, Emalie," Eleanor said in a quiet voice. "To work for something so long and hard and to see it snatched from you is not something easy to accept."

"No, Your Grace," was all she could say.

"Give him time to adjust to his new circumstances before you judge him."

"And what of my new circumstances, Your Grace?" Emalie bit her lip after the words escaped—her circumstances were the cause of all this.

"You would have faced much more unpleasantness if John had had his way in this and William DeSeverin sat in that seat, my dear." Eleanor inclined her head toward her betrothed. "A woman faces this no matter where she weds."

Although she knew it was the truth, Emalie did not like it at this moment. She had lived with the hope that her father would take her wishes and feelings into consideration when choosing her husband, but the practical side of her knew that she was simply dreaming. A woman married to bring property and money to her husband and to give him heirs; feelings and dreams had no place there.

"I understand, Your Grace. If you have no objections, I would retire to my chamber."

Escape was the only thing she wanted to do. Well, not the only thing. She would like to scream her anger and embarrassment out, but that would simply increase both for her. She waited for Eleanor's nod and then rose from her chair. She was surprised to see the count rise, also. Ah, she needed his consent now, as well, to leave her own hall. Her stomach tightened and tears threatened as a wave of desolation passed over her. But the only thing that was constant in her life of late, her people and their support, watched and waited for her every move and reaction. She could no more fail them than she could hold back the coming night.

"My lord?" she asked, tilting her head slightly to him as she turned to face him. "With your permission, I would retire."

He closed the short distance between them with two steps and lifted her hand to his lips. Even the tension that filled her did not prevent her from noticing his breath as it tickled the fine hairs on her fingers. If his gesture was more than the usual perfunctory one, she could not tell, but she did not remember ever noticing the details of one or another until this one.

"Until tomorrow then, milady."

He lowered her hand from his lips and placed it on his forearm, intent on guiding her from the dais. But his eyes caught her gaze and she could not breathe. Amusement, anger, suspicion and fear. She read them and recognized them as the same feelings coursing through her. Something else coalesced in his gaze—his eyes darkened and became more intense than before.

Desire.

An overwhelming need to run struck her and she fought to take a breath. The moment passed and he looked away first, turning them toward the steps from the raised platform to the floor. She was glad for his support, even though she tried not to grip his arm for balance.

Desire was not something she had thought about in this bargain. She did not know Eleanor's reasons for summoning this particular courtier to her rescue and she did not know his reasons for accepting such a call. His arrogant and irritated attitude in the solar, and his apparent dismissal of her from her oversight duties, made her believe that he was here for the property and riches. It made her overlook the aspect of marriage that had brought her to this point—procreation. Her shiver brought his attention and he paused in his escort of her through the length of the great hall.

"Is something amiss?" he asked in a low voice. More shivers pulsed through her at the tone of it.

"Nay, milord, all is well. You need not leave the queen to escort me to my own room. I know the way." If she was abrupt with him, she had not intended to be so. But his nearness and his voice made her uneasy, even more so than she had felt before meeting him. Now he was here, he was her husband and he was in charge of her and all she owned.

"Very well, then, milady. I return to Eleanor's side as you suggest. There is much I need to discuss with her."

He released her hand and waited for her to leave.

Anger flared once more as she realized that he would discuss matters with the queen that concerned her and that she would not be included. Delaying her departure no longer, she walked the rest of the way through the hall. She was so disturbed by his dismissal that she was in the corridor leading to her room before she realized that Alyce trailed behind her. Her maid hurried to get to the door first and, once opened, Emalie rushed into her chambers.

The wind whipped his hair and stung his eyes, but he remained in the full force of it. Refusing to seek refuge behind one of the towers, Christian stood on the battlements of Greystone Castle and looked out over the surrounding countryside. The light of the full moon flowed like quicksilver over the rolling hills and valleys, causing everything in its path to shimmer. Closing his eyes, he allowed the power of the cool gusts to wipe away the tension within him.

Too many hours within walls caused his gut and his skin to tighten. He needed time outside, being buffeted by whatever nature threw at him, in order to regain control over his fear. Would it ever leave him?

He had thought that just leaving the prison cell and riding away would have freed him, but it had not. He believed he could scrub away the scum accumulated after months without bathing and filling his stomach with food after suffering deep hunger would relieve the anguish of those months. But it had not. Even having his honor restored by the king's command did not lessen the dread that he would be returned to those dire circumstances. And the king's demand that Geoffrey stay behind only served to intensify those fears.

Mayhap after he carried out this task for the king

and his mother, he would feel more in control of his life. There was, however, a niggling feeling that there was much more here than anyone was saying.

Why was he chosen to receive this estate, and the titles and woman that went with it? Did Eleanor's fondness for his mother really explain it? And surely there were neighboring noblemen who could have been called upon to take control of this demesne. Richard had mentioned his brother John. Was he the threat here? Well, that answer he knew—absolutely yes.

He turned his back to the wind and walked the length of one side of the castle wall. Guards passed him on their rounds and more watched him from the corner towers. He nodded to each as they passed and studied their faces and their habits. He would speak to Sir Walter tomorrow about the troops and their commanders. Now that the betrothal agreements confirmed his power here, he would call some of his own men from Langier to come and serve him here. He would feel more secure once his own retainers arrived. Turning his attention back to the surrounding landscape, he thought of the one who was at the center of this puzzling situation.

Who was this woman, now his betrothed wife? How had she fallen into John's net? Or was her involvement with John of her own volition and Richard wanted her under the control of his own man? He would discover John's role in this as Richard had commanded and then mayhap Geoff could join him.

Of course his brother's condition would prevent him from traveling at this time and probably for some time, until he recovered from the deprivations of their imprisonment. God and king willing, Geoff would join him by Michaelmas. He did regret that his own return to Chateau d'Azure would not come until next spring at the soonest. But he had made a bargain with the king and he would hold up his end of it. And then he would be truly free.

Mayhap not completely free; he would, after all, have a wife to contend with. Other men had married and survived and he chuckled with the certainty that he would as well. A noise drew his attention and he watched as that very same wife walked onto the ramparts opposite his position. Christian stepped back into the shadows and simply observed this mysterious woman who was now his.

The lady made her way to the end of the parapet and placed herself in the force of the same wind that had buffeted him a few moments before. As he watched, she closed her eyes and turned her face into the strong breezes that passed over the crenellated wall. A quiver shot through him as he recognized the motion as the same one he made when the tension inside him grew too strong. He had taken several strides toward her before realizing his intent. Stopping before she saw him, he knew he did not wish to intrude on her private moment.

Studying her face as the moonlight illuminated it from above, Christian wondered over Eleanor's refusal to explain the countess's circumstances. Their private talk had been as frustrating as the one prior to the betrothal announcements—only cryptic comments and a growing feeling that he was entering a lion's den. Trouble was, he did not know who was the lion...the Plantagenet prince or the woman he was to marry in the morning.

As if she had heard his thoughts, Emalie turned and looked at him. Their gazes met and he was once more assailed with the feeling that, in some way, they were kindred spirits. But alike in what way? Before he could look away, she dipped her head in a subtle salute, turned from him and walked back to the door that led to her hallway. Her maid stood in the doorway waiting for her and, without any delay, the women descended the stairs and disappeared from his view.

Christian faced the wind once more and tried to quiet the sense of fear within him. Once they were married and the queen left, he would discover Emalie's secrets and carry out his duty to the king. Once he gave Richard the information he demanded, Christian would be safe and his honor, name and wealth would be restored permanently as promised. And once he was firmly back in control of his life and destiny, he would…

He shook his head in confusion. He had lived so many months just trying to survive each day that he had never thought about what would happen next. Without his father to guide him for the first time in his life, Christian was unsure of how to move on in this life he was gathering.

Turning out of the gusts, he walked to the doorway and entered the keep. Pushing his windblown hair from his face, he sought warmth in his chamber. He closed the door, tossed off his cloak and poured himself some wine from a waiting pitcher. Swallowing deeply, he felt exhaustion taking control of his body.

There were simply too many things to worry about, too many uncertainties to face in the coming days and months, and Christian did not have the physical strength to face them all with the confidence he needed. He decided then and there that gaining back his stamina was his first priority. Once he felt stronger, he could face these many challenges. Then he would face his duties to his king and his honor.

Collapsing on the bed, he could not even pull himself back up. Tomorrow would be another trying and long day and he needed to rest. Tomorrow, he would plan out the rest of his life. Tomorrow, he would be married.

Sleep overtook him and the room faded into darkness around him.

married.

Chapter Six

Although the long, soft strokes of the brush through her hair usually calmed her, this night Emalie believed that nothing would. Alyce had even taken to watering her wine since dinner so she would gain no relief there, either. Now her heart pounded in her chest and she startled at every noise in the corridor outside her mother's chamber door.

No. Not her mother's. Now this was her suite of rooms.

Emalie could have moved into these chambers after her mother's death and surely after her father's, but somehow it had not seemed the right thing to do. She'd remained in the rooms where she'd grown up, where she'd been a daughter. Now she was a wife and belonged next to her husband. Eleanor's servants accomplished the move with the swiftness and thoroughness expected of them and she now sat awaiting her husband's arrival.

Husband.

They were truly married now, although her memory carried only glimpses of the ceremony and the Mass that had followed. Because this was being done as expeditiously as possible, most of those who swore their fealty to her and now to her husband were not present. Only those knights and women of her household were witnesses and they were not many in number.

Alyce's slow and steady movements continued, but the desired effect did not happen. Emalie tried to remember saying the words that bound her to Christian, but the day was a blur in her mind. The only clear remembrance she had was of counting the links on the golden chain her father had given her on the last anniversary of her birth as she watched the men who had sworn to protect her turn over their allegiance to her husband, now the Earl of Harbridge. It had been her mother's favorite and she wore it today as she did every day—to remind her of her parents and her duties to the people of Greystone. Duties that included giving up her people and soon her own self into his control, and hopefully into his care.

Emalie shook herself free of her reverie and thought about the duty to come this night. He would take her and make her his wife in all ways. And he would know her truth. The room darkened and began to close in around her. Try as she might, she could not catch her breath.

Alyce must have sensed the change in her, for she stopped what she was doing and draped a warm shawl over Emalie's shoulders.

"There now, milady. All will be well." Alyce clucked as she wrapped the length of wool tighter around her.

Emalie dared not look at her maid for fear of crying. Tears had threatened all day but now, wracked with worried anticipation over her coming wedding night, her eyes burned. Any reply was lost when the expected

knock came on her door, but it was at the doorway that
joined her room to her husband's and not at the hallway, which she had expected. Emalie stood and faced
it.

Eleanor entered her room, followed by Eleanor's
priest and then him…Christian Dumont. Eleanor
walked across the room and took Emalie's hands in her
own and, with a nod, dismissed Alyce from the chamber. A soft look entered the queen's eyes as she examined Emalie from her head to her toes, which were
visible below the thin gown she wore.

"We are almost done, Emalie," Eleanor whispered
in a voice so low that no one else could hear.

Emalie curtsied slightly to her in response and lowered her gaze, waiting.

"Christian, your mother would be proud of you this
day even as yours would be, Emalie." Eleanor took
Christian's hands and encircled them around Emalie's.
"I am pleased to see two families who have been so
important to me finally joined together in wedlock."
Eleanor sounded very pleased with herself over these
arrangements, almost as though she had planned them
for years. "Father, will you give them your blessing
now?"

Emalie caught Christian's gaze as he looked up, both
startled by Eleanor's actions. There should be a bedding ceremony and then the blessing. There should be
witnesses so that no doubts of the validity of the marriage could be raised. Eleanor just smiled at them both
and nodded at her priest, who raised his hand and made
the sign of the cross before them.

Emalie did not hear the words he prayed. She could
hear nothing but the beating of her heart as the moment
she dreaded approached even more quickly. Soon there

was quiet in the room and Emalie realized that Eleanor had dismissed even the priest now. Unable to move, she stood with her hands still clasped in Christian's. He seemed as baffled by these proceedings as she.

"I informed those attending your wedding celebration that I would stand as witness to the bedding." Eleanor looked from one to the other and nodded. "Now that Father has issued his blessing on your marriage and wedding night, I will retire."

"Your Grace?" Emalie took a deep breath in and continued. "Should we? I mean…what is it you want us to do?"

Undressing before this man would be difficult enough, but with a witness? She had never attended a bedding before. She had only heard whispered tales of the undressing and examination that a newly married couple had to endure so that no objections to their physical suitability could be raised later. Eleanor gazed at her first and then at her new husband.

"Since there will be no repudiation of this marriage by either of you, I see no reason to do anything but wish you well and leave."

Eleanor turned from them and walked to the door leading to the hallway, pausing with her hand on the latch before opening it. "And there will be no disavowal in the morning, will there? Christian? Emalie?" Not waiting for their responses, Eleanor pulled the door open and stepped into the hall. "I will be gone before you rise in the morn, so I will say my farewells now, my dears. Be kind to each other."

And with those words, and after all her machinations, the dowager Queen of England, Duchess of Aquitaine and dowager Countess of Anjou left them alone. To begin their married life. Emalie shuddered at what her husband's reaction would be when he found she was no longer a virgin. He watched her for a moment and then released her hands from his. She wondered what to do next.

"May I have some wine?" he asked in his native language.

"Of course, my lord. Would you sit while I pour some for you?" Emalie answered in the regional French he'd used. After pointing to a bench near the hearth, she filled a goblet for him and refilled her own and then carried them to him.

He accepted it from her with murmured thanks and sat down and stared into the fire for a few minutes. Not knowing what to do, Emalie stood at one end of the hearth, placed her goblet upon the mantel shelf and waited.

"So it was you who visited me while I bathed?" His voice broke the silence and she turned to face him.

"Yes, my lord. I brought you an herbal potion for your bath."

"You have my thanks. 'Twas very soothing." He stood and approached her. "But this is what I remember most." She remained motionless as he reached out and lifted her hair from the edge of the shawl she clutched tightly around her. He slid his fingers through the length of it, gently, drawing it over her shoulders, and then looked into her eyes. His fingers grazed her neck and face, sending shivers through her. The breath she had finally found was lost once more as his hands touched and teased her shoulders and the tops of her breast.

She needed to warn him before this went any further. If he discovered that she had lost her virtue after he consummated their marriage, he might be angrier than being warned first. But the touch of his lips on hers drove any words or explanation she had planned right out of her mind. He moved his mouth over hers, stepping nearer still until he wrapped her in his embrace. His kiss was gentle, like the touch of his fingers on her skin, but persistent, and soon a wave of heat moved through her body until she felt sweat trickle down between her breasts.

Completely unexpected, this feeling of being held by him, of being kissed by him, undid her. She had tried to prepare herself to mate with him, to allow him his marital privileges, but never did she anticipate such a physical reaction from her own body.

'Twas not that she was without experience, although, other than a few kisses, she had no memory of what William had done. She only knew from Alyce that she would not feel a virgin's pain again so this mating should not be difficult for her. Now, with the heat pouring through her, and his kisses becoming more insistent and impassioned, she thought that she might even tolerate this, but first she must warn him of what he'd find when they mated. Drawing her face from his, she sucked in a gasping breath.

"My lord. Please."

"Emalie," he said in a whispered voice. "So sweet."

"I need to speak to you, my lord," she begged as she pulled from his embrace. The room around her could not be cold and yet the loss of heat from being in his arms made it feel chilled indeed. She watched the expression on his face and in his eyes change as she stepped back from him. Disappointment appeared in his gaze now.

"You have my attention. What is so important that

it can not wait?" His tone carried a sharp edge and Emalie worried about broaching this subject. Mayhap there was another way?

"My lord, I beg your tolerance and patience," she began as she lowered her eyes. "I had thought that I could simply acquiesce to the demands of this marriage."

The silence between them grew until she was forced to look up at him. Meeting his gaze and expecting to find disbelief or even anger, she was surprised instead to find a measure of acceptance or understanding in his expression.

"Am I so onerous that you find it, as you say, impossible to acquiesce to your duties?"

"Oh, no, my lord! 'Tis not you. Just that this marriage and its arrangements have happened in such a short time and with so little notice to me that I can hardly believe myself married." A sad smile crossed his face and so she pressed on with what was probably a hopeless request. "And I suspect that you were surprised by this as well?"

"Surprised? Why would you say that? Marriage is expected of those in our class. The partner and the date of the ceremony are the only questions left awaiting an answer."

Emalie glanced over at her goblet of wine and reached for it. Sipping it, she tried to regain her calm and focus her thoughts on the thing she hoped to gain from her new husband. Unable to discern a proper approach, Emalie decided to simply ask.

"I would ask that we postpone this..." Unable to say the words, she motioned between them with her hand. "Until we know each other better."

A choking sound drew her attention. Christian

coughed a few times as though he had swallowed his own wine the wrong way. He wiped his eyes and looked at her.

"Lady? You are jesting? A marriage is true only after it is consummated and I will not jeopardize my claim—"

"Your claim to my lands? My title? My people?" A wave of anger filled her and it was impossible to stop the words.

"Aye, countess," he answered, his voice filled with sarcasm. "What was yours is now mine. And I want no question to be raised about my right to all that was granted to me."

Realizing her mistake, she stepped back and knelt before him. If she had to humble herself to him to gain a reprieve, so be it. She had done so before to protect what was hers; it would not be so very painful to do so once more. She needed time before he found out the truth of her dishonor. No, not dishonored…she would never consider herself as that. Nothing she had done, nothing she had tried to do, would ever deserve the outcome she had reaped. She had not given away her honor; she still carried it deep within her.

Taking a deep breath, she whispered, "My lord, I meant no challenge to your rights as my lawful husband. Truly. As my husband, all I have is yours. I am yours."

She heard his breathing and wondered at his response. She waited for him to say something before continuing, but he said nothing.

"I have recently lost my father and have faced many trials in trying to keep my estates and my people from ruin. Please, my lord, give me a bit of time to accustom myself to our marriage."

She felt his hands grasp her shoulders and pull her to her feet before him. Raising her eyes to him, she waited for his refusal. Even she understood the need to claim her, but her fear of what he would do when he discovered her lack of virginity had driven her to this.

"I will go to my room, Emalie. You have your reprieve."

"But, my lord, what of...?" Confused over his quick agreement, she thought to ask him about Eleanor's order that there be no repudiation of their vows.

"Do not worry about your reputation—I will mark the sheets so that none question that the deed has been done."

Christian walked from her to the side of the bed, rolling back his sleeve as he moved. After he pulled the bedcovers back, he drew a knife from his belt and made a small, precise slit in his forearm. He held his arm out over the bed and allowed small drops of blood to fall onto the white sheets, marring their cleanliness forever. She gaped as he assessed the amount necessary and then pressed his other hand over the wound to stop the bleeding.

"Now no tongues will wag on the morrow."

She stood there, speechless, unsure of what to say and unable to force a word out of her mouth.

"In a way, this is a blessing of sorts."

"It is, my lord?" For her certainly, but for him? There would be time to explain to him, in some way, what had happened to her. She did not think she would ever reveal the name of the man who had taken what Christian should have had, but she owed him some accounting of her actions.

"As you said, this marriage was a surprise to me.

Although I came here to carry out some order of the queen's, I did not expect to gain a wife, more titles and more lands. This reprieve of yours will give us some time to learn about the other and to accommodate ourselves to this marriage.''

His words agreed with hers, but there was something underneath the words themselves. She sensed something questionable, something dangerous…just something else there. Mayhap this was a blessing after all. If he could see her as a capable chatelaine, a calm and sober woman and a dutiful wife, mayhap he could forgive her lapse of…behavior? Time might be exactly what she needed.

"I agree, my lord," she answered. "Many men and women of our class do not have the opportunity to acquaint themselves with their spouses before marriage. This could indeed be a blessing.''

Emalie watched once more as the fire lit his face and many emotions played across it. She wasn't certain that there would ever be enough time to really know this man. A strong feeling of betrayal emanated from him and she worried about the effect her own news would have on him. Would he be able to accept her sin or would he make her pay dearly for her lack of virtue? Either way would be in his power as her husband and lord and there would be no one able to protect her if he sought to punish her. She had only the queen's words to give her hope.

"I will retire to my own chamber now, my lady. I will rejoin you in the morning to make our appearance before your people.''

She watched from her place by the hearth as he walked slowly to the door that opened to his room. Did this simply postpone what would happen? He turned to face her once more before leaving her chamber.

"I would ask that you share this arrangement between us with no one else."

The only person she could speak to about such intimate matters was her maid Alyce. Alyce knew everything about her and would go to her death before revealing any of it to anyone else. Alyce had proved herself to be trustworthy even in the face of John's threats and intimidation.

"Not even the woman Alyce, if you please."

A bittersweet smile crossed his face as he spoke. Did he read her thoughts now? She nodded at him and he left without another word, leaving her confused and overwhelmed by her body's reaction to his slight touches and passionate kiss.

Emalie gazed around the room and stared at the drying stain on her bedsheets. Christian's mark on her sheets was almost exactly the size of the one left there the night that William had taken her virtue. Alyce had shown her the sheet before burning it to protect her. Now here was this fake one proclaiming her purity to any who would see it.

A part of her wanted him to know the truth. A part deep within her twisted with guilt over deceiving this man brought to save her people. Another part of her, trained well by her father, recognized that Christian Dumont, *le Comte de Langier* and now Earl of Harbridge, had his own price to do what he was doing. For in her limited experience, no man, especially not a nobleman, did anything that did not fulfill his need for power, land or titles. That she may be recompense for some task or past glory from the king did not surprise her.

Emalie circled the room, blowing out the candles and trying to calm herself before sleep. She crept into the bed, hearing the ropes creak under her weight. Settling on one side and trying to keep her sleeping gown from the stain, she closed her eyes and waited for sleep to come. A thought came to her even as she fell under sleep's power—he had shed his own blood to protect her.

But knowing that her monthly cycle was already late by many days, she wondered if his attempt would be successful?

Christian strode over to the hearth in his chambers and poured more wine for himself. Sitting in a chair near the fire, he pondered his actions, still not believing his luck this night. Clearly she was an innocent and had not understood his situation. For in asking him for this delay, she had saved him from revealing his truth—that he could not have consummated their vows this night. In spite of a measure of desire, his body had indeed betrayed him.

Taking a deep drink from his cup, he remembered her face as he spoke the words granting her boon. A flash of relief first, followed by suspicion, then relief again had filled her expressive eyes.

So, she was relieved not to have to face that particular duty this night? Was it simply maidenly reticence that caused her to make her unusual request? Placing the goblet down, he rubbed his eyes and stretched his arms.

Emalie had turned out to be so much more than he had anticipated since discovering the nature of his duty to Richard. Surprise, amusement, respect, and even a little desire had filled him at each of their encounters.

He knew full well that his refusal to turn the chatelaine's keys back over to her angered and embarrassed her, yet she kept her dignity and did not berate or challenge him in public. His first inspection of the records and conditions of the keep revealed that she was clever and efficient in her handling of resources of the demesne and those who depended on it.

He smiled as he remembered the disgruntled look she had worn when he laughed out loud at their first meeting. So intent on his discussions with Eleanor in the solar was he that he never considered that it was the countess standing in attendance on the queen. Emalie had witnessed his every reaction and word to the news that he would wed and never did she betray herself. She could not, however, contain her feelings when he had laughed as he was formally presented to her by the queen. A breach of protocol, but one that he could not control.

The reaction that had given him hope was the one that had coursed through his body when he saw her standing by the fire in her chambers. The flames once again revealed her womanly curves through the gown she wore and once he had lifted her hair from the entrapment of the woolen shawl she held like a shield around her, its silky feel encouraged him to touch it and her. Barely grazing his knuckles over her skin had caused a blush to spread up her neck and over her cheeks. As he watched her respond to his touch, Christian had hoped that all would proceed as it should, but it had not.

He was blessed and cursed with a wife who seemed to be all the things a noblewoman should be—capable, efficient, demure in public and passionate in private. He could understand after watching her for just one day how a woman like Emalie, with her titles and riches, her accomplishments and abilities, and her subtle sexual charisma, could become the center of a plot by John and his cronies. The man who controlled her gained a large portion of England—well-maintained, productive estates that would provide for those attached to them. The man who took her got her riches, as well, and titles with which to earn even more. The man who married her had a wife whose earthy allure and health promised many heirs to carry on his name and honor.

Emalie Montgomerie was the perfect wife for a man like him—suitably titled, wealthy and of marriageable age. All the things that had made her the perfect target for John's plans. For now, he had her, controlled her and her wealth and lands. And he would continue to do so at Richard's command until the truth was known.

Controlled as long as they both kept secret their delay of the consummation of their vows. Her request had canceled his need to explain his physical difficulties and had saved him an incredible amount of embarrassment. But it had also given her a true reason for repudiation in spite of Eleanor's demand that there be none. Mayhap his temporary difficulty was not the blessing he called it?

Another thought troubled him. If his wife was involved with John's attempts to wrest control of England from Richard, he had just provided her with an escape from this union. What would Richard say to that? However, had he the need to extricate himself from this union, he could do so now in good faith. He would be able to swear on his honor that he had not consummated the marriage.

It was a possibility, although a narrow one, that he would need this later, and bloody sheets could be explained and the physician appointed to treat him by the king could attest to his physical limitations. Not that he would want that known, of course, since it would put a doubt on his ability to produce an heir for his estates and titles. But it was good to have an escape route planned when one went into battle.

And he felt as though this was the battle of his life, even more important than his daily struggles to stay alive while in prison, for the life he had saved was nothing without his honor. And fulfilling this task set before him would regain his honor.

Christian stood and stretched once more before snuffing out the candles left burning around his chamber. Of necessity he would leave his door closed this night, since anyone passing could glance in and see that he did not sleep with his bride. Taking a few deep breaths in and forcing them out, he tried to let go of the tension in his body. In the next few weeks, he would eat and sleep and train with the knights to regain his strength and his form. And when he was once again himself, he would discover his wife's secrets and decide whether or not to take her to his bed and claim her for himself…a wife in fact, not only in name.

Dropping his robe to the floor, he climbed into his bed and lay on his side, awaiting sleep. It came, in his physically exhausted state, quickly.

Chapter Seven

Emalie knelt in the chapel and thanked the Lord she had survived her wedding night. She knew, of course, that simply making it through that particular night and its peculiar change of events was no guarantee of future safety, but she would take this reprieve and make the best of it.

The morning had found her chamber filled with those who wanted to witness the priest bless the couple and who wanted to see the proof of her lost innocence. The mark on the sheet was suitably sized and apparently satisfied those who saw it. If Alyce or Sir Walter were surprised to see it, they gave no sign. Her husband had scrambled from the bed, gifted her with a kiss on her cheek and then disappeared into his chambers. As her women surrounded and took care of her, Emalie remained lost in her own thoughts. Soon, she found herself in the hall breaking her fast with her husband. The morning continued to move around her at some surreal pace and when Christian announced his plans for the day, she had asked to accompany him.

"My lord, I would join you and show you my...your

lands.'' She rose as he did, intent on being the one to guide him through the keep and village.

"Nay, my lady. Please consider this a day of rest. Sir Walter and Fitzhugh will be more than adequate for my needs.'' He lifted her hand to his lips and lightly touched it. "I am certain that riding would be somewhat uncomfortable for you.''

The nervous laughter and the deeper chuckling from the men spread through those watching and listening and told her that word of the bloody sheets had been shared and their marriage was believed consummated. She was safe, but at what cost?

He stepped back and turned away from her, motioning to the two men nearest to follow him. Anger and pride straightened her spine and she took a step toward his retreating figure.

"My lord? I would ask your leave to ride along with you. I assure you, I will not hold up your progress.''

Christian stopped and turned back to her. Although the smile never left his face, she saw the intensity in his eyes and knew she had overstepped herself. Her body's first reaction was to back away from him as he approached.

"The queen has gone as she told us she would and I am familiar with the uproar that comes with both the arrival and departure of one of the royal family. I am certain that there is much to do here to reclaim the household as our own. See to that, my lady.''

He nodded at her, his gaze never leaving hers. The challenge was clear in his voice and his stare. Without thought, she began to reply and was stopped by his whispered warning.

"Acquiesce *in this,* Emalie,'' he said in an undertone so that no one could hear his words but she. "Do not force me to embarrass you before those you call yours.''

Blinking at his words, Emalie's breath held at his threat. What would he reveal to her people? She could not take the chance.

''The morning's weather looks promising, my lord,'' she said, loud enough for her words to carry through the hall. ''I am pleased that you can take advantage of such a day to see Greystone at its best.'' Then, lowering her head, she eased into a deep curtsy before him.

''Fare thee well, my lady,'' he said as he turned and walked away from her.

She rose from her curtsy and found that her legs shook. Once Christian was gone from the hall, she sought the quiet of the chapel. And she had spent a good hour in prayer before her maid sought her out.

''Milady, he means to hear grievances later today.''

At first, Emalie was not sure who Alyce spoke of. Then the reality sank into her consciousness. Her new husband, the Earl of Harbridge, would supplant her in this important duty. Hearing the complaints of her people and dispensing justice was something that Emalie had done since her father's death. Desperation filled her at the thought of someone other than a Montgomerie carrying out the lord of the manor's duties.

''Did you hear me, milady? He is planning to…''

Emalie understood completely and clearly, probably even more so than her faithful servant. Christian was moving to consolidate his position now that he was Earl of Harbridge.

''He has the right,'' she whispered.

She had known this moment would come; sooner or later she would have married and her husband would have taken control of her estates—this was really no surprise to her. The only unexpected part was that it happened so quickly.

The only way to stop him would be to repudiate their vows, but that was simply not a possibility. Eleanor had found this man for a reason and Emalie was not prepared to risk her people's lives to avoid giving up her control.

"But milady, 'tis your right to hear complaints." Alyce's brows shifted into a frown, most likely waiting for Emalie to react more strongly to this encroachment on her rule over Greystone castle and village.

"No longer, Alyce. No longer. Now 'tis my husband's right."

The older woman clamped her lips shut as though trying not to reply. Shaking her head, Alyce nodded and stepped back after deciding not to argue this any longer. Her servant turned and left the chapel without another word.

It was a good thing, too, since Emalie could feel her own emotions raging within her and she did not think she could answer more questions. Bitterness at her fate and the loss of her father pulsed through her, making her stomach churn and her eyes sting with tears. A sense of loss pervaded her spirit—her parents gone and now she would watch as her power was eroded bit by bit by this man brought by Eleanor.

Looking up at the altar, she wondered if the Almighty was there, as the priests taught. And if He was there, was he listening to her prayers? Prayers sent daily begging for protection, for understanding and especially for acceptance of her new circumstances. Some requests, it would seem, had been heard, others ignored.

Her hardest task was yet to come and Emalie real-

ized she needed to yield to her new husband's attempts
to become the Earl of Harbridge before her people.
Those who lived and worked at Greystone must come
first, as her parents had taught her. As a noblewoman
and as a Montgomerie, she had responsibilities to carry
out and this marriage was the first step of many. If
Christian was to protect her and her people, he needed
to be accepted by them and seen by those who threatened the safety and well-being of Greystone as a com-
petent warrior who would not be defeated.

Emalie bowed her head in respect and then walked
out of the quiet stone room where she often sought
comfort and a respite from her duties when they overwhelmed her. As Christian had said, a visit from roy-
alty, especially a protracted one, caused many problems
for a household and she needed to right things within
Greystone's keep and village. For now she would give
her attention fully to that task and try to put her other
worries from her mind.

Emalie had been correct—the usually unsettled
weather in this area had cooperated with his desire to
tour the village and surrounding properties of Greystone Castle. The sun had become an ally and broken
through the clouds enough to make the day warm and
dry. Unfortunately, his body betrayed him once more.

Christian looked at his escort with envy—Walter
was a robust man, filled with life and endurance. Without meaning to, Christian rubbed his hand down his
chest and felt the bones now so close beneath his skin.
He would need to live on his reputation as a tournament champion and warrior until he regained his
strength and form. God willing, with food and training,
he would feel more himself quickly.

It was only midmorn and he was exhausted. Walter had led him through the village and toward some of the outlying properties first. They'd visited several larger farms, all belonging to the Montgomerie family, and now his. Well-fed children ran from the houses to greet him as he was introduced to the tenants and to some of his new vassals. Herds of cattle and sheep grazed in pastures, fattening for the kill. The fields were filled with abundance, crops of all kinds that would fill their larder through the winter and feed the people.

As Fitzhugh opened the records at each stop to show him the harvest and planting and the costs of each farm, he was struck again with the abilities of his new wife. Apparently not contented with letting her steward and castellan work without guidance after her father's death, Emalie had stepped in and made many decisions about the running of her estates, decisions that seemed both well thought out and successful. A wife fit for a nobleman with many estates.

But at what cost? How had her properties escaped John's pillaging? Why did Richard suspect her? He felt as though he was working in the dark without clues or information to guide his efforts. His attention was drawn to the sound of someone clearing their throat.

"Aye, Sir Walter?" He acknowledged the man with a nod.

"Would you care to take a short rest, my lord? The heat grows stronger now," Walter asked in a gruff voice.

Christian rubbed the sweat from his brow with the back of his hand and nodded. Given an excuse, he would take it, for he was not far from falling from the mount he rode. The small group of men directed their horses off the road and into a copse of trees. Dismounting, each man took out a skin of wine or ale and refreshed himself. Looking through the trees, Christian walked into the shadows to relieve himself.

The sound of rushing water gained his attention and, when done with personal tasks, he followed it until he found a fast-running stream. Kneeling beside it, he scooped water with his hands and splashed his face, head and neck. Then he drank of the water and let it cool his throat.

"Although we are still on Harbridge lands, it is probably not a good idea to stray alone from the road into the woods." Walter stood but a few yards away.

"Outlaws? Here?" Christian wiped his mouth and face with his hands and turned to face Walter.

"Lawlessness still reigns the edges of Harbridge, my lord. My lady's father was not completely successful in that regard."

Christian stood and faced Walter. "And tell me of the late Earl of Harbridge. What kind of man was he?"

"A fair man, my lord. One who considered his properties and the people who served him as his responsibilities."

"Unlike many?" Christian probed.

"England has become a dangerous place since Richard was captured. Many lords turned a blind eye to all that happened around them and the common people suffered."

"Why has it become such a place?"

Walter stuttered at first then explained. "The infighting of the Plantagenets has hurt all those who serve them, from villeins to lords. Surely I tell you nothing that you do not already know?"

Of course he knew this, but Christian wanted to determine what this man so integral to the running of the estate believed. The Plantagenet games emanated from his own country and he knew well of John's land-grabbing efforts over the last several years. Since Richard cared little for the dreary, cold land of England, he had looked away from John's antics. It was only during Richard's imprisonment, when John began using England's resources to pay Richard's enemies, that Eleanor began exercising more control. Or trying to.

Christian began walking back toward the road as they talked. "And why did Montgomerie never make suitable arrangements for his daughter? Especially with so much danger surrounding them?"

"He did, my lord," Walter answered quickly then he paused. "But that was no concern of mine."

"One would think that as castellan, everything that affects this demesne is your concern."

"I still think you should ask the lady about that, my lord."

Christian heard the insolence in Walter's reply and looked back at the man. Walter would not meet his gaze. Obviously torn between his former lord and the new one, the castellan chose discretion. Deciding it was best to find out how far the man would go to protect his lady, Christian asked, "If I ordered you to tell me what you seek to hide, would you, Sir Walter?"

The older man rose to his full height and did not attempt to hide his disdain. "Nay, my lord. I will protect my lady at all times."

"But she does not need protection from me." Irritation entered his voice and he did not try to lessen it. Let the man hear his anger.

"So you say, my lord."

Silence grew between them. Christian faced Sir Walter and crossed his arms over his chest. Even in fit form, he could not match the man's height or bulk. But power was in his hand.

"I could have you removed from your post, even from Greystone itself. What say you now?"

Walter squinted as the sun's rays broke through the branches above them. He took in a deep breath and exhaled loudly.

"Aye, my lord, you could do that and more, if you chose to. But I still say that you should ask the lady these questions and not me."

A measure of pride glinted in the man's eyes as he stood his ground against these inquiries into his lady's history. Christian weighed this against any possible efforts to force disclosure and knew he had lost the challenge. He turned and walked the distance to his horse. Mounting, he called out to the men. "We ride on now."

With a flurry of activity, the small contingent of guards mounted and moved onto the road. Fitzhugh and then Walter took their places in the lead and the group moved down the road to their next destination. Although he knew the guards were confused, he said not a word to them or to Fitzhugh, who glanced surreptitiously in his direction and Walter's.

There was more to the Lady Emalie and her availability for marriage. Had there been someone else before him? Another betrothed? And what had occurred to stop that marriage? Unfortunately, there was no one else within Greystone he could ask, for he feared they would all be just as protective of Emalie. And he would have disclosed more about his mission than he should.

Realizing that retreat was at some times a strategic move, he decided to observe more and question less until he was more secure in his position. He would begin his new approach this afternoon while he held manor court...or he would if he survived long enough to return to the castle.

Chapter Eight

He was limping badly by the time he entered the hall. Slowing his pace did not help, nor did holding himself erect and imagining the humiliation of having to pick himself up from the floor. It was sheer determination that moved his feet forward to the table on the raised dais. And it was pure stubbornness that he would not permit himself to call a halt to the proceedings and find his bed.

He must be seen as hearty and able to defend what was his. Scavengers could smell weakness and he would not bring them to Greystone. A lord not able to carry out his responsibilities did not deserve to have them. And his honor, already assaulted and trampled upon, would not allow him to surrender in this.

Christian dragged his weakened body up the several steps and sat down hard on the large chair at the center of the table. Lucky for him, a large pillow cushioned his descent and did not cause him further harm on landing. An efficient servant handed him a goblet of wine which he drank in one long swallow. A platter of cheeses, cold meats and bread followed, but he could not decide if he was more tired than hungry and so he sat for a few minutes just trying to stay upright.

Some villagers gathered in the hall in anticipation of his hearing of grievances. Christian fought to appear awake, but the effort simply added to his exhaustion. Fitzhugh's approach forced him to turn.

"My lord, would you prefer that we cancel today's proceedings?"

Christian, in truth, would have liked nothing better, but his headstrong nature would not let him. "Nay, Fitzhugh. We will hold the manor court this day as planned."

Fitzhugh did not argue with him, but he bowed and nodded to several other servants standing nearby. A few guards drew near to the dais and took positions on either side of the steps leading to the table.

"My lord?" Fitzhugh stood next to him once again and leaned down. "Would you like to eat before we begin?"

Christian could hardly believe the words that left his mouth, but he could only blame his fatigue. "Nay, Fitzhugh. Let us begin now, for the sooner begun, the sooner finished." He roused himself and held out his cup for more wine. This time he tasted the vintage and found it wanting. Mayhap he would send word to his estate and have them send several barrels of his best. Putting the cup down away from the documents that the steward laid before him, Christian examined the parchments in preparation.

There were a few requests from villeins and freemen regarding proposed marriages, grants of land and disputes. He had watched his father hold court many times and felt at ease. A young man sat at the end of the table, quill, knife, parchment and ink at hand to record the decisions as they were made. Fitzhugh had a guard go to the door of the hall and call out the announcement that the lord was present and would hear from those who had grievances.

As a throng of people entered, Christian wished he had canceled this. He was nigh to passing out and wondered if his decisions would be sound ones. A passing thought to call for Emalie tickled his mind, but he motioned for Fitzhugh to begin.

Two hours and two dozen decisions later, Christian finally gave in to the demands of his body and told Fitzhugh to end it. Although he thought he had made logical and fair settlements and resolved many questions brought to him, he did not want to continue and lose his ability to reason.

He now faced another challenge—getting up from the table and walking from the room. He had never felt so alone and nearer to defeat than this. Christian stood and the chair beneath him was immediately pulled away by an attending servant. Taking a deep breath, he walked the few paces to the end of the dais and, in spite of a stalwart effort, stumbled down the steps. When he thought he would fall to the floor, Fitzhugh called out.

"My lord? I know you are still unfamiliar with Greystone. Please allow Henry to show you the way back to your chambers and serve you as you need."

A boy, young but strong looking for his size, appeared before him and Christian decided that laying a hand on the boy's shoulder for support was far more appealing than landing on his face among the rushes on the floor. Christian made it out of the hall and down the corridor, but was almost daunted by the sight of the stairs before him. If he placed more of his weight on young Henry than he wanted to or more than he could bear, the boy never gave any indication.

As they approached his chamber, the hallway began to swerve and sway around him. Even his death grip on Henry's shoulder did him no good, for his legs began to shake and his vision blurred. Finally they reached the door and Christian entered. He took hold of a chair and waved the boy off.

"Henri, *pardon moi,* Henry. Please tell my lady that I wish not to be disturbed."

Henry bowed and backed out of the room, pulling the door closed behind him. Just as he thought to tell him not to close it tightly, the darkness surrounded him, pulling him into the void.

Emalie sat at the table, hands clasped in her lap, waiting for Christian to arrive for dinner. She was feeling quite proud of her self-control and of the accomplishments of her people today. Her cook had prepared delicacies sure to please her husband's sophisticated palate, recipes gleaned from Eleanor's own cook who had recently held sway over Greystone's kitchens. After the initial clash for power, the two cooks had become fast friends and exchanged many formulas for culinary masterpieces.

Control over her own behavior had come at a high cost today. After watching him return with Sir Walter and Fitzhugh and seeing him begin the manor court without even inviting her to be present, Emalie had returned to her chamber. Witnessing him in her father's place had ripped a hole in her heart and forced her to her bed, incapacitated by tears and grief. How long had it been since she had held her father's lifeless body in her arms and known that her life was now going to be so very different than when she had awoken that day?

Due to her father's unexpected death she went from daughter to orphan, from partner in the management of her estates to ward of the king and from lady to countess. And she liked none of the changes, then or now.

And the pressure was changing her—from confident woman to an emotional creature who cried at any small upset. Would she ever feel as though she was herself again? After seeing this man begin to take over her duties and her power, she instinctively knew the answer.

Now she found herself resentful that he could not arrive at dinner on time. Alyce had urged her to go easily with him, to allow him time to accommodate himself to Greystone and their way of doing things. In truth, it was a difficult thing to do while under the close scrutiny of those living within the keep.

Murmurs filled the room about his obvious absence and Emalie endured the curious stares of those closest to the dais. Sir Walter and his wife Rosalie were seated near her at the high table and they looked just as uncomfortable as she felt. Emalie motioned to one of the servants and whispered to him to seek out her husband and "invite" him to dinner now.

She lifted her goblet to her lips and hoped the wine would soothe her nerves. Instead, a bitter taste flowed over her tongue and she grimaced. Immediately, her attentive steward was at her side.

"Milady? Something is amiss with your wine?" Fitzhugh's brows gathered in a frown. He took all complaints very personally and the wine was his particular area of expertise.

He had started out as the vineyard master on one of

her more southerly properties and had guided the cultivation and harvesting of the grapes and the production of the various wines used by her households. He had even created the wine she drank now as a special blend for her to mark the fifteenth anniversary of her birth. And the wine he brought to table had never tasted so badly as it did now.

"Mayhap this is an old keg? It seems to have gone to vinegar."

He looked for her permission before taking her wine and sipping it himself. Another frown crossed his brow. "It is the same as it was yesterday, milady."

"I noticed a difference in it last evening as well, but forgot to mention it to you, Fitzhugh."

A ripple of soft laughter echoed through the hall, and when she realized what last evening had been, she could feel the heat of a blush creep up her neck and onto her cheek. Only the return of the servant she'd sent looking for her husband kept her from reacting to the embarrassment of the moment.

"Well, Henry. Did you find my lord?" Her voice trembled, probably from a bit of resentment and a bit of embarrassment at the ribald comments she could still hear.

"Aye, milady. He is in his chambers."

"Did you invite him to our meal?"

"Nay, milady." The boy shifted from foot to foot and kept his gaze lowered to the floor rather than meeting hers.

"Why not, Henry?" Impatience must have entered her voice, for Fitzhugh came forward once more and whispered something to the lad. The boy nodded once and again and then looked up at her.

"Milord said he did not wish to be disturbed."

"When did he say this, Henry?" She turned in her chair to face him.

"When I escorted him to his chambers, milady. Earlier this afternoon."

"Well then, Fitzhugh, if my lord husband does not wish to be disturbed, I see no reason to hold up our meal any longer. You may tell the kitchen to begin serving the food."

Fitzhugh hesitated for only a moment, but it was a moment too many for her in her current state of mind. She glared at the steward until he carried out her order, and it was indeed an order and not to be ignored or misunderstood.

Servants rushed forward carrying platters for those at the high table and those below. Haunches of beef, game birds dressed with seasonings and covered in pungent sauces, roasts of mutton, all crispy and hot, were delivered and the smells of the well-prepared foods filled the hall.

Soon all were eating, except for Emalie, who found that her appetite had fled once more. The enticing smell of her favorite dishes now seemed offensive somehow, as though tainted and unappealing. Breaking off a chunk of bread, she chewed it while the others ate the heartier fare. She sat quietly, not even trying to converse with the others.

This rude behavior on Christian's part was a puzzle to her. Why was he doing this? Sitting court in her hall, she could understand. It was part of his need to gather everything in Greystone and in her Harbridge estates under his control. Or maybe he was just uncomfortable here? He had arrived under orders of the king and been married within a day. He had no one from his household with him to serve him and had none of his own vassals or guardsmen.

Emalie took a sip of the ale that now replaced her bitter wine. Mayhap he was just standoffish, as most French and Angevin nobles were to English subjects of the Plantagenets. Putting the cup down, she wiped her mouth with her napkin and stood, waiting for the servant behind her to pull her chair away. When others at the table began to rise, she stopped them.

"I wish to retire early this night. Pray, continue with your meal and enjoy the entertainment I have arranged for your pleasure."

Although every one of those at the table knew she had made all these efforts to please her husband, they would never contradict her words to her face nor behind her back. Stepping away from the table, she walked down the steps and out through the hall, fighting back more inexplicable tears the entire way. Finally out of the hall, she climbed the stairs to the top floor and made her way to her chambers. Passing her husband's door, she spied young Henry standing silently before it.

"Has he spoken to you?"

"No, milady. Not since he ordered me from his chambers."

"Has he not called for food or drink?" She walked closer to the boy to hear his whispered words.

"No, milady."

"And is he alone?" Another suspicion entered her mind. If she had denied his physical needs would he take another to satisfy them?

"I wouldn't know, milady." Henry looked away, clearly understanding her question even at his young age.

"Go to the kitchen and have them prepare a tray for my lord. Bring it here when it is ready."

"But, milady. He said *you* were not to disturb him."

She paused, fighting to keep her surprise and hurt contained. She would reveal nothing of what she felt to this boy.

"I have given you an order, Henry. Go to the kitchens now."

Although he hesitated for a moment, the boy bowed and left, leaving her to contemplate her next move. Emalie leaned close to the door and listened for sounds within. If her husband had mentioned her in particular in his order not to be disturbed, it seemed logical and somehow respectful that he would not want her to know of his assignations. It did not mitigate her anger, but it made her curious about not asking for food. Those involved in bedplay usually needed food and drink to bolster their strength.

She waited for the tray to arrive and, with it, her excuse for entry. But a small, niggling thought kept entering her mind. She shook it off and leaned against the wall. There it was again—a slight shiver ran through her and she knew that something was not right. She lifted the latch of the door even as she knocked lightly on it.

"My lord? Are you within?" she called out in a low voice. "My lord..."

Pushing open the door slowly and quietly, she could see the empty bed first and then, as she stepped within the chamber, she saw him slumped on the floor. Rushing to his side, she lifted his head gently and saw that he was still breathing. The heat emanating from his skin and body told her the problem—he was ill, very ill.

Letting his head rest once more upon the floor, she rushed from the room seeking help. She directed the first servant she saw to bring Alyce and Sir Walter to the chamber and returned to Christian. Turning him until he lay flat on the floor, she then pulled down the bedcovers so that he could be placed there without delay when help arrived.

Although she knew only a few minutes passed, it seemed like hours until she finally heard the clamor of approaching people in the hallway outside the chamber. Sir Walter entered first, followed by Alyce and then others. Within moments, her husband had been placed on the bed and her herb chest was on its way to her, along with other supplies she might need.

Alyce efficiently cleared the chamber of all but herself and Sir Walter and then waited for directions. Emalie placed a cold compress on Christian's brow and wiped his face and throat with a rag dipped in herbs and cool water. For the first time, he stirred beneath her hands.

"I...have...been...ill," he whispered in words forced out.

"You *are* ill, my lord. Lie quietly and let me try to rid you of the fever."

He grabbed her wrist as she reached for the compress on his head and held her still. "I have been ill," he repeated, and he tried to rise from the bed. He pushed his hair out of his fever-glazed eyes and collapsed before she could ask Walter for help.

Looking at him with a healer's eyes, Emalie saw once more the signs of illness that she had first seen while he slept in his bath. Whatever his affliction had been, it had taken its toll on him. Now the fever was back upon him and needed to be treated.

Realizing that fever was more effectively treated when the whole body was bathed in cool water, she began to unlace his tunic and the linen shirt beneath it. Her hands shook as she unbuckled the belt at his waist, but she noted that the holes used now were not the well-worn ones farther out in the leather. Her husband had lost weight since wearing this belt and these clothes.

"Milady? Would you like some help with that?" Alyce asked softly from her place next to Emalie. "Why do you not see to the brews you will need and Sir Walter and I can take care of this."

Emalie nodded and saw that her truth was known to both of them. How had they known? They should have expected the bloody sheets. Christian would have needed to confirm his claim should the need arise. Had she given herself away by word or deed?

She walked to the table, opened and searched her chest of herbs and powders and prepared a beverage for him with watered wine, herbs to lower the fever and others to give him strength. The sheet had just been placed over him when she finished. It took a long time to get the drink down his throat in small amounts, coaxing it swallow by swallow until he finished it. Smoothing his hair out of his face, she laid his head back down and adjusted the pillow beneath it.

"He has already lost so much weight, he can not afford more from this fever. Tell the cook to prepare a beef stock as soon as possible."

"Aye, milady." Alyce curtsied and left the room quietly.

"You were with him all morning, Walter. Did you see any sign of this illness?"

"He looked tired, milady, that is all."

She looked at her faithful castellan and then at her husband on the bed. "Did he say anything to alert you to this?"

"We spoke of the estates and the harvests and the strength of our fighting force." He paused and met her gaze for a moment. "And he asked about your father and about you."

"And what did you tell him of my father and of me?"

"I refused to answer his questions and told him to speak to you."

"Walter, that was dangerous. We know him not. He could have had you removed from Greystone for defying him."

Emalie stood and filled the cup with more wine. Her hands shook now at the thought of the actions her husband could take against a recalcitrant vassal. She needed Walter here, she needed him with his responsibilities intact and she needed him safe.

When the drink was ready, she sat next to her ailing husband and began forcing the brew into him again. "Pray, please tell me how he reacted."

"He told me all the ways he could punish me for disobeying him and then he walked away."

She stopped and looked at him. "I do not understand. Why did he allow you to refuse him?"

Footsteps and voices approached the chamber, so he whispered his words.

"I think 'twas a testing, milady. I think he was assessing the loyalty of those here and he got his answer in my refusal."

Emalie wiped some of the wine off Christian's chin as it spilled from his mouth. Her efforts to get him to drink were partially successful, but he would need much more in order to rid his body of this fever. Laying his head down, she looked at Walter.

"He looks starved. Look how his bones show through his skin here," she said, pointing to his chest and his shoulders. "It takes some time to lose this much fat and muscle. What could have done this?"

Walter walked over to her side and looked more closely. "How do you know how much he had?"

"The queen talked about his fitness and his success at tourney. A man can not win without strength and size." She heard Alyce's voice outside the door and finished her comments. "I suppose we will have to wait until he can speak of it…if he will speak of it."

Alyce entered with more supplies and Emalie was caught up in the care of her husband. Luckily, it was not as serious a fever as she first thought and it responded quickly to her various treatments. After a long night, the morning arrived and her husband woke, weakened but hungry.

Christian felt as though someone had hit him repeatedly over the head with a hammer. His mouth was dry, but his scalp was sweat dampened. Efforts to lift his head from the pillow seemed futile. His attempts did not go unnoticed.

"My lord, you are awake?"

Emalie fussed over him, adjusting the pillow and the sheet. Glancing around the room, he saw the remnants of a healer's treatments—bowls, a chest of herbs, mixing accoutrements and a roaring fire in the hearth.

"What happened? I only remember returning here after…" His words drifted off as his thoughts did. He remembered struggling to remain upright in his chair as he heard the complaints and requests of the villagers.

He remembered struggling up the stairs with some help from a boy. And everything went dark after he entered his chambers.

"Henry said you gave orders that I was not to disturb you. I ask your pardon for invading your privacy against your orders." Emalie lowered her gaze and would not meet his.

"My lady, from the look and feel of this, it would seem to be a very good thing that you did so. I will not punish you for this transgression."

His weak attempt at humor was not successful, for his wife paled at his words. Since her color did not look its best, he felt somewhat ashamed by the results of his jest.

"Peace, my lady," he said, raising his hand between them. "'Twas a poor try at humor on my part."

He grinned and he feared that with his weakness, it was more of a grimace than a true smile. Shifting in the bed, his skin shivered beneath the sheets and he realized he was naked but for the covers. He tugged the bedclothes up higher around him, trying to cover the sores and gaunt figure that was his body.

She must have noticed his discomfort, for Emalie rose from her seat by the bed, went to a trunk placed along the wall and reached inside. She brought a clean shirt to him and turned away while he sat up and pulled it over his head. Settling back down, he watched a blush fill her cheeks as she faced him over the bed.

He thought of how to begin, of what to say, to explain the physical condition she had witnessed during her care of him this past night. Christian also needed to find out who else had seen him during the night.

"You look exhausted, my lady. I thank you for your

care. It has obviously been successful for me, but at great cost to you.''

She lifted her hand and pushed her loose hair back from her face and over her shoulders. Every movement of hand and face was graceful, flowing without evidence of the exhaustion she must feel if she had been by his side through the night.

''And please pass my gratitude on to the healer whose ingredients were so helpful to you.''

She blinked several times and then stared at him. His brain was muddled and he did not seem to be able to say the correct thing in this strange situation. He had not expected to wake up naked with his virgin wife standing over him. But then, nothing in his life had been within his expectations over these past several months. He let out a breath and tried once more.

''I have been ill and it seems that the illness has not left me as completely as I had hoped. I do not mean to insult you or yours here with my words or actions.''

''I thought you were doing just that last night by your refusal to attend dinner.'' Almost deceptively soft, her words were filled with hurt, a hurt that he had not intended to cause. Before he could speak, she continued. ''I should have recognized the illness in your gait and in your face.''

''You? You are the healer?'' This was astounding— was there no end to her talents and abilities?

She drew back and he realized he had done it yet again. He took her hand just before she moved too far away from him.

''My mother had some measure of healing talents, but the bulk of the work was done by our herbalist. If I misunderstood…''

''Nay, my lord. I, too, have an herbalist in charge

of the gardens and preparing the herbs and concoctions. He is the truly talented one. I fear that yesterday and last night have simply taxed my strength more than I realized. I am not usually so sensitive to words and actions.''

He noted a sense of sarcasm in her words and felt some relief and nodded at her. ''My lady, since you have begun these treatments, tell me what I must do to heal and be well.''

''Your illness, my lord? Tell me what caused this.'' Her gaze moved down his figure from head to toes and he felt as though she could see through the sheet and shirt that covered him.

Uncomfortable with revealing any details of his imprisonment to her, he hedged his words. In spite of her efforts, he did not know her, and her actions and motivations were all to be scrutinized.

''I do not wish to speak of it now. You have seen the results of it...tell me how to regain my strength.''

If she was surprised by his refusal, she did not show it. Instead, she launched into a list of suggestions about how to return to his past vim and vigor. Many of them were the same as recommended by Richard's physician, but she improved on even those with several of her own. A knock at the door interrupted their conversation. Emalie's maid entered with a tray and handed it to her lady. A few whispered words were exchanged and then he was alone with his wife.

''You may begin with this, my lord, and then you should rest. I will send young Henry to you to assist you in...other matters.'' He was certain she blushed at this reference to personal hygiene and functions.

''You should rest as well.''

''There are tasks that must be done, my lord. I will rest this evening.''

She placed the tray on the table and helped him to sit up. Although he accepted her help with the first few spoonfuls of the hearty broth, he soon waved her away with thanks for all she had done. She turned and walked slowly to the door, glancing at something on the shelf near the trunk of clothes. He wondered if she realized that she sighed while looking there. After a slight pause, she left, closing the door behind her.

He sat up straighter and tried to see what had affected her so. 'Twas only his belt, rolled and stored there. Then he knew what she had seen—her ring of keys. He sank back and finished as much of the meal as he could, while thinking on his arrangement with the king.

A part of him wished he could simply accept this marriage and Emalie as part of the king's largesse. A place deep within him longed for the peace and tranquillity of well-run estates. Another part of him, that place within where memories lived on, desired a welcoming wife and family and sons.

He lifted the tray from his lap and put it back on the table. Henry had not yet arrived and, truth be told, he wanted nothing more right now than to go back to sleep. Sliding down on the bed, he wondered if he should be honest with her and seek his answers that way. Mayhap if she knew her estates and people were in danger of being lost, she would reveal all to him.

Nay, in his experience women did not think that way. And if she were involved with John, he would be acknowledging his own position as Richard's spy. 'Twas best to wait and watch. And his wife would have to accustom herself, as difficult as he knew it would be for her, to his control over Greystone and everything that belonged to the Earl of Harbridge.

Including Emalie, the Countess of Harbridge.

Chapter Nine

If Emalie had thought that the sight of her key ring, *her keys,* lying on the shelf with his belt was difficult to accept, it was nowhere near as painful as what she faced over the next few weeks. Removed from her duties, she had little to do except observe as her new husband consolidated control and began to gain the acceptance of her people. Walter was his almost constant companion, as he studied the ways of Greystone and made changes he deemed necessary.

She hurt too much to look at it objectively. Every adjustment made to accommodate him and his desires about how or when to do something and whose duties remained the same or varied tore at her heart and her memories of life before him. Emalie had become so accustomed to discussing the administration of the estates with her father that not doing so left a gaping hole in her life and in her soul.

In his favor, she would admit that he was scrupulously polite, always came to dinner and had followed each of her recommendations aimed to improve his health. 'Twould seem to be working, too, for he was gaining weight and stamina with each passing day. And he was abiding by their agreement not to consummate their vows. Actually, other than dinner or a chance meeting, she saw and heard little of him.

Emalie stood and walked away from the embroidery hoop and paced across the solar to look out the window. A warm breeze passed over her. She closed her eyes and enjoyed its soft touch on her skin. Mayhap she had spent too much time indoors. These melancholy feelings were not something she was familiar with in her life. She was usually just too busy to sink into this self-examination. She needed to do something.

Glancing back at the women working attentively on their sewing and embroidery tasks, she felt so out of place. Even at her mother's behest, she had never spent much time in this room. 'Twas only since the queen's stay that she showed up here on a regular basis. Now, with all that her husband oversaw, she feared this would be her residence for some time. Watching Alyce, she waited for her maid to look up from her work. A good brisk walk outside might lift her spirits, and the sunbeams playing over the ground beneath the window drew her to them.

"Alyce, I will return anon," she said as she crossed the room to the door and opened it. The other women in the room stood as she passed them. Waving them down, she stopped in the doorway. "The day is too fair and beckons me out. Will any of you join me?"

Murmurs and soft laughter met her words. 'Twas obvious that the other women were quite content to work in the quiet of the solar and not go outside at all. Giving them one more chance to accept her invitation, she left. In a way, she welcomed being alone for a time. Making her way through the hall, she nodded to those who greeted her and tried not to see their sympathetic glances. All in Greystone knew how much she had lost even as her husband gained, but, she told herself for the hundredth time this week, 'twas the way of things.

A guard opened the large door leading out to the courtyard and Emalie walked down the steps. Enjoying the warming bursts of wind and sun, she walked briskly around the keep to the outside gate of the herb garden. Work was what she needed to divert her thoughts and worries. There was no sign of Timothy, the gardener and herbalist, so she found the leather apron always left hanging on a nail near the gate and strode down the main aisle, examining the various patches and beds of medicine and cooking herbs. He was most likely within the keep in the workroom or outside the walls gathering those plants that grew better wild than cultivated in the gardens. Kneeling down near an overgrown bed, Emalie reveled in the quiet hard work of clearing weeds from around the plants and soon lost track of time.

Alyce's calling finally broke into her reverie and she stood. Her hands and the edges of her sleeves were coated with the dark rich earth of the gardens. Unable to resist, she lifted them to her nose and inhaled the heady aroma of the fertile muck.

"Milady, the lord calls for you. Visitors are arriving." Alyce rushed to her and untied the straps of the apron, tsking over the coating of dirt on her. "He said to make haste."

"Do you know who comes to Greystone, Alyce? Did my husband say?" Emalie hurried to remove the apron and shook as much of the dirt from her hands as possible. Using water from a bucket kept near the cistern, she washed as best she could and followed Alyce inside. This time she took the back stairway up to her chambers.

In spite of her bulk, Alyce moved quickly and efficiently and, within a few minutes, Emalie's hair was recaptured under a veil and coronet, the dirt and sweat had been washed from her and she wore a fresh gown and tunic. With a deep breath, she hastily left her room and used the front stairway to the great hall.

The laughter and chatter of many people reached her on the second landing and she quickened her steps. Just as she entered the room, she witnessed her husband grab one of the men, a man much younger than himself, and pull him into a hug. Emalie stopped and watched this group of strangers. She realized that they were unknown to her but obviously very familiar to Christian. 'Twas then that she noticed her people stood away from this group, aloof and watching these exchanges of greetings. Since the group was speaking in their own dialect, most of her household did not understand it.

Christian looked at Fitzhugh, and her steward nodded in answer. Without other directions, two of the newly arrived guards assisted the younger man and followed Fitzhugh out of the hall. Her husband watched the man's departure with concern in his expression and then turned back to the group, moving through it, greeting each one personally, whether they be men or women. And the group was a mix of people—some looked noble in bearing and dress, some looked coarser. They were old and young and in between. As he finished, he caught sight of her and called her to him.

"My lady, come meet my retainers from my other estates."

They bowed and curtsied respectfully as she approached. Christian took her hand and led her to the front of the group. Then he introduced her to them.

"This is Emalie Dumont, my wife and Countess of Harbridge and Langier."

It struck her then, as he used those words, that just as he had gained the rights to her properties, she was now lady of his. When she looked at those before her, she noticed that they were also stunned by this declaration, but probably for a different reason than she.

Christian nodded at one of the men and he came forward before her. "This is my oldest friend, Sir Luc Delacroix. Luc, greet my wife and present yours to her."

Sir Luc escorted a woman to her and then both dropped in bow or curtsy before her. Taking her hand in his, the knight lifted it to his mouth and touched his lips briefly to the back of it. He was a handsome man, rumpled from traveling and wearing a mail coif under his hauberk, but his smile was full and genuine. The woman beside him was a surprise to her—not the usual pale French beauty, but a dark and exotic one. Her coloring was like none she had seen before and Emalie could not help but ask.

"Where does your wife come from, Sir Luc?"

The group quieted and she felt as though she had done something wrong. If she had, the knight before her gave no indication. He raised his wife to her feet and then smiled once more.

"My lady, my wife is from the Holy Lands. May I present Fatin Delacroix to you?"

The lady Fatin bowed her head again and waited for Emalie to acknowledge her before rising completely. She might be from a foreign land, but she understood the custom. Emalie had never met anyone from the Holy Lands before. Could this woman be a Jewess? Would a good Christian knight marry one of those people? Or even one of the other peoples who lived in the East? One of the infamous Saladin's people?

The silence grew around her and she knew her husband was waiting for her response to this woman, to this foreigner, for some reason. She had been raised and trained well enough to know how to do this, regardless of what she thought of the visitor.

"Lady Fatin and all of you, welcome to Greystone. Come to table and refresh yourselves." She pointed back to the tables at the end of the hall where servants were already preparing for them.

The tension was broken and the group followed her and Christian to the tables. Luc and Fatin sat next to her husband and soon were deep in conversation. She waited to be included, but it did not happen.

Not hungry, she picked at some bread and tried not to be offended. 'Twas obvious that he and his friends had been long separated and this reunion was both unexpected and welcomed.

A pang of jealousy filled her, for other than Fayth of Lemsley, she'd had no friends. Fayth was the daughter of one of her father's vassals and they had spent much time together as children. But, she sighed, less so since her mother's death a few years ago.

Without intending to, her sigh drew attention from those around her. Sir Luc spoke first.

"*Pardonnez moi,* my lady. 'Tis been too long since we shared table with Christian and we forgot ourselves."

Handsome and charming. Like many of the knights who accompanied Eleanor on her journeys and yet so unlike, for she detected no arrogance or false modesty in him.

"No offense was taken, sir. I was lost in my own thoughts, I fear, and not paying the attention I should have."

There was a certain repartee involved in conversation that she had learned during her time with Eleanor. With so few visitors from outside England, she had little practice with it. At least these knights from her husband's lands would give her that.

"Our thoughts were only to get here as quickly as possible and we did not send someone ahead to warn you of our coming, as guests should. But with Geoffrey weakened by the travel..."

His words trailed off and he turned to Christian who shook his head.

"Geoffrey? Was that the young man who left earlier? Is he your squire, my lord?"

Hushed chuckles and shushing spread throughout the group. One and all looked to Christian and she waited to be told of her error, for it was clear she had supposed incorrectly.

"Geoffrey is my brother," Christian said quietly, but his soft tone did nothing to lessen her embarrassment. If she could have slid down under the table and away from the scrutiny of her husband's people, she would have. Emalie could feel the heat pulsing in her cheeks and could not think of a word to say in response to this gaffe.

She knew if she reached for her cup, everyone would see her hand shaking, so she clasped them together on her lap. The silence grew and grew until it seemed to scream at her from all around.

He had not shared any of the details of his life with

her in these weeks since their wedding—she knew nothing of his family, other than the few details shared by Eleanor. Christian had never mentioned his own lands, until today, and never mentioned any siblings. What would his people think of his refusal or failure to make his family known to her?

The urge to escape was great and growing stronger and Emalie knew she must take her leave. Realizing that no one else could remedy this situation for her, for what could her husband say to explain her lack of knowledge, Emalie stood and addressed her husband.

"My lord, with your leave, I would like to check on Fitzhugh's arrangements for your guests."

If Christian wished to argue with her, he did not. Not hearing a word of dissent and not looking at him for any indication of refusal, Emalie picked up her skirts, nodded her head in a quick bow and left the table.

She found Fitzhugh and learned he already had the servants organizing the rooms needed and moving luggage so that the chambers would be ready for their guests quickly. She looked about for Christian's brother and found him in a small chamber near the stairs. It took but one glance to see that he was suffering from the same illness as his brother but not faring as well in his recuperation. A cough wracked the boy's body as she watched.

Since no one else seemed to be watching him, Emalie entered the room and helped him sit up. Holding him as the coughing continued, she laid her hand upon his chest and felt the wheezing within. In her thoughts, she prepared the necessary brew to ease the cough and strengthen his breathing. Once he quieted, she would gather the ingredients.

His breathing, though harsh and rasping, calmed a bit and she let him lie down once more. Emalie smoothed his hair back from his face and felt as though she were looking at her husband, some years ago. The resemblance between brothers was strong—hair, eyes, facial structure—all marked them as brothers.

And interestingly, both shared the same illness. Although 'twas clear that the younger fared much worse than the older, the signs and symptoms were the same. The treatments would be as well, except that she would add several others to this one's. Geoffrey slipped into an exhausted sleep and so she left the room. Christian was waiting for her in the corridor.

"My lady," he began, but she ignored him. Anger at her embarrassment in the hall grew within her. Emalie turned away from him and walked in the other direction. It would take longer to reach the workroom, but she could escape him.

"Emalie," he said, taking her by the arm and pulling her to a stop. Surprised by his action, she gasped. No one had ever handled her in this manner before. He released her quickly and instead blocked her path with his body. "I would speak to you."

She waited, not moving, not meeting his gaze. Staring down at her own clasped hands, she tried to calm herself. What could her husband say at this time?

"I believe I owe you an apology." When she did not respond, he continued. "Since Fitzhugh carries out most of your former duties, I did not have you informed about the approach of visitors. I beg your pardon for not alerting you to their arrival in a more timely manner."

If he had used a dagger, his words could not have hurt more. 'Twas very clear that he thought of her as a guest rather than his wife and had no need to tell her anything of importance. Still staring at her hands, she fought to contain her pain and the tears that now gathered in her eyes.

"And since he has performed most efficiently, you may return to whatever you were doing before this interruption."

The force of his words rocked her back on her heels, like a blow across her face would have. Trying to control the anger and humiliation was nigh to impossible and her temper got the best of her.

"Did you never think to tell me of your brother, my lord? Did you not think that *a wife* might be interested in knowing of her husband's family?"

"I did not think he would be coming here so soon, so I thought to tell you of him later."

"Are there others in your family who may arrive unexpectedly, my lord? A mother? A sister? Another brother? A wife should know these things."

His voice dropped in tone. "There is no one else, Emalie. Geoffrey and I are the last of the Dumonts...at least until you give me an heir."

Unable to soften her stance, she asked one more question. "Is his illness the same as that which plagued you, my lord?"

He stepped back from her and raised himself to his full height. New muscle filled his tunic, new strength filled his muscles. He was gaining vigor with each day and the presence of it so close was a bit unnerving to her.

"I have said that I will not discuss my illness with you and that has not changed. That Geoffrey suffers from the same matters not to you. Simply treat him as you did me."

He raised his arms over his head and stretched them out. She could not help but look. Then a terrible thought entered her mind—mayhap she should have told him the truth when he did not have the strength to hurt her. Alarmed, she bent down and escaped his block.

"Aye, my lord," she called out as she walked swiftly away from him. "I will get my medicaments now."

After a few strides, she gathered her skirts and ran the rest of the way down the corridor, ignoring any and all. Without thought, she headed for the one place where she could gather her control and her thoughts before facing him again.

"That was poorly done, brother."

Christian turned at Geoffrey's voice.

"I thought you asleep." He reentered the small room and approached the bed. "How do you feel?"

"Not as well as you, I can tell. You must be feeling much stronger if you can torment a lady." Geoff tried to sit up but gave up the struggle after a few moments.

Christian looked at the doorway and realized that Geoff could see and hear everything that passed between him and Emalie from his place on the bed. He grinned at his brother.

"Actually, I feel well enough now to train. And soon so shall you."

"If your ladywife gives me the correct brew and not the one she probably now has planned for you." Geoff laughed, a weak chuckle, but it was wonderful to hear. "Is she truly your wife?"

Not in all ways, he thought but did not say. But soon she would be, for with his returning strength came his desire for her. A desire that was pushing him to act on it and claim her in his bed. A desire that warred with his concerns of her loyalty. A desire and a wanting that interfered with his attempts to decide what place she should occupy in his life.

And since his efforts to determine her true character had turned up nothing untoward, he was now thinking about making the marriage a true one.

"Aye, she is my wife, given to me with lands and titles and riches by the king."

"At Chateau d'Azure, you would only say you had duties to carry out for the king in exchange for our freedom and our name. You said nothing about marrying."

"I knew nothing of the marriage when I arrived here. I was taken by surprise as much as you were by finding it out. Here now, enough talk of this. I came to make certain you are being well cared for."

Geoff laughed softly at him. "Aye, my lord, I am well." His face then grew serious. "However, from where I lie, your words hurt your wife's feelings most grievously. If you wish to do something, attend to her."

"Hurt her? Nay, she is but troubled over the changes I have brought here."

"You never did have an understanding of women, Christian."

"And for one so young, you claim an impossible knowledge of them, brother. Let it be for now and rest. I will visit you later."

Christian pulled the boy's cover higher onto his shoulders and mussed his hair. It felt incredibly good to have Geoff here with him. Walking out of the room, he wondered at Richard's actions. He had said Geoff could not join him for several months and yet, here he was. Sometimes Christian's head spun as he tried to trace and understand the machinations of the Plantagenets' mother and sons. And trying to discern Richard's true aim under this was impossible for him.

Was his brother correct? Had his rightful attempts to bring Greystone Castle and village under his control somehow hurt Emalie? Those in their social class knew the workings of a modern marriage, for whether in England or his native Poitou, the woman brought titles, land and money and the man controlled all of it.

But he had heard some rumors of her unconventional upbringing by her father, who treated her almost as a son. Oh, not in physical training, but in her control over the planning and records of their estates. Even the priest sang her praises, an accomplishment almost unheard-of. Mayhap this was the time to return to her the chatelaine's keys and control over the household that she once exercised? He would continue in all the lord's duties, of course, and make all the important decisions as was his role as lord.

He would seek her out later and make certain she understood his vision of how their marriage and their estates would work. For in that moment, he had decided to keep her and make theirs a true marriage. Once she knew that and they consummated their vows, she would know her place and all would be well.

Now that he had settled that, Christian sought out Luc for some swordplay.

Chapter Ten

She was tired.

It had been an extremely long and difficult day and she had decided to retire early and soak in a hot bath before bed. Alyce had prepared everything and assisted her and even now sat behind her brushing her hair in long strokes before the fire's heat.

Now she tried to let go of all the turmoil the day had brought. In spite of her exhaustion and her recent ability to fall asleep instantly, she felt completely awake and not ready to sleep at all. Noises and voices raised in talk came through the wall from her husband's chamber. She did not know who was in there now, but it sounded like male voices. After some laughter, the room next to hers was quiet once more.

The knock on their shared door was unexpected. At her nod, Alyce went to answer it, but Christian pushed it open first. With a motion of his head, he dismissed her maid. Much to Emalie's dismay, Alyce never even looked in her direction for her permission to leave.

"My brother and Luc and his wife have all had at me this evening, my lady. I came to give you a turn."

There was some levity in his voice and when she met his gaze, she even saw some amusement there.

"What were their complaints, my lord?"

"First, let us deal with mine." Christian walked slowly toward her, his manner reminding her of a wildcat stalking its victim. The hair on the back of her neck stiffened and she waited for him to reach her, unable to move away.

"Yours, my lord?" Damn, but she could hear her own voice tremble.

He reached out and grasped her hands, guiding her to stand. Then he tipped her chin so that she would look at him.

"We have been married for almost four sennights and I have yet to hear my name from your lips. Say it, Emalie. Say it for me." His voice lowered to a whisper, a very throaty commanding whisper and one she could not resist.

"Christian," she said softly.

"Again," he ordered.

This time as she opened her mouth to say it, he covered her lips with his and kissed her. He moved slowly and softly against hers and then pressed more firmly. Just when she thought it was over, she felt his tongue slip inside her mouth. He ignored her gasp and touched within. Heat built there, with every move of his tongue, and then spread into the rest of her until she was pulsing from it.

She felt his hands move into her hair and slide through as he wrapped the hip-length locks around his fists, holding her closer still. Her own hands moved restlessly on his chest. He lifted them to his shoulders and put his arms around her, drawing their bodies into tight contact.

The strength of his arms was new and had not been there during their last embrace. Good food and exercise had brought this about. Even as she tried to focus on her thoughts, her mind refused and went wandering. Her body turned traitor and reacted to his hot, wet kisses—the pulsing grew within her and centered on that place between her legs, which became hot and wet with moisture. And her breasts…her breasts felt heavy against his chest. Their tips ached and tingled with some unfamiliar urge to be touched.

As if he had heard her thoughts, his hand slipped between them and touched one of her breasts. Her body arched, pressing the sensitive tip into his hand, and he groaned as he closed his fingers around it. Her thin robe did nothing to slow his path or to lessen the sensations created by the friction of his fingers.

Their mouths still touched and now he teased her tongue to meet his, sucking on it gently. She had no idea that such touching of tongues could be so pleasurable. Once John had forced her into a kiss and pushed his tongue into her mouth, but in no way did that kiss resemble this one. Shaking her head at the memory, she tried to pull away.

"Ah, my fair Emalie," he whispered against her lips. "Do not go yet. Let me…"

His words ended with his lips once more over hers and she felt the tugging and tingling caused by his fingers. Every movement against her nipple pulled a string within her until she wanted to scream. Just when she thought that she would, he slid his hand away and moved to her other breast. Within moments, they both felt heavy and throbbed against him.

He moved his mouth from hers and began to lick and kiss down her throat, untying her laces until she stood bare chested before him. The cool air in the room did nothing to slow his ardor and, indeed, made her nipples even tighter. He looked at her with passion-glazed eyes before leaning to kiss her shoulders and even lower. Her knees buckled at the heat of his mouth and he lifted her and placed her on the bed.

Kneeling next to her, he slipped her gown off her shoulders and then licked each place where his fingers had been. Her neck, her shoulders, the soft plump rise of her breasts and then the nipples. She moaned against it. Her body stiffened as his mouth nipped and sucked and licked the buds he had made so sensitive. Again, close to screaming, she fought to control the myriad of feelings tearing through her. She clutched the bedcovers in her hands, fighting against something she did not understand. He lifted his head from where he teased and taunted and spoke to her.

"Emalie, I apologize for hurting you."

"My lord?" He frowned and touched his tongue to her nipple once more, sucking harder and harder until she groaned. How could she think when he did that? Oh, he wanted his name used. "Christian?"

"In granting your reprieve, I believe that I have hurt you. For in not knowing me and I not knowing you, I continue to trample on your feelings."

"My feelings, my lo—Christian?" How could she bring any thoughts together now? If he would move away and give her some room to breathe, mayhap she could think. Instead, his hand massaged her belly and began an infinitely slow movement toward the place that ached and throbbed the most.

"I know that it has been difficult to stand by and watch me take over your lands and your people. Although it is the way of it, I know you had hoped for something different here.''

This was not fair. His hands and mouth were creating fire within her and his words confused her. She did not want to think. She heard the apology he offered and would accept it later, when her body was cooled and her head was clear.

His fingers inched down closer to the tuft of hair and she held her breath for his touch there. Instead he offered her more words.

''I will try to be more considerate of you in ruling our estates, Emalie. I will try to ask for your ideas. I will—''

''Touch me, please, my lord,'' she begged through clenched teeth. The screams lay just within her control, but she did not care. His touch had caused such a desire within her, she knew only that he needed to hurry.

He lifted himself away from her and pulled his robe off, baring him to her sight. She reached up to touch him, but did not get the chance. He lowered his head to her breast once more and she felt his hand sliding down to her thighs. Closer and closer he moved, until her thighs fell open to his touch. She ran her fingers in his hair, for his mouth never left her breasts and she knew she did not want him to stop.

Then his fingers slipped between the folds of heated skin and touched something that made her scream out. Her body tightened and arched beneath his hands and mouth and endless waves of heat and pleasure coursed through her. From his fingers and his mouth and out to every part of her, she throbbed and shuddered from within. As the vibrations continued and she watched him climb between her thighs, the passion of the moment clouded her thoughts.

She watched as though from afar as he lifted her hips and spread her for his entry. Every warning that should have gone off did not. She simply waited, aching and trembling, for him to fill her and end the charade between them.

Her heart pounded and her breaths were shallow and panting. He leaned over her and kissed her softly on her lips once more. She felt him positioning his manhood and waited for endless seconds for his entry and his reaction.

It did not happen.

The pounding on her door became louder and louder and finally a woman's voice shouted over it.

"Milady? Milady?"

"Go away," he growled in a loud voice as he held himself still. Emalie laughed and frowned at his animal-like sound of possession.

"My lord? Chris? Are you in there? Hurry, Geoff is worse," Luc called.

At the mention of his brother's name, Christian changed before her eyes. He pushed away from her and slid off the side of the bed. Grabbing his robe, he pulled it on and rushed to the door, leaving her alone and naked on the bed. Opening the door just a crack, he listened and then closed it.

"Luc says that Geoff is having a coughing attack and can not breathe. Can you help him?" She had seen his face covered in laughter, in anger and even in passion. But right now, a deep fear played over his features.

Still unable to calm her racing heart, Emalie scurried to the end of the bed and put on her heavier robe. Every part of her shook and she struggled to get the robe on.

His hands brusquely pulled it into place as she tried to think of what she needed.

"Go to him and I will be there anon, my lord."

He nodded and pulled the door open completely. The servants who stood there gawked at her through the doorway until Alyce began shouting orders and cleared everyone from the hall. Emalie began to bring some semblance of order to her hair, and Alyce was pushing and pulling woolen stockings on her legs and tying them above her knees. A quick hunt in her trunk located a new chemise and, soon, it was on her under the robe and she was on her way to the room where Geoff lay.

The commotion in the hallway outside his room was considerable and many of those newly arrived were among the observers. With a loud announcement, Alyce cleared a path for her and she entered the room. Geoff was still coughing and his coloring was terrible. He struggled to take in a breath between coughs, but she could see the spasms in his frail chest. She went to his side, but Christian would not let go of him.

"My lord, you must let me see to him."

"Please, Emalie. Save him?"

His familiar use of her name startled her; she was unused to hearing it from him. One of the servants entered with her chest and she went to work. Christian stood aside and did only what she asked him to do—assisting where and when she needed him. He allowed no other to touch his brother.

Within a few minutes, she had his coughing lessened and his facial color had turned from blue to a pale white. Not good, but much better than blue. When he could sit, she poured steaming water over a collection of leaves and had him breathe in the aromas given off by them. Holly and hollyhock leaves were known to aid breathing and lessen coughs.

Soon Geoffrey was breathing better and not coughing. Emalie mixed up a number of herbs and poured them into a cup of warmed wine. This would keep him calm and breathing through the night, another one would stave off these dangerous attacks. Within a few days, the coughing should be under control.

Whether too exhausted or simply not inclined to fight, the young man did everything as she directed him. Soon he lay sleeping peacefully, and the only sound in the room was the occasional crackling of a piece of wood in the brazier. Emalie sat and watched the rise and fall of the boy's chest, satisfied with her efforts to ease his breathing.

"Come, my lady." Christian held out his hand to her. "I will escort you back to your chambers."

Although her first impulse was to refuse and not face the completion of what had been begun earlier, she truly wanted to stay and watch over the boy. She shook her head.

"My lord, by your leave, I would stay here for a while longer."

"You look exhausted, Emalie. You can be called if he has need during the night."

"My lord…Christian, please. By the time I am wakened and arrive, his coughing can be out of control once more. I would like to be here until I am sure the herbs have done their job."

He looked torn over what to do, but with a weary shake of his head he gave her permission to stay at his brother's bedside. Soon all were gone except her, and she settled down for a quiet stay.

Chapter Eleven

He was meeting with Luc in the solar early the next morning as planned, to discuss the defensive needs of the keep, when the call came. Not from Geoff's room as he had expected, but from Emalie's chambers. The servant would only say that he was needed above.

He raced up the flights of stairs and arrived winded from the run. Luc was at his heels the whole way. Christian cleared the hallway himself with a furious bellow and was met at the door by Alyce.

"How is she, Alyce? What happened?"

"She was coming to the hall from my lord's brother's room and passed out. Sir Walter brought her here."

"Have you called someone? Who takes care of the healer?" He looked helplessly from Alyce to Luc and back again.

"I have called a woman from the village, my lord. She is within now."

He reached for the door, but Alyce stepped in front of the latch and Luc grabbed his tunic from behind.

"She will come out when she is done, my lord. Give her some time."

"Emalie is probably exhausted from caring for my brother. She will be fine." He said it as much to convince himself as them. The sound of talking within eased his concerns. Emalie must be awake.

This was probably his fault. After taking advantage of her innocence and introducing her to physical pleasure, the strain of caring for her brother had been too much.

The door opened and a woman even older and grayer than Alyce emerged. Pulling the door to a quiet close, she looked around the corridor until she saw him and then nodded at him. So thin she looked emaciated, Christian did not know whether or not to believe that this woman was also a healer.

"My lord," she said with a slight bow. "I am Enyd from the village."

"Is she ill?" Christian asked, looking past the woman to Emalie's room.

"No more or less than any woman who is breeding, my lord. She will be fine after a bit of rest. I will check on her in another sennight."

"Breeding?" he asked. He knew what the word meant, but it could not apply in this situation. They had been married long enough, of course, but until last evening had never had a physical relationship at all. "Breeding?"

"Felicitations, my lord. As hale and hearty as milady is, she'll give you many healthy heirs." Enyd left without another word.

He turned to her maid, who must know the verity of this, but Alyce had taken advantage of his surprise to slip into Emalie's room. Suddenly Luc was smacking him on the back and offering glad tidings to him. It

took but a look to still his friend's outburst. And as he
stared into his friend's eyes, the truth struck him.

His wife was pregnant.

It could not be his child.

The walls around him began to move and a steel
vise seemed to close around his head and his chest.
Bursts of light shattered his vision and he put his hand
out on the wall to steady himself.

She had cuckolded him.

She had given herself to another man and now bore
proof of her sin.

Humiliation and dishonor would once more be his
and his family's to bear because of her. Everything
within him screamed for vengeance. His honor demanded action and his rage grew within him until he
could almost not contain it.

"Chris? What is wrong? The midwife said she is
fine." Luc tried to offer help, but he could not. Luc
did not know the basis for his shock and dismay.

He felt the rage ready to explode and knew he
needed to separate himself from this place or everyone
within would know the truth. He pulled from his
friend's grasp, ran down the stairs and out of the keep.
Making his way to the stables, he called out orders to
saddle up one of the mounts and, within minutes, he
was charging out through the gates, going toward some
unknown destination. He gave no thought to the mail
he should have worn or the escort he should have
taken. Only one thought filled his mind.

Emalie was pregnant with another man's seed.

Every one of his most terrible doubts had been confirmed. He had been right to take away her duties and
responsibilities. He had been right to replace her ways
with his own. He had been right to request his own

men to come and work this estate with him…to guard against betrayal.

Unanswered questions burned through his mind in spite of running a treacherous path away and north from Greystone. He was forced to use all of his strength and concentration to control the horse beneath him. Finally, when both he and the mount were ready to collapse, he pulled to a stop. He continued on foot, following a stream to a lake, allowing the horse to cool off. But even feeling as though his body had been dragged this distance from Greystone, he could not cool his rage.

Then the plan behind this struck him—Eleanor had known. Richard may have, as well, but Eleanor had definitely plotted this. Her words on their wedding night came back to him. *There will be no repudiation of this marriage by either of you.* It had not been a comment, it had been an order from probably the most devious and experienced of all the Plantagenet players.

Richard may or may not have been a part of the planning, but he had certainly played into his mother's hands. For what reason, he knew not, but a mere noble-man could not guess at the intricate ploys and plots of the royal family. Richard, John and Eleanor were all each other's staunchest supporters and bitterest ene-mies, changing sides, it sometimes appeared to outsid-ers, at the whim and will of the wind.

Christian tugged at the reins, guiding the horse to the side of the shallow lake to drink. Kneeling nearby, he splashed the cool water on his face and sipped some from his hands. When he could breathe once more, he hobbled the horse and sat under a tree.

Emalie. What had been her part in this? Who had she lain with? Whose babe did she carry now?

He rested his head in his hands and almost laughed at the irony in this situation. He had sold his soul to regain his and his family's honor and now stood to lose it anyway, once the truth was known. Dishonor and the horns of the cuckold loomed before him. Disaster could be the only outcome of this and now he and his brother were in great danger.

Another contradictory facet struck him about this— he had found out the secret, or part of the secret, of Emalie's involvement with John and he could not reveal it to the king. Now he did laugh out at the irony. For a feeling deep in his gut told him that John did play a part in Emalie's dishonor; he might even have fathered the child.

What did he do now? Christian pulled at several strands of grass and twisted them around his fingers. Did he follow Eleanor's obvious desires and not expose Emalie's dishonor to all? That would mean keeping and recognizing the child she carried as his own and, if it were a male, as his heir.

If he exposed her guilt, he would bear the brand of the cuckolded husband and would be forced to put her aside and seek a new wife. He would probably lose all claim to Greystone, although there was a chance he could retain some or part of it at the king's command. After all, his own lands came and went by order of the king. But the dishonor attached to her would spill back on him.

He stood and brushed the dirt and grass from him. Ah, this was not to be borne! All he had worked for, all he had begged and bargained for was at risk now because of the weakness of one woman. A woman he had to face upon his return. A woman who held his and his brother's future in her lying, deceitful hands.

Loosening the straps from the horse's legs, he regained his saddle and turned back the way he had come. He would face her with her sin and then decide which path to follow. A nauseous feeling filled him as he realized that his life and his honor were still not his own and that either choice he made would force him to play into the Plantagenet game where no one but they could win.

Pacing did not help. Neither did praying or sewing or simply worrying. He knew the truth of it and, by God, she feared him now more than she had that first night. Inwardly, she cursed her cowardliness, for it had been at the root of all this. And she waited…for his return and her punishment.

At this point, the story of his finding out she was breeding and his leaving the castle grounds at a breakneck speed on an unfamiliar mount were still separate stories. Gossip had it that he left because he was so upset by her illness. More said that he had yet to discover the cause of the illness, although breeding was a foregone conclusion by those of Greystone. The appearance of Enyd settled the bet for those of such a nature.

Until he came back, Emalie remained secluded, claiming ongoing illness. Unnerved by his lack of response and his precipitous departure, she had sent Walter and Luc out after him. It had been several hours since they'd left and, this time, without word was wearing on her nerves.

A commotion outside the solar's windows drew her attention and she stood to look. Staying back just enough to see and not be seen, she watched as Christian rode through the gate, followed by both of their retainers. None of them looked anything but tired and miserable. As each one approached the keep, a boy from the stables took their horses and led them off. Christian looked neither right nor left and seemed not to hear any words spoken to him. Instead, he stared at the window where she stood and, although certain she was out of his sight, shivers down her back told her that he knew she watched.

Crossing from the windows, she sat in one of the high-backed chairs near the brazier and waited. She sipped a tea made of chamomile and other herbs, trying to calm the storm that raged inside her. The one she faced when her husband arrived would tax her greatly, so she used this time to calm herself as best she could.

The minutes dragged on and on and then, without warning or sound, he stood inside the door. She watched his approach, deciding that confrontation would not be in her best interest. The jangling of keys drew her attention to his hand. Her keys. Christian walked forward until right in front of her, and held out his hand; the sound of the keys banging together was discordant and disturbing.

"I had thought to offer these back to you last night. After my brother and Luc carried on at me so over my behavior toward you, I believed that it was time to let you take back control over those duties that a ladywife should have, especially one of such character and upbringing and capabilities."

The urge to grab for them was great, but the cold look in his eyes when she finally met his gaze stopped her. She shuddered at the anger there and waited.

"I actually berated myself for not taking your opinions and advice under consideration." He laughed harshly and raised his hand. Thinking he meant to strike her, she shut her eyes and prepared for the blow. The sound of the keys hitting the wall behind her startled her.

"You would have been smarter to simply have let me bumble my way through our wedding night. God's truth, as ill as I was, I might have missed your lack of a maidenhead altogether."

It was difficult to meet his gaze, so much anger filled it. But at the same time, she could not look away. He reached out, grabbed her by her shoulders and pulled her to her feet. Then, as if he could not bear touching her, he dropped his hands and stepped back.

"Did Eleanor know when she summoned me here?" he asked, his quiet voice belying the rage she felt emanating from him.

"She suspected it might happen, my lord. That is why all haste was made in bringing you to Greystone."

"So, she knew of your dishonor and chose to keep it secret from the man she decided should be your husband?"

"'Twould appear so, my lord."

"Did she know the name of the man who you gave your virtue to?"

Emalie tried desperately to control her own anger. She had made some bad decisions in her attempts to retain the Harbridge estates and titles, but never once in this had she lost her honor or given away her virtue. She bit her tongue to keep the retort within her.

He stepped closer now and asked again. "Did the queen know who fathered your bastard?"

She winced at the words. He was bringing even more ugliness into this than had been brought so far and his biting words unnerved her.

"Aye, she knows."

"I would have the name of the man who lay between my wife's thighs before I did."

She said nothing. He was deliberately being crude now, but she would not sink to that.

"The name, Emalie. I want his name now."

She fought the urge to sink to her knees and beg his forgiveness. Taking a deep breath in and forcing it out, she made herself remember that she had not asked for the treatment she had received. And, if truth be told, she was more a victim in this than he.

She shook her head in refusal to his demand.

"Is it that so many climbed in your bed that you can not tell which one's seed you carry within? Like a common wh—"

The slap surprised them both. She did not remember lifting her hand in answer to his insult, but the imprint on his face and the stinging of her palm made it clear she had slapped him.

"I am the Countess of Harbridge and have never sullied a vow I made, my lord. This unfortunate act took place prior to our marriage, prior to me ever knowing of your name or person, and I will say no more of it than that."

He laughed at her, as though he could not believe her words or actions. "Unfortunate act? Is that what you call it?" He snarled the words back at her.

"I made some bad decisions, but what was done to me was not at my request or with my permission." She kept her voice low and steady, trying not to aggravate this tempestuous confrontation any more.

"You would cry rape? And have me believe that your virtue was taken and not shared freely?" He turned from her and walked to the table. Pouring a goblet of wine, he drank it without pause. Then he stared at her, awaiting a reply.

"I do not think you will believe anything I say about this, my lord."

"Too true, lady. Too true," he said, walking to stand before her once more. "I do not see all the strings yet, but without a doubt, I am a puppet in this. The more I struggle to see this clearly, the more the lines cross and tangle."

She could feel the anger seeping from him suddenly. His appearance changed, too, as weariness overtook him and made him so much less a threat to her physically. Realizing that he was not yet recovered from his own illness, she almost reached out to him. He saw her move and stepped away, again disdain for her touch evident even with the exhaustion.

"We will not speak of this again after we leave this room. I will give no indication that anyone but myself is the father of the babe you carry and neither will you."

Emalie gasped at his words. She had expected disclosure and punishment. Even death would have been within his right for a treacherous, unfaithful wife. Acceptance was not the response she anticipated.

"Why, my lord?" she asked.

"Because to do otherwise would hold my name and my family up to ridicule and dishonor. And I have paid too much for my honor to expose it to such defamation as an annulment or even a divorce."

She nodded, unable to speak.

"You will behave always with the decorum expected of my countess, and do not give me a reason to doubt your fidelity again." When she would have agreed, he held his hand up, halting her words. "You will go nowhere within or outside the keep or castle without an escort. I will assign guards and a maid to you. They will remain with you at all times unless I am present myself.''

A prisoner. He was making her a prisoner. Within her own home.

''My lord, what must I do to make you see that these arrangements are not necessary?''

''Tell me his name.''

She was the one to turn away now. She could not do it. Even to gain her freedom from his restrictions. For to allow the name of the man to pass her lips and be forever attached to hers would do more damage than had already been done. Her refusal to admit her virtue had been taken had saved her people and kept them safe until the queen could intervene, and she would not fail them now.

Of course, considering what would happen to her, she wasn't certain that the queen's choice was a better one. But she relied on the queen's extensive experience and knowledge to guide her and if Eleanor thought that this man, the Count of Langier, offered more to Greystone's people than her own son, then so be it.

''So be it,'' he said, echoing her own thoughts. He walked to the door and pulled it open. Several of his own warriors stood in the hall. ''My lady is not well and would retire. Luc, please escort the lady to her chambers and stay until I arrive.''

Although his friend looked as though he wanted to argue, he said no more and simply held out his arm to her. When she would have accepted his escort, Christian leaned in close to her and whispered so that none could hear his words.

''After the news of your condition has made its way

through Greystone, I do not wish to hear of it from you until you bear whatever it is you carry within. Then I will decide what is to be done with you and it.''

She stumbled at his words and his knight took her arm and steadied her. The anger was back within him now. She could feel tears burning in her throat and eyes and kept her head lowered and her gaze on the floor before her.

The sound of the keys as he retrieved them from the floor and attached them to his belt mocked her as she left. And the worst part was that she knew he did it apurpose.

Chapter Twelve

"Milady?"

The new maid stood behind her and whispered words in her ear. Marie was her name and, true to his word, she was with Emalie every waking moment of the day. Alyce still served her, but Marie stood witness to every move she made and every word she spoke. And she reported directly to Christian. If Emalie gained no other satisfaction in this, at least she knew that the reports must have bored Christian to tears, for such were her days now.

She nodded and waited for Marie to speak.

"My lord suggests that you retire now."

Emalie looked over at her husband and saw that he was watching her intently. He was not drunk yet, but would be soon. It was now his practice to stay at table long after she'd left and drink himself into a stupor. Then, as gossip declared and she had witnessed once from the doorway, one of the younger servants, usually Lyssa or Belle, would help him to his room. It was always a noisy process and she knew that it was intentional on his part. Much laughing and knocking about in his chambers followed their arrival there and, try as she might, it was nigh impossible to block out the sounds from her side of the wall.

Tonight, though, it was difficult to convince herself that this was for the best. Her people knew something was wrong between them. Alyce had whispered warnings to her for days. This was definitely not how she had hoped her life would go. She had hoped for so much more with the man she married.

"Milady?" Marie said again.

"I am not ready to retire, Marie," she said loud enough for him to hear.

"But, milady," Marie began to argue.

"My lord, you are gracious in your concern, but I am not yet ready to go to my room." She moderated her voice so no hint of the challenge within her statement was heard. "I wish to walk."

Without breaking from her gaze, he nodded. "You may walk then, my lady. Your escorts will see to your safety."

It was a calculated chance on her part, but it had been days since she'd been permitted anyplace in the keep except her room, the chapel and the solar. He'd even refused her permission to work in her gardens or workroom or to visit with Geoffrey. She rose and left the table, walking through the great hall and toward the stairs.

"Milady, this way…" Marie followed close behind and began to direct her to the doorway that led to the courtyard.

Emalie stopped and faced the woman. "You may serve me at *le comte*'s command and you may report back to him, but you do not order me. Remember your place and remember who I am."

One of the guards snickered at her rebuke and Marie's face filled with color, obvious in even the dim light of the landing. "But he said..." She hesitated.

"My lord said I may walk, he did not say where. So I go where I wish. You may accompany me as he has commanded you to or you may go and tell him where I go. The choice is yours."

Emalie wished she had controlled her outburst, but she was on edge tonight. Without another look at the woman, she began climbing the stairs, floor by floor, until she reached the hallway that led to the battlements. One of the guards stepped in front of her and opened the door. She turned onto the narrow path and followed it around the perimeter of the keep.

Lost in thought, she walked briskly around until she had made one circuit. As she was about to begin another, she looked at those who accompanied her. Marie was shivering and the guards looked completely bored with this duty.

"If you wish, you may stay here in the guardhouse. You do not need to follow me around." When Marie looked as if she would argue, Emalie continued. "I am in plain sight at all times. Stay here."

Marie must have been very cold, for she stayed in the shelter of the structure. With each step away, Emalie felt better. Reaching her favorite viewing spot, she turned into the wind that always buffeted these heights and let it tear at her. Layer upon layer of tension left her as the somewhat warm summer gusts passed over her. As always, her hair loosened from its braid and coif and tangled in the breezes. It felt wonderful to her.

She looked off in the distance and saw the well-tilled and maintained fields of wheat and barley. It would be harvest time soon and from the little she heard, it would be another bountiful season for Greystone. In most years, the overflow from this village was divided up among her other properties so that there was enough for all. Cattle and pigs would be readied for slaughter and preserving, again distributed through all her estates.

This year, however, she would play no part in seeing it done. She would be kept out, had been kept out, of all the discussions pertaining to running the estates. She wondered if he knew of plans to enlarge the village barn this year? Had Fitzhugh made suggestions to Christian as he always had to her? Did Christian consider ideas not his own?

Frustration filled her once more and she turned into the wind again. Uselessness was not part of her being; she needed to be busy. Soon it would be too late, for her body was already changing. She feared that when Christian was faced with the reality of her carrying someone else's babe, he would become even more hostile and controlling.

Her hands slid down over her belly searching for change. Other than her breasts growing larger, she could tell no other differences within her. A few mornings of ill stomach and a few bouts of light-headedness were her only symptoms so far. The midwife said all was progressing well toward a late-winter birth.

Feeling stronger and refreshed, Emalie decided it was time to go to her room and paced the walkway once more, stopping at the guardhouse when she finished. Realizing that Geoffrey had not yet made an appearance at dinner, she asked one of the guards about him.

"André, how fares my lord's brother?"

The guards exchanged glances and then looked at her.

"Is he well? He should be out of his room and fighting any restrictions by now."

Emalie did not like the lack of response and the strange looks exchanged between the men. She should look in on him and decided to do just that...now. Knowing they would try to stop her, she walked to the door leading below and entered the keep. Without hesitating, she picked up her skirts and increased her speed on the steps and soon arrived on the first floor. Hearing their protests from behind her, she hurried down the hall leading to his room.

Just as she reached his room, her guards caught up with her.

"Milady," André said, reaching out and grabbing her arm. "You can not go in there."

The other man took her other arm and pulled her away. "My lord has ordered you away from here."

If not so stunned by their words, she would have fought their grasp. But another voice entered the fray. Walter came barreling down the hall.

"Remove your hands from her. You have no right to touch her," he yelled as he pushed into the guards. Gaetan released her to defend himself and she found herself flung onto the floor by André as Walter attacked both men. Scrambling away from the brawl, she watched in horror as the fight turned bloody.

"Halt!"

Christian bellowed the order, but it took a minute for it to take effect. He stood outside Geoffrey's room with his hands on his hips. He spied her on the ground and hurried to her side, helping her to her feet with a tenderness and concern that surprised her. But, once steady, he released her arm quickly.

"What goes on here, Gaetan? How has the lady ended up in the middle of a fight?" He crossed his arms over his chest and waited for his man's reply.

"She ran from us and was on her way to your brother's room, milord. Against your orders."

"She? You would speak of your lady in such terms?" Walter challenged.

Gaetan began to stutter out an answer, but Christian waved him silent. "Walter, what do you here?"

"I was returning to the hall and saw your men take hold of the lady. I tried to stop them."

"And if they were acting on my orders? What say you to that?" Christian had lowered his voice.

"I do not believe you wish your lady manhandled by those you assign to keep her safe, my lord." Walter's glare was obvious to even her and she waited for Christian to take action against him.

"'Tis true enough, Walter. They may have misunderstood my orders. I will meet all of you directly in the hall to explain my wishes."

Nodding at him, the three men and Marie left the corridor. Christian turned to face her now.

"I did not know of your order, my lord."

"And if you did, would you have obeyed or defied it?" His tone was quiet, but no less dangerous than if he had yelled it.

"I seek to treat your brother's illness, my lord, not to defy your wishes."

"If I could only believe you, lady. But I trust you not and I trust you alone with no man. So the guards and Marie will stay as your companions."

She simply nodded at him. "May I see your brother

now, my lord?'' Her intent to discover Geoffrey's condition had not changed.

''Nay, my lady. He sleeps and I do not wish him disturbed.'' He stepped next to her and offered his arm. ''Come. I will see you safely to your chambers before I speak with the others.''

She did not place her hand on his arm as expected. Instead she crossed her arms over her chest and faced him. ''He should not be asleep, my lord. He is a young man and should be out chasing the maids for a kiss.''

''What know you of young men and their activities?'' he said, glaring at her. ''Ah, was your paramour a young man, then? Did he take you to some secluded place and ply you with his kisses?'' His words ended with a snarl.

She sighed, for this would always come between them. And even revealing the man's name to him would not lessen his rage.

''My lord, please let me see him. The concoctions I left for him should have had him free of his bed and ready to return to his regular food and drink. Please,'' she begged, laying her hand on his arm.

Concern for his brother overrode his objections as she thought it would and he nodded his permission. Standing back, he let her lead the way into Geoffrey's room.

''I need my herbs, my lord. And mayhap Timothy's assistance.''

She walked to the brazier and moved a kettle of water over the flame to heat. Rolling up her sleeves, she took a linen cloth and dipped it into a basin of cool water on the table. Pressing it to the boy's forehead, she wiped the sweat from his brow.

She knew that Christian was battling himself over

what to allow her to do. She also knew without a doubt that he valued his brother's life above almost everything else. He had never spoken of it to her, but it was clear in his words and his actions. Geoffrey was most important to him.

"I will send for your chest and for Timothy. Will you remain here?"

She nodded without looking at him and heard the door open. Realizing that this might be her only time to speak to him privately about another concern, she turned and called to him.

"My lord? You will hold manor court on the morrow?"

"Aye."

"I have heard that Nyle the chandler has asked permission to marry again. Will you grant it?"

"Not that it concerns you, but aye." She almost smiled at his blatant attempt to put her in her place.

"His first two wives have died very young, my lord."

"Childbirth?" His voice caught a bit as he offered the most common reason for a woman's death.

"Nay, my lord. Their deaths have more to do with his fists. I would ask that you not sentence another girl to that."

"But her parents have consented to the marriage."

"He pays well for brides and silence from their families when they end up dead."

He frowned and nodded. "I will think on your words." He turned to leave.

"That is all I ask, my lord."

He spun around and gave her the strangest look—one that combined disbelief, surprise and acceptance of some measure. A moment later he was gone. She turned back to Geoffrey and spent the next two nights and days struggling to loosen the fever's grasp on his frail body.

That is all I ask.

Her words turned round and round in his thoughts and his irritation grew. Intent on not letting her interfere with his plans for Greystone and on not letting the truth of their marriage be known, Christian had pushed her away again and again. He avoided the solar when he knew she was there. He avoided the hall and even his place of refuge, the battlements, when she walked there.

Now he stood staring at the entrance to her gardens where he allowed her to work during the mornings. She had saved his brother's life, he did not doubt it for a moment. She had labored for two more days and nights after forcing her way into Geoff's room and, with everything she had, fought the fever that sought to claim his life.

Then, without a word, she had returned to her room and the restrictions he'd placed on her movements and activities. He had lessened them the next day. She could spend time where she wished as long as she was accompanied by the guards and Marie.

Guiltily he remembered watching her from the hall as she ministered to her brother. He had come and stood at times when she did not know he was there. He would like to have convinced himself that he feared she would do something bad to his brother, but he could not fool himself that much.

The truth was that he was completely and utterly intrigued by her. As he had been from the moment they met. As he had been with each new fact he learned of her history, her abilities, her management. And at each time when other women would have cried or fretted or begged for fripperies or jewelry, Emalie asked only to serve her people.

She had begged him for herself only once, that night when he went to her room, intent on having her. As he pushed her further and further toward physical pleasure, she had begged for his touch. Even the memory of it inflamed him now and his body reacted to it. He, they, had been so close to joining their bodies that he could remember the frustration when interrupted. He had ached for hours afterward and his desire to fill her had not lessened with the news of her pregnancy.

Even when filled with rage over her deceit, he had been tempted to take her over and over again, claiming her body with his own so that she was marked by his smell, his sweat, his seed. The animal response within startled him, for he had never been a man driven by the physical needs within him. But she did that to him.

Since the day he had discovered her secret, he had battled his lust for her. He had tried to spend himself on other women: women available to him because he was lord here and women who were pleased by his attentions and his desire for them. It had not worked, for they soon left his chambers with a coin for their unsuccessful efforts.

Wine did not work, either. He needed to drink enough to make him sleep and even then he was tormented by images of her as she had been that night in her chamber. Naked. Arching into his hand. Kissing him back with passion-filled eyes and a hot mouth. He shuddered now as his groin tightened and his cock hardened.

''You are frightening away all the females of the

place with that look, my lord.'' His friend stood before him, laughing.

"Luc, I have been waiting for you." Christian shifted his long tunic and resettled his belt on his hips.

"Waiting for me and lusting for her." Luc laughed again as he smacked Christian on the back soundly. "Does she know you stand before her gate with desire for her in your eyes?"

He looked around and began walking away from his wife's garden.

"I think mayhap you mistake me for you and your wife. I have heard stories..." Christian laughed now.

"I am a fortunate man, my lord. My lovely Fatin needs me to keep her warm on these terribly cold English nights."

They both laughed. Christian had heard Fatin's complaints over the cold weather—any place would be cold after spending so much of one's life in the heat of the Holy Lands. Luc had revealed that she now scandalously wore breeches beneath her gowns to keep her legs warm.

"Come, give me your report."

They walked a distance until they reached one of the stable yards. Leaning against the rails of the fence, Christian waited for the information Luc had gathered.

"It took some time and more of your coins to discover that your lady was correct. Both of Nyle's wives died after brutal beatings."

"Did you check the rolls? How were they listed?"

"As having died of lung fever. But apparently the damage done to both of them was so extensive that they contracted lung fever due to their injuries."

Christian let out the breath he was holding. "Of

what age were they?'' He didn't know why he asked, only that he needed to know.

''The first was ten-and-three, the second was ten-and-five.'' Luc added, ''This new one he wants is ten-and-four.''

''How did she know?''

''How else, Chris? She tended their injuries.''

He stared across the yard at men working a new stallion. His ability to control his own warhorses was almost regained and then he would have them brought from his home.

''If she is given credit for one more good deed, I swear she will be nominated for sainthood even before her death.''

''Is there no way to heal this rift between you two?''

''No.''

''Would you tell me of it?''

''No.''

He could not bring himself to discuss his wife's sin with anyone. Not even his lifelong friend, with whom he had shared danger and success and even a few women along the way, could know of this.

''There were three more fights this week between our men and hers.''

''And I have been doused with hot soup and bad wine and somehow the spoiled meat ended up on my platter at dinner last eve.''

''Are you getting their message yet, my lord?''

''I think the bedsheets still coated with lye were my first clue, Luc. And my tunics sewn together. And probably the several near-misses during training with the new bows.''

''Can you not call a truce in this? Lives are at stake.''

Luc did not know how close to the truth his jest was. Until Christian learned the name of the man involved and ascertained whether Emalie was a willing participant, nothing could be done. He shook his head. "No truce is possible, nor retreat."

"You know that she intercedes on your behalf with her people?"

"What?" Another blow to his self-esteem. The wife he punished spoke for him?

"She has made it known that these changes are for the good of Greystone and that your assigning guards and a new maid to her were for her protection due to recurrent illnesses during her pregnancy."

"Damn her!" Christian swore under his breath. "Anything else?"

"I fear that I am now one of her admirers, my lord. I will beg your pardon now."

He wanted to smash his friend's face into the dirt. The thought of knowing that someone had taken Emalie before he married her and not knowing the identity of the man was driving him insane.

In coherent moments, he knew his reaction was simple jealousy and envy and possessiveness, but that did not lessen the rage that exploded within him every time he thought about it. If she would simply admit to it and tell him the name, he could breathe again. He would be able to stop looking at every man in Greystone wondering if he were the one. Imagining her in bed with another man, writhing with the passion he knew was within her, was eating his gut.

"Why?" he said with a sigh.

"Simple, my lord. She defended my Fatin."

"Fatin? Was there some problem?" Luc and Fatin had not had an easy time of it, since returning from the

East. A good Christian knight did not marry an infidel and bring her back to God-fearing Europe without some obstacles. Rescuing her from the massacre that had killed her master had been the easy part of their lives together. Living as man and wife under the watchful and invasive eyes of the Church had been more difficult.

"Your lady has banished one of her serving women from the solar. Lady Emalie heard her call Fatin an infidel and threw her out."

Christian rested his head on his arm. He felt as though he were being pulled in two opposite directions. Part of him wanted to put this behind them and accept her and all she offered as a wife, even if it was a challenge to him to live with the thought of her bearing another's child. But a darker part wanted to scream and roar in pure jealousy and not settle until his honor had been regained, until she acknowledged her error, her sin, and begged his forgiveness for her deceit. That part did not want to accept anything less than her complete acquiescence in all things—he wanted her unquestioning support for all he did within Greystone and he wanted her in his bed surrendering all that she was to him.

Raising his head, he laughed bitterly to his friend. Only something drastic could break this stalemate.

"Report to me if you hear anything more," he said.

"Aye, my lord." Luc bowed and left Christian there alone.

Chapter Thirteen

He was restless this night. The winds were high, telling of a storm brewing. Thunder rolled and crashed in the distance and spears of lightning flashed in the sky. No rain yet fell, but it would. The smell filled the air with the promise of it.

Christian paced the confines of his room for nearly an hour and then decided to seek out Luc for a game of chess. Walking down the corridor past Emalie's chambers, he noticed that no one stood guard in the hallway. Checking her room, he found it empty. It was late for her to be wandering and he began to wonder where she could be.

As he walked through the great hall toward the wing where Luc and Fatin stayed, he saw Marie. Calling her over, he asked about Emalie.

"She is in her workroom, my lord. Your brother said you gave permission and that I was to meet her there in an hour."

Completely at a loss, he nodded at the girl and she left. Looking around the huge chamber, he wondered where she could be. And why was Geoffrey involved?

Emalie was gone.

That dark part within him seethed in rage. Where could she be?

She was meeting her lover.

The accusation screamed in his thoughts and fed the anger that coursed below the surface in his veins. His hand slid down to feel the dagger he wore on his belt, as he knew he would kill them both when he found them and no one could gainsay him.

Turning, he fled the hall while trying to think of where a woman and man could meet without witnesses. Once those in the keep settled for the night, and they were nearly done doing so now, it would be easier to find them.

Remembering where he had found her unexpectedly, he went to the stairs and took them up to the battlements. If someone knew the pace of the guards on their tour of duty, it was easy enough to avoid being discovered in one of the many nooks of darkness along the wall.

He pushed through the heavy door and climbed out onto the walkway that encircled the keep. At once the winds tore at him, warning of the approaching storm. He smiled grimly, a storm, aye, but mayhap not the one expected from above. Nodding to the warrior stationed at the doorway, he decided on a deliberate pace and forced himself to it so that he did not become as obvious as he felt. Surprise would be his manner, the anger within him would serve as his weapon.

Following the path far above the ground, a niggling of rational thought teased him.

What if she were not with her lover?

But where else and with whom else could she be? Remembering her refusal to identify the man who had taken her, his stomach rolled and the bile within threatened to force its way up and out. The man who had taken his wife was there and his wife was probably with him right now. Fury surged, his vision narrowed and sweat gathered on his brow and dripped down his face. His honor demanded that he find her, now, before anyone else discovered her sin.

Finally completing his route around the battlements, he wiped his brow and tried to catch his breath. His heart hammered in his chest as he tried to make his thoughts more orderly, more full of sense and not the raging emotions that filled his body and his spirit. He had to find her.

Entering the stairway, Christian followed it all the way down to the main floor and the now empty great hall. Inspecting the area, he realized that another convenient area for trysts were the stables. He himself had spent many a passion-filled night, during the years leading up to his knighting, with a willing lass in his father's stable. That must be where Emalie was meeting her lover.

Deciding that the quickest way was through the kitchens, Christian made his way through the darkened hallway and soon entered the series of rooms where all the food was stored and prepared. Seeing no one, he went through the back door and into the courtyard.

Once outside, he walked quietly and quickly to the stables, sneaking inside without making a sound. Listening for any noises, he heard none and found no one within the stalls. Rushing to the end of the row, he realized that he was alone but for the animals there. Then he heard their voices, outside next to the building.

"Geoffrey, you must go back. The storm approaches and you can not get wet and become ill once more."

Her whispered words to his brother set his blood boiling.

"Emalie, come back with me. Mayhap he does not yet know you've gone."

He? They could only be speaking of him. And it was too late for them to worry about discovery.

"I must do this. Please go back."

Apparently his brother decided to obey her request, for Geoffrey walked away from her and passed by the alcove where he stood listening.

Emalie waited only a moment and then ran on, using the darkness for cover. He remained for a short time and then followed her around the chapel, through a gate and into a darkened courtyard. Then hearing her soft whisper again, he stopped and waited.

He had found her and, without thought or hesitation, he drew forth the blade from his belt and prepared to send her and her lover to hell for heaping more dishonor on his name. Taking a deep breath, he approached her from behind. The crackling of dead branches brought down by the winds informed her of his presence. Lightning lit the sky as he stalked her.

"My lord?" she asked as she turned to face him.

She paled as she spied the dagger in his hand, but when she looked into his eyes, her face lost all its color. He moved in closer, his sweaty palms and his pounding heart adding to the tension coiled within him.

"Move aside, *wife*," he ordered as he advanced closer and closer. Did she still seek to hide her co-conspirator from him?

"Is there some danger, my lord?" Without regard to her safety, she came toward him. He turned the blade in his hand and waited to see who was with her. When he was about to see past her, he took a breath and raised his hand, ready to avenge his honor.

No one was there.

Emalie stood before a grave site with flowers in hand. Pushing his hair back out of his eyes, he read the carving on the stone where she stood.

Gaspar Montgomerie, Earl of Harbridge
Beloved Husband and Father

Her father's grave?

She looked at him with terror-filled eyes and stuttered out some words. "'Tis been a year."

She had come out to her father's grave to mark the anniversary of his death and he stood with knife drawn over her.

Christian staggered back away from her and fled. Horror at what he had planned to do filled him as he ran out of the enclosed cemetery and into the back courtyard. Overwhelmed, he sought comfort in the only place he could.

Her hands trembled as she placed them on the door and pushed it open, not certain of who or what would greet her. As she walked back to this chamber, Emalie had lost the battle to convince herself that her husband had thought her to be in danger. The hateful stare and expression of complete fury terrified her as she watched him enter the graveyard where her father lay buried. His eyes were like slits and his breathing labored. She had seen this anger in him only once before—the night when he'd discovered that she was pregnant. He had no weapon in his hand that night.

It had taken several minutes to calm herself down and several more minutes to convince herself that she should return. As ever, duty won out and Emalie knew that she must face her husband.

Startling at a noise in the corridor behind her, Emalie pushed the door as quietly and carefully as she could and peeked into the room. It was empty and there was no sign that Christian had ever been here. She walked to the hearth, stooped closer and stirred the coals to life, hoping to remove the unseasonable chill from the room. As sparks flew, she rubbed her hands together and began to pace the room's limits.

Why had she tried to sneak out now? She shook her head as she thought of her husband turned berserker. His manner toward her had changed over these past few days and he had even approached her and initiated conversations with her, something he had not done since that night. Mayhap he would have granted her request to visit the graveyard. Fearing his inconsistency of late, she had made her own plans and would now suffer the consequences.

For her people's sake, Emalie prayed daily that his anger over being trapped into this marriage would lessen and his actions toward her recently had been a hopeful occurrence. Even though she knew he did not yet trust her, she still believed they could suit each other well and serve her people's needs.

But the man who had followed her this night, knife drawn and on the attack, was not the one who would save her and her people from Prince John's plans. He could not fill her father's place and put those who served him first in his consideration. Emalie sighed and sat down on the bed, the squeaking of the ropes echoing in the room. What could she do now?

Shaking her head, she loosened her hair from its braid and dragged her fingers through its length. Alyce already slept and Emalie saw no reason to wake her, when she was quite able to undress and ready herself for bed. Looking around the room, she spied her trunk and tried to decide if undressing and waiting for Christian's return was the best idea. Her contemplation was cut short by the approaching footsteps outside her chamber. She held her breath as a knock sounded.

"My lady?" a voice called out softly. "Are you within?"

It was Sir Luc, her husband's vassal and friend. She rushed to open the door.

"What is it?"

"Is all well?" He tried to peek over her to see into the chamber, making Emalie uneasy.

"Aye, all is well."

"My lady, one of my men reported seeing Chris... my lord running through the courtyard. I thought—" He paused, coughing and clearing his throat. "I thought that mayhap something was awry."

"I have just returned to these rooms myself, Sir Luc, and have not spoken to my lord husband since dinner. I know not where he is or what he does."

Her voice trembled as she spoke the words. Had she revealed her own worry to her husband's retainer? Perhaps Sir Luc was the very person to find Christian and determine what ailed him?

"If I might ask a service of you?"

"Anything, my lady," he said, bowing slightly to her.

"Could you find my husband and make certain he is well?" At his nod, she continued. "Discreetly, of course."

"Of course, my lady." Luc stepped back and left without another word.

Now all she could do was wait. Either Luc would find Christian or Christian would reveal himself. Whatever happened, Emalie knew it would be a long, sleepless night for her. She closed the door slowly and looked around the empty room.

As soon as he returned, this would be her prison once more. Instead of adjoining chambers shared by lord and lady, she appeared destined to be this room's only occupant. Her eyes burned with tears as she thought of her parents' loving relationship. Certainly that was far different from most of their class, but one that Emalie had prayed she would find with her own husband when the time came. Now that dream and many others were in shambles because of the very thing that she fought to protect.

Could she have done it differently? Emalie sat once more on the bed and stared at the flames that flared now and again within the hearth. Had she been too ostentatious about the secure and successful circumstances of her estates and her people? Had her own pride in being able to keep her people safe and well fed brought the ravenous royal scavenger into their midst? She knew of so many estates and titles that had been plucked up and given to cronies of John Lackland. And women, too.

A shudder wracked her as she remembered his lecherous grin and the touch of his tongue on her hand, defiling something as simple as a greeting. His very presence in a room made her want to scrub herself clean of his taint, but at those moments when blurred images of *that night* crept into her consciousness, the urge to vomit became almost uncontrollable. Emalie lay back on the bed, trying now to ease the roiling within her and to clear her thoughts. Breathing deeply, she closed her eyes and tried to picture something pleasant in her mind.

Dark eyes, glistening with lust and triumph, stared back at her. Gasping against the memory, she fought against the torrent of sounds and glimpses of John and William, the feelings of terror, the smells of wine, male sweat and spent lust. She tried to clarify them, separate, sort them, but was unsuccessful. As always, the blurry feeling of something put in her wine clouded the memories as it had muddled her senses that night. The bile rose in her throat and she scurried off the bed, finding the chamber pot without a moment to spare.

Some time later, exhausted from her physical condition and her emotional state, Emalie crawled onto the bed and collapsed. The tears that had threatened before now flowed freely as she mourned the loss of her parents, their dreams and hers. She would never know the same marriage bond that her parents had shared. She would be bound for the rest of her days to a man who thought that what had been done to her was her fault, her dishonor. She was wed to a man who would hold *that night* against her for the rest of her life. In this, and in his defense, she knew he was no different than other men, but she had hoped for more, had prayed for more.

As she felt the sleep of complete fatigue taking hold of her, she prayed in her thoughts as she did every night, as she did every morning at Mass. She begged the Almighty to let her gain some amount of love for the child she carried within. Emalie did not want to see her child as proof of her dishonor and to look on it with loathing when it was finally born. She prayed for

an acceptance of her circumstances. She prayed
for love.

Surrendering to her exhaustion, Emalie drifted off to
sleep.

"'Tis not the same quality as is served at your tables, my lord, but I believe it will do for our purposes
this night."

Christian dragged his hands through his hair and
looked up from the corner where he sat. Luc carried
two battered metal mugs and a large wineskin, obviously filled to the top.

"I do not think that the chapel is the appropriate
place for drowning our cares and woes in wine," he
answered, climbing to his feet to meet his friend.

"Ah, but did not our own good Lord drink of it at
his Last Supper?" Luc asked as he held out a mug to
Christian. As he took it from him, Luc pulled the cap
off the wineskin with his teeth and poured a healthy
measure into each cup. Replacing the cap on the skin,
he motioned Christian to sit again. "I am certain that
He will have no ill feelings toward two of his faithful
imbibing a bit in his house."

Christian sat down where he had been and drank the
wine in one long swallow, never tasting the quality or
lack thereof as it filled his stomach. Wiping his mouth
on the back of his sleeve, he leaned his head back
against the cold stone of the chapel wall. Luc swallowed a mouthful or two of his own wine and walked
a few steps away, retrieving something from the floor.

"Yours, my lord?"

Luc turned the dagger handle end out and handed it
back to him. Securing it in his belt, Christian held up
his cup for more wine. Luc sat next to him on the floor,
put his own cup down and refilled the mug for him.

"Remember, my lord, we have but one skin of wine and no guarantee that I can find more for us."

Taking a deep swallow of the wine, Christian gazed at his friend. Had word of his outrageous behavior already spread throughout the keep? As if his thoughts had been read, his friend met his stare and spoke.

"Fear not. No cry has gone out about the mad Earl of Harbridge brandishing a knife over his wife and then fleeing into the night." At his raised eyebrow, Luc went on with his explanation. "One of our own servants, in the stables for his own purposes, saw your... encounter and informed me."

"My wife?"

"Is safely ensconced in her chamber. I sought you there and found her instead. She bade me find you and determine if all is well." Luc paused, taking a drink of wine before continuing. "So, is all well?"

Christian put his mug on the floor and stood, pacing the confines of the chapel. He knew Luc was there as a friend, but he did not want his friend to know the extent of his circumstances.

"The countess...Emalie..." he stuttered.

"Aye, Emalie is the countess." Luc laughed sarcastically at him.

"Do you goad me?" He walked over to Luc and kicked dirt from the floor at him.

Luc dusted off his leg and laughed again. "Soft words and wooing you with wine was not working, so I thought other actions were needed to spur you."

Rubbing his eyes with the heels of his hands, he looked at the man before him and wondered how much he could tell him. Too many knowing the full sordid story would increase the chances of it becoming known too far and wide. It could endanger the entire matter in

which he served the king and put his own honor
at risk.

"Emalie is part of a bargain I made with the king."

"Chris, most wives are part of some bargain made
between two parties. It is the way of things for men of
your rank and mine."

"There is more to this than a simple agreement to
merge lands and wealth, Luc. More that you do not
know." Christian paused once more, uneasy about saying the words to anyone.

Luc looked away from him and drank from his cup
again. On looking back, his friend spoke in a soft voice,
made no less effective by its quiet tones.

"Your ladywife carries a child not of your making."

Christian sucked in a breath. How could Luc have
known this truth?

"That also is not so unusual, Chris. Men have been
known to marry women already breeding, to give them
name and protection."

"Widows known to be breeding, aye. Women carrying their seed, aye. But she is neither and the child
within her has not my blood! And without my knowledge."

Luc gave a grim smile. "Ah, now I understand. You
have been caught in the games of king and prince and
mother, even as your father was."

"How did you know of my wife's condition? Was
it common knowledge to all but me?" Christian felt a
wave of shame pass through him. Was he the only one
fooled into believing her a virgin? Did all of her people
know of his role or had she cuckolded him even as he
protected her reputation with *his* blood on *her* sheets?
How many laughed behind their hands or in their hearts

at the display of those sheets the morning after their wedding?

"I have never lived among people so closemouthed about their lady before. If any here knows the truth of her dishonor, they speak not of it freely or even among those of us who came with you."

"How then did you discover it?" Christian's head was reeling from the wine, and the events of the night.

"A few unguarded murmurings when the pregnancy was announced to you by the midwife. Again, one of our own heard and passed it on to me."

"And you never thought to tell me that you knew the truth?" Closing his eyes, Christian hung his head. Breathing slowly, he waited for his friend to answer.

"I did not want to force you to acknowledge or deny this. I thought you would be better if you thought everyone believed that it is yours."

"But everyone apparently does not believe. How did you know these murmurings were the truth?"

Christian looked up and watched as Luc finished his wine and stood. Following his friend's path with his gaze, Christian waited.

"I saw your condition the day you arrived at Chateau d'Azure. You could not raise your arm let alone your cock. I suspect it has only recently regained its strength as you have regained yours?"

"And you hoped to spare me from shame? What do you think your words do to me now?"

"Chris, I do not disparage your manhood. For God's sake, I have gone wenching with you too many times not to know your prowess in bedplay. I have seen too many women leave your chambers sighing in satisfaction to question your abilities to tup them well. But I saw you, I saw what Richard's deprivations did to your body. No man could expect to perform in the marital bed until some measure of healing and health had been gained.''

He nodded at Luc. His friend's assessment was completely accurate. He had not known how near to death he and his brother had been until they left their prison and traveled home. He wondered now how he had survived the trip from Poitiers to England. He was only now beginning to feel more secure in his health and his strength.

''And now, Chris? What do you do now? Can you turn back on this bargain with Richard?''

''Not and keep the honor it has brought back to me. 'Twas the reason I agreed to this arrangement sight unseen.'' Christian stood and dusted off his legs.

''And you have regained your honor through this?''

''Aye, my honor, my name and titles, my land and wealth. All has been returned to me since I agreed to carry out this task for the king.''

Something in the words rang false to him, but he did not want to think about that now. He was once again the Count of Langier as well as the Earl of Harbridge, honor and wealth restored to him.

''And tonight? The encounter with your wife?''

''I thought she sought out her lover, the one who dishonored her. I could not control my rage at the thought of it.''

''What would our old weapons master say of that, I wonder? I would think that the training you received for the battleground would serve you well in this, too.''

'''Losing control means losing your life' is what he taught us. I will regain my control over this, Luc. No one will be in danger from my anger.'' At his look of disbelief, he added, ''Not even my wife.''

"I will leave now and let you return to your lady-wife. I am certain she will feel much relief in knowing that she will not find you brandishing a weapon over her head again."

His friend picked up the wineskin and empty mugs and turned to leave.

"Luc. My thanks for your candor tonight. And for the wine."

"Make peace with this, Chris. You have all that you wanted and then some, from this bargain with the king. Accept the good and bad or it will destroy all that you gained."

Luc made a quick bow in the direction of the altar table in front of the chapel and left. Christian knew his friend was correct—he needed to come to some acceptance of this. His life could not continue in these alternating bouts of anger and control. He had to let go of this rage and accept that he had made the bargain and would have to live with the ramifications of his decision.

Looking around the empty chapel, he knew what he had to do. Taking a deep breath, he took the first step toward what he hoped would be a more acceptable marriage and life. He had given his word to the king and he would stand by it.

His honor demanded no less than that from him.

Chapter Fourteen

The sounds of the approaching dawn pierced the silence around him and he looked out the small window in the chamber to see how much longer it would be before the sun rose. He had been back for over an hour but had chosen to wait for Emalie to wake on her own. One glance at her face showed the evidence of his rash behavior—swollen eyes and nose and tracks of tears on her cheeks. But the acrid odor of the used pot in the corner shamed him more effectively than he thought possible.

Christian sat on a stool away from the hearth and simply watched his wife sleep. Other than a quiet hiccup or occasional sigh, she made no other sounds or movements. He wondered if this was how she always slept or if this was out of the ordinary for her. If his explanation worked, mayhap he would discover that and more. For now he bided his time and waited as patiently as he could for dawn's light and noises to awaken Emalie.

Soon the sounds of a stirring keep surrounded him from outside the window and inside the keep. It would be a short time until Alyce rose and came to serve her

lady. Standing quietly and making his way to the outer
room, he shook her and told her that Emalie still slept
and she was not to be disturbed. Confident that that
should give him some measure of time and privacy, he
returned within and sat back down.

He noticed the signs of her waking in the slight
movements of her arms and the tilting of her head.
Since she faced the hearth, she would not see him unless she turned over. Emalie let out a quiet yawn as
she turned onto her side and rubbed at her eyes. His
gaze followed every movement she made as she
stretched leisurely and then slid her hands down over
her stomach. She had not opened her eyes yet, but her
lips moved, the words not said aloud. He wondered
what she'd said.

His eyes were drawn to the slow movement of her
hands again. She circled her belly over and over, re-
peating some words under her breath. His curiosity
gained control over his attempts to remain out of her
sight. Even softly, his voice seemed to split the silence
of the room.

"What is it that you say? A morning prayer?"

Emalie gasped and sat up in bed, staring at him. So
many emotions crossed her face that he scarce knew
what to say first. Seeing the fear grow in her widened
eyes and pale face, he only knew he must say something.

"My pardon for frightening you," he began, as he
watched her swallow several times. Her gaze now
moved over him, from head to feet and back again, as
though she thought him some specter from her dreams.
"Both now and last night."

He stood and took a step toward the bed. She edged
ever so slightly away from him. Each step he took

closer moved her nearer to falling out of the bed. He stopped.

"Have a care, Emalie."

Her hand slipped over the side and as she grabbed for a handhold, she lost her balance. Without hesitating, he reached across and took hold of her, preventing her from falling. Once secure in her position, he released her and sat on the bed.

"I have asked your maid to leave you undisturbed for now so that we might…speak on matters between us."

The silence surrounded them and he waited for her response. Other than the calling of some birds outside the window, nothing broke into the moment. Her eyes cleared as she shook her head, sending loose tendrils of her hair.

"I am listening, my lord."

Her tone revealed nothing to him of her thoughts or feelings. He would need to move on from here.

"These few months since our marriage have been difficult ones. Although I know we've both been raised to expect a contracted marriage, I now realize that our expectations of this marriage were completely different."

A slight nod was all she gifted him with. He continued.

"I observed my father when he married Geoff's mother and took over control of her estates. I thought his ideas and methods were sound and successful and sought to follow them here. As I mentioned to you one evening several weeks ago, I did not intend to come here and trample on your feelings." He hoped to see a blush or some sign that she remembered what else had happened that night between them. She gave no such indication.

"You and Geoff have different mothers? But you look so much alike."

"Aye, my father married Geoff's mother after my mother's death. Apparently the Dumont blood runs deeply in both of us."

She nodded more this time at his words, but her face was still blank.

"In my father's case, he was wresting control from his wife's family. I fear I followed his example too closely and did not give you a chance to cooperate with my efforts."

He stood once more and made his way to her side of the bed. Looking down at her, he reached up to touch her cheek. He could see the struggle as she held herself still and allowed his touch.

"I think I resented your extraordinary successes here and on your other estates. 'Tis a feat quite unknown for women. And when one and all proclaimed your abilities and talents, even old Father Elwood, I confess to feeling jealous of you."

"But, my lord, I…"

"Nay, please let me finish before I lose my way." He pulled a stool over to the bedside and sat next to her. "I was beginning to see the foolishness in my ways when I learned of your condition. After abiding by your request and then almost…well, I confess that I felt myself losing all to the rage inside. I struck out at you in anger and sought to control you more when I could not control myself. And in spite of my worst behavior, you answered each challenge laid at your feet with a dignity and grace I could not help but admire."

He took her hand in his and raised it to his lips.

"Emalie, I beg your forgiveness for last night. I can not promise that the anger is gone, but I will promise that I am no threat to you any longer."

He saw tears well in her eyes and she swallowed several times before finally speaking.

"'Tis I who needs beg forgiveness, my lord. You were correct that I have deceived you from the first."

"I fear that we were both dragged into this by Eleanor, for her own reasons. Who can understand the Plantagenets? Emalie, I would like to propose that we begin again. It is the only way for us to honor the pledges we made together. I believe I would welcome your advice." Christian stood and helped her to stand. Reaching down, he unhooked the ring of keys from his belt and handed it back to her. "I would ask that you consult with me before changing anything that I have ordered changed since my arrival."

"Oh, aye, my lord." Her tear-filled eyes now glistened with excitement. "I will be certain to do that."

"I will leave you to rest now for I am certain that neither of us slept well last night."

"My lord, thank you for doing this," she said, holding out the key ring. "I know that it was difficult for you coming here and being surprised every step of the way."

He nodded at her and began to pull the door open. He would ask once more and then mayhap the knowledge would put his demons to rest.

"Would you give me his name?"

The joy left her face and her mouth trembled. "I can not, my lord."

"If I knew, then I would not see you in my mind in bed with every man I see here in Greystone."

She walked to him and placed her hand on his arm.

"If I speak his name, you will forever link him to me and never see anything else."

This was not what he hoped for and she must have sensed it, for she continued. "I will assure you that I have never spoken of him to anyone else and never will. Can that not suffice between us?"

Mayhap that would be enough. "No one else knows who fathered your child?"

Sadness filled her face as she spoke. "A very few know, my lord, and they would keep that secret until their deaths."

Although certain that he could name those few, he did not. 'Twas better left unsaid. His pride and his honor could be preserved in this.

"I will accept your pledge then, lady."

He turned and pulled the door open, leaving by the hallway. As he walked toward his own chamber, he heard sounds that did not sound like resting. He smiled, mayhap this would work out for the best after all.

The next weeks and months were like a dream to her—the one she'd always had, but now it was coming true for her. With the return of her responsibilities, Emalie had once more become a vital part of running Greystone and her other properties. As summer ended and the harvest was completed and stored, life settled down into a comfortable routine.

Christian was still arrogant, sometimes even a prig. Nothing could change that. But he asked for her opinions and he followed her advice. The day he asked her to sit court with him was the day she realized that she was falling in love with her husband. She cried for a long time after he sent word inviting her to sit beside him to hear the grievances and requests of their people.

Luckily she had several hours to regain her composure before she was expected to appear, but even that was a close thing.

Geoffrey recovered and thrived and soon was involved in exactly what she had said young men of his age should be—he was obsessed with the young women of the keep. Although Emalie tried to look away from his activities, she knew from gossip that at least one of the laundry maids and one of the kitchen maids were meeting him in the stables on a regular basis. His most endearing quality though was his unswerving loyalty to his brother.

No matter what task he was assigned, Geoff did whatever Christian asked of him. And Emalie knew that the most difficult one was yet to come, for Christian had mentioned to her that he planned to send Geoffrey back to their estate in Poitiers in the spring. She was not sure who would miss him more when he was gone.

Emalie stood and walked to the window of the solar. Sitting for too long was bothering her so she decided to walk outside before their meal. The early-morning sickness that had frequently plagued her had stopped, but some smells and tastes still brought on nausea. And while lying abed this morn, she felt a movement within her for the first time. 'Twould not be long until her shape grew larger and changed and her activities would be curtailed.

Alyce followed her everywhere now and they walked out into the courtyard and, after catching sight of Christian working his horse near the stables, she decided to watch. Although it was nearly Saint Matthew's Day and Michaelmas shortly after, the weather stayed warmer than usual. Christian had remarked that their vineyards were enjoying the good weather and his wine master foretold of an excellent harvest and quality.

Christian was practicing with the horse he used during jousts in tournaments. Although he had no need to earn riches by competing any longer, he did not want his horses to lose their edge and so he and Luc worked with them on a regular basis. Emalie shielded her eyes from the glare of the midday sun and watched as her husband demonstrated how he had become a tournament champion. Watching during this practice time, Emalie felt a bit jealous of those who had seen him competing in the real jousts, for his ability to be one with his mount and control the horse under the pressure of attack was obvious.

He noticed her when they took a break and rode to where she stood. He lifted his helm and bowed his head in greeting.

"My lady, how do you fare?" he said, smiling.

"I am well, my lord. And you?"

"I am pleased with my efforts this day," he said, looking over at Luc as he approached them. "Especially since I have unseated Sir Luc the last four times we have fought."

Luc pulled his visor up and glared at Christian, making Emalie laugh. How much like children these two were! "My lady, believe not this slander. Your husband has used trickery in his attempts to beat me."

"Trickery, my lord? I would not have thought it of you." She joined in the teasing.

Luc smiled smugly at Christian. "I knew your lady would disapprove of such methods."

Christian dismounted and walked over to the fence.

A squire ran to him to take his weapons and helmet. Luc stayed on his horse and waited.

"If Sir Luc would keep his mind on his weapons and not on his wife's b—"

"My lord!" she and Luc cried out together.

"'Tis not my fault that he is easily distracted." Christian laughed and nodded to his friend. "Fatin has long been his weakness and a good fighter will focus on his opponent's defects."

The two were about to have a battle of words over their prowess as warriors, but a messenger called to Christian from the gate. Waving him forward, Emalie waited to hear the news he brought. Dispatches were a common occurrence between their many estates, but this messenger was not known to her.

He bowed to them both and then handed his letters to Christian. He stood waiting for any response to the information contained within. Her husband unfolded the larger vellum packet and read the words. He held on to a smaller piece as he continued to read. Then he turned to Emalie.

"Lord Durwyn of Lemsley invites us to his daughter's wedding in a fortnight. What think you of this?"

Happiness filled her at the thought of seeing her friend. Fayth's betrothal had been one of the last things her father approved before his illness and Emalie had waited and waited for a wedding date to be announced. Before she could answer, he laughed.

"I can see by your expression that you believe this a good match?"

"Aye, my lord. Fayth and Sir Hugh are well suited for each other."

"I fear that is not a convenient time for us to travel there, my lady. What with the weather about to change and the preparations for winter upon us…mayhap we should send our felicitations to them and visit at another time.''

She could not think of a way to argue with him without arguing. Her thoughts jumbled as she tried to put words together that would not insult him or be demanding, but would make him understand how much she wanted to go. She was about to speak when she looked up and saw the repressed smile that made his lips twitch.

''My lady, I but tease you about this. I have heard you mention Lord Durwyn and his family many times and would not think of keeping you from them at this time.''

Emalie looked at him and felt her heart almost burst within her chest. And suddenly all she could do was cry. The sobs came from deep within and as she stood helpless against the power of them, Christian wrapped her in his arms and rocked her as she wept. A few minutes later, as her tears were spent, she raised her head from his chest and took a deep breath trying to calm herself.

''Your pardon, my lord. I seem to be a maudlin mess these days.''

He held out a piece of linen to her, but his arms still encircled her. And the strangest thing was that she did not want to leave his embrace. Glancing around, for she knew the impropriety of standing so in public, she noticed that they were alone. Even Alyce was nowhere in sight.

''Do not fret, lady. I know they are tears of joy for your friend.''

''I have not seen her in these last few years since

my mother's passing, my lord. 'Twill be good to spend some time with her.''

"We can stay a few additional days at Lemsley if you wish."

The tears threatened once again and she blinked them away. He thought they were for her friend. He had no idea that they were for him. "As you wish, my lord."

"Come," he said, touching a soft kiss to her forehead. "Let us go and give the messenger our answer and then you can read the message from Fayth herself." He held out the smaller packet to her. "You will have preparations to make."

He released her and offered his arm to escort her to the hall. Laying her hand on his, she walked at his side, trying not to be overwhelmed by either his embrace or his kiss. He had not touched her other than to escort her since the night in her chambers. She remembered the torrent of feelings he had caused that night with the touch of his mouth and his hands. Something inside her responded to just the memories of the heat and the aching and the throbbing and soon she felt as breathless as she had when he'd created those waves of passion within her.

Emalie wondered if he realized that he had kissed her. And her stomach did a little flip when she thought of how she wished he had touched his mouth to hers. She was tempted to look at him as they walked, but she hesitated to show how flustered an embrace and a kiss had made her. The worst part was that she wanted more.

Did husbands seek pleasure with wives who were breeding? He had not sought her bed yet, even though they had made peace between them. She had heard no more rumors and gossip about Lyssa or Belle sharing his bed, but that could simply mean he was being more discreet than before. Confused, she knew there was really no one to ask such a question of and she was unwilling to discuss the concern with him.

Mayhap she could ask Fatin? Fatin had an understanding of men and how they thought. Her comments during their conversations in the privacy of the solar were both enlightening and entertaining. Emalie decided to think on it before broaching this private a matter.

As they reached the hall, she knew the next several weeks would be busy as she prepared for the trip and then traveled to Lemsley. And for the first time in a very long time, she was contented with her life.

Chapter Fifteen

The air around him took on a sudden chill as the sun began to slip lower in the sky. Even though it was close to the equinox, dusk would not darken the day for a few more hours. Still, that did not protect travelers from the change in the temperature when midday had passed. Christian felt behind him to make certain that his cloak was nearby. A few more hours of riding would bring them to their destination and a warm place to spend the night.

His attention was drawn by the sound of Luc clearing his throat, and a bit too obviously to ignore it. Glancing back in the direction that Luc nodded, he saw that Emalie was not sitting well on her mount. Squinting through the shadows of the tree-lined path, he could see that his wife was fighting sleep. He cursed her stubbornness under his breath as he pulled the reins and guided his own mount back to hers. Positioning himself next to her, he called to her softly.

"My lady."

Instead of the response he wanted, her head drooped lower.

"Emalie."

Not wanting to startle her into a fall, he moved in closer, grasped her forearm and used his leg to steady hers. Her eyes fluttered open and then her gaze cleared as she woke from her light drowse.

"My lord? Did you call me?" she asked as she moved herself back into the center of her saddle.

Christian was struck at the innocence and beauty in his wife's face as she shook off sleep's grasp. And the realization that he wanted to see her wake in the morning surprised him. Like a punch in his gut, desire for his wife flared once more.

"If you are tired, you should ride in the cart with your maid." He tried with all his strength and resolve not to let his craving for her show. In spite of their truce, he could not let himself want a woman who carried another man's seed.

"I will be fine, my lord. My thanks for your concern."

He watched as she pushed her hair off her shoulders and then reached for her cloak when it fell behind her. Startled by her actions, her horse sidestepped and she shifted to one side. Without thought, he reached across the space between them, grasped her at the waist and lifted her off her mount and onto his lap.

"My lord, truly, I can ride my own mount," she whispered to him in a voice no one else could hear. "This is not necessary."

Emalie leaned forward and reached out to grab the cloak that now dragged on the ground next to them. Fearing that she would feel the physical proof of his body, he scooped her up and settled her more comfortably across his thighs.

"You were about to fall to the ground. You are safer here."

She leaned away as far as she could and gazed at him, confusion evident in her eyes and in the way her forehead crinkled into a frown. She began shaking her head at him as though she would refuse and then looked around at their entourage. He watched as the realization that they were being observed sank in and as his wife once again became a dutiful, demure woman.

"As you wish, my lord."

Her words were soft and full of surrender and he could feel her tremble in his arms as he gathered her close to him. She had never approached him of her own volition or expressed a willingness to, and what bothered him most was that with each passing day he wanted her more.

Christian tried again to convince himself that he did not want her. However, his initial thoughts of putting her aside had been banished, for in truth, they dealt well with each other now.

But his body, now strengthened with ample amounts of food and exercise, taunted him with a weakness and a desire for her that only one thing could satisfy. And he would not allow that to happen. He could not.

So why did he now hold her close enough that he could smell the fragrance of the soap she washed with? Every turn of her head released the scent of roses and honey that tortured him with the need to bury himself within her. He leaned down closer and inhaled her very essence, still fighting to turn his thoughts away from those desires.

"Why do you not ride in the cart?" he asked as he guided his mount forward and back into his place in the double line of riders. She gave him no answer. He

squeezed her gently and said again, "Why not ride in
the cart with your maid?"

Without looking at him, she whispered her answer.
"The rocking of the cart…makes me…ill, my lord."

It was the babe she carried that made her ill. Many
things could make a woman who was increasing ill—
smells, motion, even foods. He knew this from observ-
ing the women of his estates and even his own family.
He remembered his stepmother complaining that the
smell of roasting pigeon made her stomach lurch while
she was carrying his brother.

Her reference to the babe, even at his behest, caused
the anger to flare in spite of his resolve. The reality of
her pregnancy was still difficult to face. He took several
deep breaths and tried to calm his anger. She had not
complained about the ills of breeding or brought anything about her condition to his attention, as he had
ordered in the solar the day he found out about it.

If he was to retain his honor and his pride, he must
swallow this bitter drink and act, at least in public, as
though she carried his seed within her. Christian knew
that custom saved him in this—no noble husband who
married for lands and wealth took an interest in a
breeding wife the months before the birth of an heir.
He thought of those men whose wives were carrying
and felt confident in this belief. Other than a few trivial
questions on an occasional basis, his role would be to
turn this process over to the women of Emalie's circle
and inquire once the birth was accomplished. However,
the words that came out of his mouth surprised even
him.

"'Tis a common enough complaint of breeding
women. Ride here a while and see if it passes."

Emalie leaned away once more and stared at him.

He would not meet her gaze and soon she turned back to face the road. After some minutes at their regular pace, he felt her body relax against his in sleep. Capturing her chin in his hand, he positioned her face on his chest and rested his own chin on the top of her head where her fragrance once more tortured him.

She slept in his arms for the next several hours, even as they made their way into Lord Durwyn's walled yard and were surrounded by the sounds of a busy keep. Christian continued to hold her though his arms had long ago begun to cramp from not moving. Amazed at how deeply she slept, he reined in his horse, stopped near the steps and gathered her into his arms, ready to dismount. It would have been easier to wake her, but something within him did not want to disturb her or this time of holding her close.

As he suspected would happen if she woke, her eyes fluttered open and she realized who held her and how. She slipped from his hold and into the waiting arms of his new squire. Damn the boy for being thorough in his duties to his lord's wife! She regained her balance once on her feet and he watched a smile light her face. Jumping from the horse, he took his place next to her and observed a whole throng of people pour out from the double wooden doors at the top of the stairs.

Protocol demanded that she stay at his side and she did, but Christian could feel her trembling with excitement and looked at those approaching from within. An older man and woman, obviously Lord Durwyn and his wife, Hertha, led the group down the stairs. A younger woman peeked anxiously around them and he surmised that this was the childhood friend of whom Emalie had spoken so enthusiastically—the lady Fayth, soon to be married to a Sir Hugh of some nearby and noble family.

Lord Durwyn continued down until he stood on the landing and then he bowed deeply before Christian and Emalie. The rest of the group followed his lead, with the women dipping into curtsies, and all remained in obeisance until Christian accepted his greetings and took him by the hand. Without a moment more of hesitation, the young woman pushed around her parents and rushed to Emalie, pulling her into a crushing embrace and squealing those words that only women understand.

"Daughter!" Lord Durwyn cried out in a loud disapproving voice. "You have not yet been presented to the Earl of Harbridge. Have you not learned anything of proper manners?"

Fayth paused for a moment and then released Emalie from her arms. Stepping back, she lowered her head and curtsied again before him. "Forgive me, my lord. I fear that my excitement at seeing Em...er...the countess, overcame my observance of protocol. I hope you will pardon my lapse and not hold my parents responsible for my behavior."

Glancing at those who listened, Christian realized that they did not know what to expect of him. Even Emalie's face was now shadowed in concern.

"Rise, please, Lady Fayth. I understand that you have been friends with my ladywife for many years. Your excitement at seeing her is certainly expected and not unseemly at all."

A collective sigh was released as he nodded to Lord Durwyn and Lady Hertha. He spoke the truth. Remembering how he had felt when Geoff and Luc had arrived at Greystone those many weeks ago, he could imagine what Fayth and Emalie were feeling. So far as he knew, Emalie had no companion at Greystone to share her thoughts and gossip with. Emalie held to her station and, although scrupulously polite to the wives of his knights and those of their joined estates, kept her own counsel.

"With your permission, my lord, we have prepared a meal for you and the countess. Would you wish to partake of that now?" Lady Hertha asked as she stepped from her husband's shadow and stood before them.

"I would dearly love a cup of wine, but I think that my wife needs to refresh herself from the journey. If you would see to her needs, perhaps Lord Durwyn could see to my comfort?"

Emalie's face lit up with joy again at this opportunity to spend some time with her friend and her parents' friends. Something inside him tightened as he watched her being led off by the two women, all of them exchanging greetings and hugs at one time. They disappeared into the keep before he even took a step, their delighted laughter echoing back to him in the courtyard. It warmed his heart to hear it.

And he realized in that instant that he wanted more from her than politeness and obedience. He wanted her to gift him with the kind of smiles and joy that she had given to Lady Fayth. And he wanted her to look forward to his presence as she had to this trip. And...he simply wanted her. A sense of acceptance filled him as he finally knew that he could no longer fight this longing to have her.

Christian looked over at the older man and nodded to him, following him into the keep. He had many questions for Lord Durwyn, questions about the land

and the upcoming winter, about his wife's family and her father's plans for her, and about the involvement of Prince John in the concerns of the Montgomeries. He had much to learn while he was here for Durwyn's daughter's wedding and he would begin now to gather together the facts of the past and present.

He had ignored the final part of his bargain with the king for as long as he dared. Christian needed to complete his task for the king in order to assure that his own honor and lands were his to control once more so that, come spring, he could send Geoff home as planned and not worry.

He followed Lord Durwyn inside and he soon found himself with a cup of some remarkable ale in his hand and food before him. After taking a few minutes to eat something, he turned to Durwyn.

"You knew the old earl?"

"Aye, my lord, I did. We fostered as boys and then as fate would have it, I was vassal to him for this land."

"When did you speak to him last?"

"Just before he took ill," the older man said in a lower voice. "Then he died so suddenly that it took all of us unaware." Durwyn lifted his cup and swallowed deeply from it.

"Why did he leave Emalie unprotected? With no betrothal arranged?"

"Emalie was betrothed, my lord, but he died in this last Crusade."

"And then?" Christian pressed on.

"He was waiting on the king. When word came that Richard would be ransomed, Gaspar planned to ask the king to set up a suitable match for his daughter."

"But Richard's release took much longer than expected and Gaspar did not live to see it.'' Christian smiled grimly at the man. ''Emalie was his only heir?''

''Aye, but it would seem that Richard found her a suitable husband as Gaspar wanted.'' Durwyn raised his cup and saluted Christian.

Christian drank in silence and wondered how to bring up the subject of the king's brother. He stood and walked to the other side of the solar, peering out the window into the courtyard below. Not as large as Greystone, Durwyn's property consisted of a walled manor house and a small village. He could see to the other side of the village from his position now.

''Has Lackland returned from his brother's side yet?'' he asked, preparing himself to assess the truthfulness of the answer given.

''As far as I know, he remains at the king's side, though if I were Richard, I think that would worry me far more than having him at a distance.''

''It will take the king years to reclaim the lands John has lost to his enemies.''

Durwyn walked to his side. ''But the king's disregard of England has left it in danger. Only strong barons and nobles can stand together against those who would ravage the land and the people.''

Christian faced him. ''Gaspar was Richard's man?''

''Until his death, my lord.''

He thought on the man's words and nodded. Gaspar had resisted John. And it sounded as though Durwyn had suspicions about his untimely death. Christian would keep this information to himself while he sought more.

Sensing the conversation was done, Durwyn invited him for a tour of the grounds. Anxious to work out the tightness in his limbs from the long ride, Christian agreed.

Chapter Sixteen

He watched her leave for her chambers after she fell asleep the second time. Knowing how worn-out she must be from the traveling and her reunion, he thought she would have retired on her own. The stubborn streak he saw this night, he had glimpsed several times in past weeks. Emalie stayed at the betrothal celebration much longer than he had expected.

Finally she had given in to Fayth's request and accompanied her above stairs. The two women walked off, arm in arm, whispering like children. He relaxed now that he knew she would not end up facedown in the platter of tarts and cakes that was served last.

Sooner than he thought, he, too, was feeling the call of sleep. His host noticed and asked one of the servants to guide him to his chambers. His steps slowed as he followed behind. After a few minutes, he stood outside the room assigned to him. Pushing the door open, he was surprised to see Emalie sitting on a stool near the bed.

"There is a shortage of rooms because of all the wedding guests, my lord."

"Since Durwyn's manor is not half the size of Greystone, I am not surprised."

"As his liege lord, he has given you, given us, the largest chamber to use."

She was nervous. They had to share this room and that bed for their stay here and she was nervous about it.

And as the tightness in his stomach told him, so was he.

"At least we do not have to share the room with Geoffrey. He snores loud enough to wake the cattle in old Foster's pens."

She laughed and stood. "I think we can manage this, my lord." She shrugged her robe from her shoulders and laid it on the stool. Lifting the bedcovers, she slid beneath them.

He usually slept naked. Deciding that some discretion was needed, he unlaced and removed his tunic and the shirt underneath it, but left on the breeches below those. Although her eyes were closed when he looked over at her, he sensed that she was watching him. Christian waited only a moment before climbing in with her.

They were not going to manage this. After admitting to himself just today that he wanted her, this was poor timing indeed. Christian shifted, trying to find a spot on the mattress without getting too close.

He settled on his side, facing away from Emalie, and tried to fall asleep. Even the silence of the room and his fatigue did not help. She had not made a sound and he hoped she was successful when he had not been. Turning carefully, to not disturb her, he found himself looking into Emalie's eyes.

She lay on her back, with the covers pulled up to

her neck. And she was wide-awake. He watched as the low flames in the hearth lit her face. The urge to kiss her was overwhelming him.

He reached up and traced the contours of her cheeks and her nose. She held her breath with every touch, but did not naysay him or move from him.

"I fear this is not going to work, Emalie," he whispered to her. He slid his fingers down onto her neck, running them along the edge of the covers she held and her gown. He smiled when he heard her breath catch again.

"My lord?"

"I want you, my lady," he said, moving his hand ever lower. He did not bother to move the covers yet, for he did not want to startle her into objection. Christian rested his hand on the swell of her breasts and waited for her reaction. 'Twas not long in coming.

They were fuller against his hand than the last time, and he laughed at how he even remembered the difference. But the tips puckered the same when touched.

"My lord," she said, placing her hand on his.

"Emalie?" he said softly.

"You do not have to do this."

"I do not?"

"Nay, my lord. I am certain that a willing maid could be found to accommodate your needs."

He lifted his hand from her and sat up, pushing the covers back. Getting out of bed, he was dazed by her words.

"A willing maid, Emalie? Is that what you think I want?"

Emalie sat up now and watched him move around the bed toward her. Her hair tumbled over her shoulder and framed her face and neck in firelit waves of burnished gold. The itch in his hands to wrap it around him grew until he could not control it—and he did not want to.

Did she now fear what they had come so close to once before? He knew she had gained pleasure from it. Did this also change now?

"Are you afraid of me, Emalie?"

She shook her head. "Nay, my lord."

"Are you afraid of what will happen between us if we continue?"

"I do not think so, my lord."

"Then why do you suggest that I find someone else instead of pleasuring my wife?"

He received the blush he had hoped for. She stammered getting the words out.

"I thought that, since you had sought out Lyssa and Belle over these past months, you would prefer someone else, my lord."

If she had not been serious, he would have laughed out loud. Prefer serving wenches to her? She had no idea that his attempts to substitute them for her had been such a dismal failure. Should he tell her?

He sat on the edge of the bed, forcing her to move toward the center.

"I want *you*, Emalie, as much now as I have since I saw you for the first time, standing over me in my bath."

"I have heard that a man can content himself with any woman when the urge is upon him."

He did laugh, then. "Who has told you such words of wisdom?"

She hesitated before answering him, but finally revealed her source. "The lady Fatin."

He smiled at the answer. If anyone knew about men,

it would be Fatin. How shocked his wife and everyone who met Luc's wife would be to discover that she had spent years as a bed slave to a very wealthy merchant near Jerusalem who shared her favors with his favorite customers. 'Twas how Luc had met her the first time.

He could not help but wonder what other bits of wisdom Fatin had shared with Emalie. "You discussed this with Fatin?" She nodded. "Why would you ask her about such things?"

"I know of her past, my lord. I could think of no other who I could ask, as you say, such things."

It was his turn to be amazed; once again Emalie had surprised him. "You know of her life before Luc and you still accept her presence? You sit at table with her and protect her within your women?"

"Some would say that there is no difference between Fatin and I, my lord."

Her words hit him like a blow. She was correct—a woman who took a man unto her outside the bonds of marriage was a whore; whether she was paid for her actions was of no import. Somehow though, assigning that name to her was not possible. And if she told the truth, the circumstances had been different for Emalie. To this day, his wife gave no indication of seeking a man's attention. Not even, to his regret, his.

"Do you think of yourself in that way?"

"I have found, my lord, that those who would call me such, if the truth was known, would care not for what I think."

He frowned at her truth. It hit him too close to the mark, for he did think like that. If a noblewoman lost her virtue, she lost all. He shook his head, for he could not honestly say that of Emalie.

In spite of her dishonor, she remained kind and gracious and caring. In spite of losing her virtue, the good qualities she carried within were still there and anyone with eyes could see it. Anyone who thought less of her for her mistake...

He thought less of her.

He had not accepted the good within her.

He could not accept and act on the honor that was within him.

Standing, he reached for his shirt and tunic. He needed to think on this. He could not make this marriage a true one until he understood the truth within each of them.

"In truth, Emalie, I came here with seduction on my mind." He wrapped his belt around his hips and tugged it tightly into place. "But your words have disturbed me and I would think on them."

"Please, my lord. Stay." Her voice trembled now. He could tell that she was worried that he was angry.

"Fear not, Emalie. I will not sleep with another woman and have not since our marriage." Her expression hardened as he watched. "Although I tried to replace you with others in my bed, I failed miserably."

"Lyssa? Belle?" Again he could see that she had to force out the names that were so distasteful to her.

"The intent was there on my part—I confess to that. But even with wine to help my efforts, I could not take another when 'twas you I wanted all along."

He leaned down and kissed her gently on the lips. He swore they softened under his in welcome, but he pulled away and walked to the door. "I will return anon. I just need some air."

Leaving the chamber quietly, he made his way down to the hall, then out to the courtyard and toward the one storage barn within the wall. Durwyn was using every inch of space for guests and those who accompanied and served them. Christian knew that Luc was sleeping there. Although he never stopped, several guards nodded their greetings to him as he passed.

Pulling open the side door, Christian stepped inside and waited for his eyes to become accustomed to the dim light given off by only a few small lanterns. The sounds of deep snores filled the large open space and were interspersed with other sounds that could only be from a certain type of activity. Seeing a loft raised on one side of the barn, he knew that it was the origination for the noises of coupling that echoed through the building.

Moving among the rows of sleeping men, he finally located Luc and shook him awake. They met outside a few minutes later and walked away from the building; Christian preferred that their words not be overheard.

"I had thought I would get some good sleep without Fatin here to keep me awake through the night," Luc complained dryly.

"Do not begrudge your friend a few moments of your precious sleeping time. Come," he said, nodding toward the courtyard, "walk with me."

Luc yawned constantly as they began to circle the manor house. Christian pondered how to ask the question that haunted him the most. After they passed the same guards for the third time, Luc stopped.

"Now. Ask it now or I am back to that miserable pallet in the barn." Luc crossed his arms over his chest and moved no farther.

He had no choice now. If he wanted to understand the feelings that raged within him, he needed his friend's advice.

"How can you keep her as your wife knowing that she has had so many before you?"

Luc's face turned beet-red and he reached out and cuffed Christian on the head. Not enough to hurt, but Christian got the message that he had annoyed his friend. They had never discussed this, even on Luc's return from the Holy Lands with a wife in tow. Luc had matter-of-factly informed his liege lord of his marriage and introduced the exotic beauty who was his wife. It was not until one drunken night when things were very difficult for them that the truth had been revealed.

"Because, you imbecile, I am content in knowing that no matter who came before me, I am the last man she will have."

"It does not bother you that she has—" He did not finish because Luc grabbed his tunic and twisted it around his neck, making words impossible.

"If you were not my liege, I would pound you into the ground right here at my feet for the insult you offer my wife." Luc released him with a push and it took Christian a few moments to regain his breath.

"I mean no insult, Luc. I seek to understand."

"I saved her from the massacre because of the pleasure she offered, but she accepted my offer to marry because we have so much more than that."

He knew he should stop, but the answer that he needed had not been given yet.

"But how do you accept the dishonor of what she did before you?"

He knew he was in trouble, for he saw the glare of Luc's eyes as his friend threw the punch at him. Landing hard in the dirt, he waved Luc off.

"Dishonor? Where is there dishonor?" Luc growled

with the words. "I do not profess to understand or accept the infidel's ways, but Fatin was raised to be what she became. There was no dishonor in it. She is a good person, a caring person, a forgiving person. That is all that matters to me." Luc tightened and opened his fists as he spoke.

From his place on the ground, Christian thought about his words. His friend was right—honor was more about how a person lived their life than a title regained through coin or service. Emalie had never lost her honor, because she was still the good woman who put her people's needs first. No night of shame could take away what she really was.

Just as no declaration by the king would restore his honor. If he had not lost it by his own behavior and deeds, then it was still his own. His lack of acceptance of Emalie did indeed threaten that which he pursued with such effort, for he could not treat the woman he had taken as his wife so dishonorably without losing it in reality.

"My thanks," he said, climbing back to his feet. "Your words have made me see the error in my thinking and in my ways." Swiping the dirt from his tunic, Christian offered Luc his hand.

Luc hesitated before reaching out his own hand. "I thought you had made peace with your lady?"

"We have, on many issues, save one."

"Come here and let me knock some sense into that thick head of yours." Luc reached out and tried to grab his tunic again. "Go, make peace with her, Christian, before you lose all she brings to you."

When he started to reply, Luc continued. "And I do not refer to titles or lands or wealth. See past that to the treasure you've received. Now go. I wish to sleep and dream of the treasure I've left behind at Greystone.''

Without another word or argument, Luc turned and left him standing in the yard.

His friend's words had made a great deal of sense to him—they felt right. They spoke to the heart of the problem for him in his marriage to Emalie. And now it was up to him to take action and make things right.

Chapter Seventeen

He was somehow different today.

Emalie was awake when Christian returned to the room after leaving so precipitously, but they exchanged no more words. He had undressed quickly and quietly and climbed into bed next to her. After waiting and waiting for something to happen between them, for some touch or word, she had been greeted by his soft snoring. It had been hours before sleep claimed her.

This morn, she awoke wrapped in his arms and almost covered by his body. She had no memory of moving toward him in the bed or of him taking her into his embrace, but it was definitely a pleasurable feeling to be so close to him.

There. There it was again.

She looked over at him and found him deep in conversation with Lady Hertha. His leg, however, was brushing against hers. And she knew it was being done deliberately. Once, earlier in the meal, he had even laid his hand in her lap as he asked a question about Fayth.

She swore that the place he touched on her thigh still bore the heat of his hand there. And her neck tingled from his breath as he whispered private questions to only her. The subject of his queries were not personal, but the manner he used was. Sometimes he simply leaned toward her until his mouth was so close to her ear that she felt his breath there. Other times, he lifted her hair away from her ear and almost touched his lips to it as he spoke.

Then she realized that he had continued to touch her at every possible moment and opportunity since this morn when she left his embrace. A kiss on the hand. His hand on her waist as they walked. His thigh against hers. The heated whispering in her ear.

And then there was the dance.

Christian surprised her by asking her to join him as the musicians played a lively tune. As they moved through the intricate steps of the dance, she realized that she had never seen him dance before. When she mentioned it, he replied that since fighting was simply a dance, his trainers had insisted he master the art of dance.

But his touches throughout were not part of the dance she'd learned. His arm brushed her breasts several times as he turned her. And he had held her much closer than necessary during the lift, causing her body to slide down his as he placed her back on her feet. With her hands bracing on his shoulders, she looked down into his eyes and a most disturbing desire raced through her. She wanted him to hold her like this when they were both naked. She wanted to feel his heated skin against hers.

Emalie shook her head, trying to break the reverie. Although she could break out of the scandalous thoughts, her body had reacted to them already. Her increasingly sensitive breasts swelled against the constraints of her clothing and sweat trickled between them, and down her back. Tiny tremors moved through her and settled deep, making an unfamiliar ache begin and strengthen.

Her attempts to be discreet in her discomfort were unsuccessful, for Christian turned back to her with his full attentions.

"I have been neglecting you, my lady," he said as he slid closer to her stool. "Here, let me serve you."

She must be losing her mind. His emphasis on the word "serve" sent more chills through her and she would swear he meant so much more than simply helping with the wine.

He held the goblet to her lips when she sipped and then placed his own mouth where hers had been. Entranced, she watched as he licked his lips to catch an errant drop of wine. Her breath caught when he looked at her mouth as though he would do the same to her lips. She was still reaching for her napkin when he speared a morsel of roasted pigeon from their shared trencher and held it out to her.

Instead of placing it before her, he held it just beyond her mouth. Then he stared into her eyes as he moved it closer and closer. Just when it was about to reach her lips, he slid it over them and then slipped it inside. She closed her eyes against the intensity she saw in his gaze and chewed. With the heat and tension building between them, she found it impossible to swallow.

"Here, my lady. A sip to ease its way."

The cup's rim was warm now from both of their mouths and she drank as he offered.

This was insanity. She fought to control the urge to beg for his touch as she had that other night he came to her room with seduction in mind. Was this also a seduction? Did he deliberately warm her and train her to his touch like a falcon in the mews is trained?

Damn her, it was working. For with each touch or kiss or warm breath against her skin, she wanted more. And damn him, she could tell by his knowing gaze that he was aware of her reactions.

Suddenly he leaned back and held out his arm to her. Standing as she placed her arm on his, he spoke to their hosts.

"My lady and I thank you for your gracious meal and entertainment. Until tomorrow…"

With a nod of his head to Lord Durwyn, and with no other words, he led her away from the table and out of the hall. When Alyce moved to join them, he waved her off.

"I will attend to my lady, Alyce."

"Aye, my lord," Alyce answered, curtsying.

"And come not in the morning until I call you," he added as they passed by her.

Emalie could not argue or question, for anticipation filled her. If her maid said aye or nay, she knew not. Emalie only knew that he would join with her when they reached their room. And that made her even more breathless. Her body was heated and throbbing already, for his deliberate touches and teasing had done that.

She did not think it, but they seemed to race up the stairs and down the hall to their chamber. He let go of her hand only to drop the bar on the door, and then he wrapped her in his arms and kissed her.

It was a kiss that promised, a kiss that teased, a kiss that added only more heat and wetness to her. His tongue touched her lips and slipped in her mouth and she could taste the wine they had shared and she could taste him. His arms encircled her and his hands reached into her hair, pulling the coif and veils from it. Soon he had slid his fingers into her hair and freed it from the braids Alyce had made so diligently. And his mouth never left hers.

Over and over they kissed until they were both gasping for breath. He lifted his lips only to take a breath and then he plunged inside her mouth again. His hands still played in her hair, holding her close. After minutes or hours or days—she could not tell any longer—he released her mouth and stepped back.

"I will play lady's maid, Emalie. Let me help with these."

He reached out and began unlacing her long sleeves from the place they attached to her overtunic. His movements were slow and always he kept his hands on her. Once untied, he slid the sleeves from her shoulders, down her arms until they dropped on the floor. Still touching her, he moved his hands over her arms, onto her shoulders and neck.

"Here now. Turn this way and I will see to your tunic."

Although she hesitated to turn from him, he guided her until she faced the fire and he was at her back. His hands moved down her back, tugging and loosening the laces until he reached the base of her spine where the dress opened. Before she could reach up to lift the tunic, he slipped his hands in from behind and pushed it from her shoulders. As the tunic fell, he skimmed over her hips and waist, her belly and breasts. Although she still wore her shift, it did nothing to lessen the sensations he caused as he touched her.

He stepped closer behind her and pulled at the laces that closed her shift in the front. His breath against her neck was hot and she felt the muscles of a man, of a warrior, at her back. All about him was hard, except for his touch. She could not help it when her head dropped back against him. He kissed her neck as he bared her to the fire and to him.

Then he began his tormenting, for he lifted her arms over her head and slid his fingertips down until he reached her shoulders. His path moved lower onto the fullness of her breasts, which ached and swelled, their tips tightened even more by his approach. His fingers moved with a feathery touch, teasing the nipples, tickling the skin and then he moved on, his path ever downward.

The muscles in her stomach tightened as he made his touch heavier, now using his hands to follow the contours of her body. He stopped just as he reached the hair at the juncture of her thighs. She waited for him to feel between them, to find the wetness he had caused, but he did not. Instead she felt his hands on her thighs and she let them open for his touch.

And he did not.

When her body trembled in readiness and in anticipation and in need, he began his efforts anew. This time, her knees buckled when he grazed the springy hair between her thighs. Taking pity on her, Christian turned her in his arms and took her mouth in searing kisses that claimed her as his own.

The feeling of being naked against him, even clothed as he still was, was intoxicating, but she wanted to feel him.

"My lord," she whispered when he finally released her mouth. "Your clothes?"

Faster than she could have imagined, he took a step away and undressed himself. He did not bother with laces or finesse, but he accomplished his task in the shortest amount of time that she thought possible. Then she truly lost her breath at the sight of this man before her, for he in no way resembled the man she remembered from the bath.

He had not only healed, he had added muscle and weight until he now resembled the warrior mentioned by the queen. His shoulders were broad and his chest rippled under her gaze. She looked further and saw that the muscles continued in his arms and, when she finally dared, his thighs. Although she tried not to stare, another part of his anatomy was well formed, too. She looked quickly back at his eyes, which were laughing at her.

"Now we are even, Emalie."

"Not even, my lord," she whispered as she glanced once more below his waist. "You appear to be much bigger…"

She never finished her words. He gathered her close and kissed her again. This time, with their skin touching, she felt something within her coil tighter and tighter. She began to imitate his touch and glided her hands over his back and shoulders and down below his hips. He was hard everywhere.

He pulled her toward the bed and they tumbled onto it. Now she could wrap around him as she wanted to, for he had positioned her on top of him. Doing so placed his manhood right under the most heated part of her. It lasted for a few seconds. Christian rolled her under him and then lifted his head.

She was ready to beg him to finish this, but he kissed her gently and then looked into her eyes.

"Be my wife?" he asked gruffly.

"I am your wife, my lord."

"As you promised? Only mine?"

Then she realized what he wanted. He wanted to consummate their marriage vows.

"Only yours, my lord," she promised.

"Only mine," he growled, entering her and joining with her so quickly and completely that she gasped. When he began to pull back, she entwined their legs so he could not leave her.

There was no stopping or slowing after that. Christian's every movement was a claim on her, as a woman and as his wife. He touched her everywhere as they moved together in the dance of passion. The powerful strokes built the tension within her until wave after wave of pleasure and release was upon her. After a few more thrusts, Christian held himself still within her and groaned out his own release.

After a few moments of quiet, he rolled onto his side, this time keeping himself inside her. She thought mayhap she dozed off to sleep. Soon though, Christian began his efforts again and this time their passion was slower and, if possible, even more agonizingly pleasurable than the first time. The third time felt simply decadent and different once again and finally took them to the edge of sleep.

As she nodded off, she heard him repeat the words he'd said throughout the night and she felt comforted somehow by the claim inherent in them.

"Only mine."

The next days went too quickly. Although Fayth was the bride, 'twas Emalie who felt like the newly wedded woman, blushing furiously at the bawdy comments and exploring the physical side to marriage. Her husband was her constant companion and they shared many a touch and caress and many, many kisses. He left her side to go on Durwyn's hunts and on the various tours, but he always made her feel, well, reclaimed on his return.

After Fayth and Sir Hugh left for his family's home, Emalie and Christian left for theirs. The trip home was completely different from the one there. She and her husband were so wrapped up in each other that she hardly noticed the passing of time or the miles traveled.

Once back in Greystone, she knew that their behavior was the subject of much discussion from their noble attendants to the servants in the kitchen. One and all noticed the change between them and Emalie was truly glad for it. She thought that he had fulfilled her dreams once he had accepted her back into her duties, but she was wrong. For now that he had staked his claim on her, body and soul, she flourished within their marriage as an equal to him. In only one aspect was there any degree of uncertainty and that was the babe that grew within her.

He was careful of her, whether they were traveling in the village or he was making passionate love to her. Always, he took care of her and made certain of her comfort over his. But he never asked about the babe or discussed it with her.

Christian was not outside the normal bounds with this. Most men never concerned themselves with their offspring; it was the wife's responsibility. In most marriages when the offspring was of the father, it made sense. In this one, she supposed, it made even more.

The weeks of summer turned to autumn and as the whole of Greystone prepared for the approach of winter, Emalie felt the touch of fear in her soul. Something was coming their way. Something malevolent. Something powerful that could destroy her and the man she knew now she loved and all that they worked for.

She prayed more, in the chapel every morning and evening, and heard the Mass as often as possible. Although most around her thought she worried over the babe's safe delivery, she did not. She prayed that Christian would forgive her when he discovered the truth about the babe and for drawing him into the Plantagenets' game.

Chapter Eighteen

The guards alerted him that visitors approached. Climbing to the ramparts of the keep, Christian watched the small party as they left the woods behind and came ever closer to his gates. His hair whipped around his face as he tried to discern their identity. He looked at the knight next to him, who shook his head. The group was still too far.

Although only November, the winds foretold of an early and harsh winter ahead. The villeins and serfs had redoubled their efforts to make necessary repairs and all in Greystone worked to prepare for the worst.

The entourage turned onto the road leading to the gate and 'twas then he noticed the royal banner. The three golden Plantagenet lions, lying *passant guardant* on a field of red—Richard's new coat of arms. But it could be any of the royal family members traveling under that flag.

The riders moved too fast for it to be Eleanor. The king was too busy regaining control of his lands on the Continent to journey to England now. That left only one of Henry's royal get.

Prince John.

"I suppose he has had enough of kissing his brother's royal arse?" Luc asked dryly. "They fight and forgive at an alarming rate."

"But their forgiveness extends not past their bloodlines. The rest of us are held to pay for our misjudgments."

Christian turned and spit in the dirt. That was how his father had lost all.

"You should greet him, Chris. He takes offense at the little gestures."

"I suppose I must. And Emalie will have heard of their approach by now. We should greet him together."

"Fatin will not be in attendance, my lord."

Christian stopped and looked at his friend. "Why not?"

"I have heard too many stories of his coveting other men's wives to allow her in his presence."

Christian nodded, realizing that Fatin's exotic appearance and earthly sexuality would draw John's attention like a fly to honey. He did not blame Luc for trying to protect her from the prince's lust, for what John wanted, John took. It did not matter if that was a woman, a castle or riches. And mere men could not naysay the Plantagenet prince.

"Unfortunately, Emalie must greet him, but I will send her to her chambers. She has been feeling ill of late." Emalie was never sick, but if this would ease the way for her to be freed from her attendance on John and his entourage, he would use it.

"Very good, my lord. They pass under the gate now—we should go."

Christian left the parapet and made his way to the great hall. As he expected, Emalie was there, directing servants to prepare refreshments and rooms for the arriving guests. If she knew who visited, she gave no indication. She smiled when she noticed him watching and held out her hand to him.

"Visitors, my lord."

"I saw them from the battlements and came to greet them."

They walked in front of the raised dais and waited there. He thought it would be best to inform her of who her guests were.

"A royal visitor arrives."

Emalie looked at him. "Eleanor?"

He shook his head. "I could not see clearly, but I believe it to be John."

Her shaking could be felt where her hand lay on his arm. He looked at her, but she would not meet his gaze. Even her breathing changed and he was concerned over the differences in her. As he watched the visitors come closer, she seemed to regain her composure.

"What business does he have here, my lord?" she asked.

"I know not, but we will find out soon. Ah, my lord," he said, bowing before the prince. "Welcome to Greystone."

"Dumont," John said, nodding his head. "I thank you for your welcome." John stepped nearer to Emalie and reached for her hand. "Countess, you look well. And *enceinte?* Charming!"

Christian watched as John bent to kiss Emalie's hand. He could feel her reluctance to his touch.

"My lord, what brings you here?" Better to find out sooner than later.

"I bring greetings from my brother the king and my mother, who could not visit."

Knowing Richard's preference for Anjou, Aquitaine

and Poitou, Christian doubted the king would ever visit his English kingdom again. Eleanor traveled to wherever she wanted whenever she chose.

"Look, William. Not only is the countess as beautiful as ever—" John spoke louder and waved to one of the men in his retinue "—she is bountiful as well!"

A large man, about his own age, dressed all in black and gray, came forward out of the group and nodded. Emalie trembled again. Something was not right. Christian noticed that Alyce had appeared at Emalie's side and Walter was standing close by, as well.

"Emalie, my dear," he said. "My felicitations on your fertility. William, what say you?"

"My lady," William said, "how do you fare?"

At first, the man's eyes were hostile and angry, but when he gazed at Emalie they softened with a concern that was not appropriate for another man's wife. For his wife. He watched as William's gaze swept downward and fixed on her growing belly.

"Have we met, sir?" Christian decided it was time to interrupt.

"We have not, my lord," the man answered without taking his gaze off Emalie. "But I know Emalie."

Christian bristled at his familiarity and at using her name and not her title. A pain began in the pit of his stomach and grew as he noticed John's glee over both Emalie's and his discomfort.

"How so?" He looked at Alyce and nodded to her. Emalie appeared close to fainting and he was afraid to think of the reason.

"DeSeverin's family and the Montgomeries come from the same part of Anjou. William has known Emalie since they were children," John answered for the man.

Seeing how pale she was, Christian knew he needed to get her away from the prince. "My lady? I see you have once more overworked yourself. Please retire until later." Emalie blinked several times and then focused on his face. He smiled at her, hoping to reassure her and called to Alyce. "Alyce, see the countess to her chambers and let no one disturb her."

Alyce moved close to Emalie and supported her steps away. Walter followed close, making certain no one interfered.

Christian invited John to the table, but the prince watched until Emalie was out of the room. He exchanged some curious glances with DeSeverin before the two took their seats. Although he had Fitzhugh serve his best wine, Christian tasted it not due to worrying over Emalie's reaction to John and William.

"When is the babe due?" John asked after he had drunk some of the wine and torn off a chunk of bread.

"The midwife says the spring. But being the countess's first birth, she says it's difficult to tell."

"The spring? I think not," John offered, raising his voice louder.

"Pardon me?" Christian looked at John.

"What think you, William? I think the countess looks to be further along than that. Do you agree that she will not make it past Candlemas Day?"

William grunted and raised his cup in a mock salute.

A part of Christian knew exactly what this was, but he refused to fall into their game without knowing the rules and the prize. Well, he could guess the prize— Emalie and the titles and lands she brought to her husband.

Before he could go any further, Luc approached his chair. Bowing to the prince, Luc leaned in and whispered. The words struck fear in his heart, but he knew that he could not allow these vultures the satisfaction of knowing how they had terrorized Emalie.

"My lord," he said to John, "there is a problem I must deal with. My steward will see to your needs until dinner."

He gave John no chance to stop him, for he stood and followed Luc through the kitchens to the back stairs and up to their chambers. Without knocking, he entered and found her on their bed, her face bloodless and her breathing labored.

"The midwife?"

"I sent for her immediately, my lord. And for Timothy." Alyce hovered close to her mistress.

And all he could do was sit by her bed and wait. He did so and, as he waited, he took one of her frigid hands in his and rubbed it. She would not meet his gaze, but she mumbled something under her breath over and over. Her words were too faint to hear.

Soon the door opened and Enyd of the village entered. He thought to argue about leaving, since he was the husband and there was not a place on Emalie's body he had not seen or touched. But this was not the time to stake his claim. He pressed a kiss to her forehead and left her in the care of the women.

Dinner was a solemn meal, for in spite of John's bids to goad him, Christian remained calm. He recognized John's maneuvers—he had used them many times in battle himself.

Distract.

Disarm.

Destroy.

With no word on Emalie's condition, he chose to ignore many deliberate attempts to question and insult

both his and Emalie's honor. Although this was neither
the time nor place, he knew it would come. Finally, as
soon as was reasonable, considering John's royal
status, he excused himself and went upstairs to await
news.

The door opened as he put his hand on the latch and
Alyce invited him inside. Emalie was awake, but
looked pale and frightened. Enyd stopped him with instructions.

"She is to rest as much as possible, my lord."

"Of course."

"Timothy has made some concoctions for her to
drink to strengthen her and the babe. Make certain—"
she glared at both Alyce and him "—that she follows
his directions."

"Will she…?"

Her stern expression stopped his questions.

"She had some contractions today and a spotting of
blood. With some precautions, all should be well."

He nodded and she took her leave. Alyce left also
and he was alone with his wife.

"Do you have need of anything? A drink? Some
food?"

She shook her head. Christian saw her eyes fill with
tears and he sat down beside her on the bed, opening
his arms to her. Without hesitation, she leaned into his
embrace. She sobbed, murmuring words of sorrow and
pleading for his forgiveness.

"Emalie. Emalie, please, you must calm yourself.
Please."

He held her and rocked her until she finally stopped
crying and fell into an exhausted sleep in his arms.
'Twas some time past that before he could slip out and
lay her down on the bed.

Never had he seen her like this, not even in the face of his fury had she lost her control. Although he knew that the pregnancy was part of her overreaction, he also suspected that the truth of her pregnancy was the other part. A truth she still would not share with him, but with the prince's arrival and her reaction to him and his crony, one that became very clear. One that he truly did not want to face right now.

A soft knock at the door caught his attention. It opened a crack and Luc peered inside. Waving him in with a gesture to keep quiet, he waited to hear the reason for this intrusion. Since Luc knew of Emalie's condition, he knew his friend would interrupt him for only something of importance.

"His Highness wants to speak with you. Now."

"Can it not wait? I do not wish to leave her alone."

"If I thought it could, I would never have come here. Chris, he ordered me to tell you he wishes to discuss personal matters with you and it must be now. It sounded so much like a threat, I knew I must tell you."

Christian slid off the bed, careful not to wake her now that she had calmed.

"Where?"

"As sacrilegious as it sounds, he requests your presence in the chapel." The disdain was clear in his friend's voice.

"Will you stay here?" He would not leave her alone.

"Fatin waits without and will stay at your lady's side. I will stand guard until your return. No one with harmful intent will enter here."

"My thanks, Luc."

He walked out into the hall and waited for Fatin to enter the chamber and Luc to take his place in front of the door. Content that Emalie would not be disturbed, he walked quickly through the keep, out into the yard and into the stone chapel.

The prince waited for him at the altar. Luc was right—it felt like sacrilege to meet this man in this holy place. Motioning him forward, Christian waited for his attack. John did not mince words.

"I have wanted Greystone, nay, all of Harbridge's properties, for some time. And until my brother and mother interfered, I would have had it, and the countess, as planned."

John paused and turned to face him. "I will offer you the same proposal I offered DeSeverin."

Although rage at the prince's audacity filled him, he knew that his survival—and Emalie's—depended on him keeping his temper in check. "And that was?"

"You may hold the title and manage the lands, but I control it all and the wealth that comes from it. Oh, and of course, the fair Countess Emalie is mine whenever I choose to avail myself of her most plentiful charms."

John knew not how close to death he was at that moment. And unwisely, he chose to continue. "William and I had so little time to train her, but I am certain a man of your sophistication has taught her much during these months. I am tempted, I must confess, upon seeing her lush breasts, not to wait for her to drop the whelp before having her."

Christian's vision blurred as fury coursed in his veins. A quick death was not good enough; he would draw it out as long as possible. He fought off the drive to kill and focused on how Emalie would survive this bastard with no one there to protect her. He took a deep breath and blew it out.

"I fear I must decline Your Highness's generous offer."

"Decline? You do not understand your situation here, Dumont. I am offering my friendship to you."

"I am Richard's man."

"So am I. I have spent the past few months showing my love for my brother and gaining his forgiveness for all sorts of imagined transgressions while he was so unfortunately imprisoned abroad."

Christian prayed that God would strike the man dead for sinning so grievously in his house, but it did not happen.

"Did I mention that he has made me his heir to receive all of England upon his death? I should think that you would want to count among those who supported me and not among my enemies."

"I thank you again for your *kind* offer, but again I must decline." Christian could stomach no more of this. He turned to leave.

"Did you know that the old earl betrothed the fair Emalie to *my friend* William before his untimely death?"

Christian stopped walking and waited for the rest of it.

"And William, as anxious as he was to wed a woman of such charms, anticipated their vows. Who could blame him? With a woman who has as much to offer as she does, what man could resist her pleas to take her? I'm certain that neither you nor I could."

He pictured his hands around the prince's neck, choking the breath and life from him. It was the only thing that kept him from doing it in reality.

"Now a child exists and William has betrothal documents and wants to press his suit to regain Emalie and his child.''

''Why would you give me this opportunity?''

''Because, Dumont, I observed you and realized quickly that you are better for this than DeSeverin. Unlike him, you have an ability to make these lands successful and thereby valuable to me.'' He heard John's steps approaching from behind him.

''So, do I support his suit or do I lose the documents to prove his claim?'' He placed his hand on Christian's shoulder. ''I leave in the morning and would have your answer on it before I go.''

Christian nodded.

''You do have one other choice in this, Dumont. If you wish, I will see to a quiet annulment and you can simply leave all of this behind. You leave with your honor intact and able to enter into a true marriage when you locate an appropriate bride.''

He started to pull away and John just laughed. ''Son of Guillaume Dumont, think well on this, for if you back the wrong Plantagenet, you could end up in the ground with those others who made that mistake.''

John passed him and laughed on his way out of the chapel as though his words carried some humor. The urge to scream and kill and vomit came upon him, but he knew from experience that he must regain control of himself or everything and everyone he cared about were in danger.

Since his determination had not changed during the dark hours that he spent at Emalie's bedside, he saw no reason to confront John with his decision. The prince would know that no word was an answer, too.

John's own words had made the decision clear to

him. John told him that if he acquiesced in this he would be free to seek a true marriage.

A true marriage.

He had made a true marriage with Emalie the night they had first joined as one. The pledges made months before were confirmed in the physical act that made them man and wife. He had claimed her as his own that night so that no annulment could undo what was now real before God and man. And more importantly, in making his decision, what was real to him.

All he could do now was wait for John's response and decide what to do when it came. He would like to have all the facts to base his judgments on, but with Emalie in this precarious condition, he could not risk it.

He doubted not that John would move quickly; he may have begun his plans while offering friendship. Shaking his head, Christian knew that John had most likely set up contingencies for both possibilities.

Without Emalie's help, he could not fight John. He was not sure that he could fight him even with her help, for what if John possessed what he claimed to have?

The most disturbing part of this now was John's insinuation that he, too, had been involved physically with his wife. He could not imagine Emalie with John, or William either, if he admitted it to himself. Was he simply deluding himself in this?

He glanced over at her as she slept. How many times had he done this since their trip to Lemsley? He found that he enjoyed sitting at her side or lying next to her in the bed and watching as she slept. He shook his head at the absurdity of it.

What man would be content to sit like this?

She sighed then, drawing his attention to her face.

The fire's light played softly on her features. The swelling of her eyes was less now, but her breathing was still ragged and not smooth. How long until she calmed?

He thought back again to the night in Lemsley when he made her his own. And even back to the night when it had almost happened. There was a sense of innocence about her sexually that was a part of her. She had not been exposed to the type of debasement that relations with John would have brought about in someone. She did not fake the wonderment as he brought her to the edge of pleasure and beyond.

If she was more uninhibited with him now during their bed play, there was still a basic freshness to her. No, he shook his head again, John's depravity had not touched her.

That did not, however, mean that the child was not his. It was always a possibility that John fathered the child, stealing that task from his willing crony De-Severin. There was most likely no way to tell to a certainty unless the child was born with some telltale marking or coloring that was clearly from one man and not the other.

Christian stood and rubbed his eyes. Dawn would be accomplished soon and this endless night would end. But, he feared, the darkness would be with them for much longer.

Distract.

Disarm.

Destroy.

John had distracted him with his sudden appearance.

John sought to disarm him with the offer that would allow him to remain as lord of Greystone but at a completely unacceptable price.

Christian wondered when John would try to destroy him and how he would wield the weapons he held—Emalie's fear and participation, DeSeverin's complicity and his own fear of falling into the same trap that had killed his father.

The pain in his gut intensified with each passing hour. Well, he thought as he decided to try to sleep, the game was underway.

God help them all.

Chapter Nineteen

Her eyes did not want to open. They hurt and felt swollen and would not cooperate with her efforts to wake. Her head pounded and the rest of her body ached as she tried to move.

"Here now, my lady. Let me help you."

"Fatin?"

"Aye, my lady. Alyce runs some errands and will return anon. I am here to watch over you."

Emalie opened her eyes now and looked around the room. The sunlight streaming in through the window told her it was full day. The night and morning had passed without her knowledge. Glancing at the table next to the bed, she saw several bottles and goblets laid out in an order she knew Timothy would have done.

"*Oui,* madam," Fatin said, reaching for the one closest to her. "I have instructions to follow under 'pain of death,' your husband declared."

Emalie pushed herself up to sit. "I would not want you put to death on my account, Fatin. I promise to obey you in this."

Emalie held her breath and drank the brew down in one long swallow. She had some idea of what ingredients Timothy would use and knew their bitter taste was difficult to conceal. Fatin offered her some wine to wash the taste from her mouth.

"My husband?"

"He goes about his duties and left word he wishes to know when you wake."

"The prince?"

Fatin's mouth looked as if she had tasted spoiled meat. With disgust evident in her voice, she answered, "The prince and his entourage left early this morn. And none too soon for me."

Emalie needed to ask. "Was anyone…hurt?"

Fatin hesitated as though she did not want to answer. "Aye, my lady. One of the village girls, but not greatly. Enyd said all would be well."

She had failed once again. Because of her own fears, another of her people suffered. If she had only kept her wits about her and made arrangements with one of the village harlots who did not mind John's particular tastes. That usually placated him during his stay and kept the innocent safe. She would have Alyce find out more for her.

"Fatin, I have a favor to ask of you."

"My lady?"

"Before you send word to my husband, would you bring Father Elwood here for me?"

"You would see the old priest before your husband?" Fatin asked.

"Please."

Fatin nodded and walked to the door.

"Your husband also said that the person who allowed you out of your bed would be put to death. Do not risk my life while I find your priest for you."

Emalie nodded in agreement and watched as Fatin

left. She must do this before she lost her courage, for yesterday she had given in to evil. Leaning back against her pillows, she waited.

A short while later, a knock at the door came and Fatin opened it after a few moments' delay. The priest who had served her family's spiritual needs for many years followed behind. Once Fatin had checked on her, she left the chamber to inform her husband, giving her the privacy she needed.

His frown caught Luc's attention and they both watched Fatin approach the stables. Luc had other things on his mind and the lustful grin on his face made no secret of them. Christian, however, was concerned because Fatin was supposed to be tending Emalie while Alyce was gone.

"My lord, the lady is awake," Fatin said, bowing before him.

"You were ordered to stay with her, Fatin. Why did you come and not send a servant?" Luc's face turned red, but Christian did not care at this moment. "I do not want her left alone," he explained to both of them.

"She is not alone. The old priest is with her. I thought to give them some measure of privacy. My lord." The latter was added more in disdain than in respect. He heard it in her voice.

"Why did the priest visit her? I said no visitors until she was out of bed. Pray, tell me not that she has left her bed."

He was already several paces on his way when she called to him.

"Your lady stays in bed, but asked for the priest herself. I summoned him before I came to you. As to the reason for his visit—who can say why those of your faith feel such a need to seek out their counsel?''

She would only share those controversial and almost heretical thoughts with Luc and him, for Fatin had a clear understanding of the danger of the words she spoke. And she had to be upset to do so. Christian stopped and faced Fatin and Luc, who trailed closely behind him.

''Your pardon, Fatin. I am overwrought in my concern over Emalie and did not mean to insult you.'' Fatin nodded, accepting his apology. ''I am glad you were here for her, especially when she has no one else she counts as a friend.''

Luc looked suitably impressed with his repentance and smiled. ''I understand your concern, my friend. When someone you love is in danger—''

''Love?'' he interrupted. ''She is my wife. It is appropriate to be concerned for her welfare.''

Certainly he had some tender feelings for Emalie, but he would not consider himself in love with her. Their marriage was an arrangement of two people who suited each other well and got along passably well. He respected her, he even liked her and, God knows, he lusted for her. But love? He shook his head at the two of them, denying the emotion that would simply complicate matters more. No, not love.

He entered the keep and made use of the back stairs, scaring at least two laundry women who carried bundles much too slowly for his pace. Reaching the top floor, he walked to their chambers. He leaned his ear against the door and heard hushed voices within. Waiting as long as his impatience would bear, Christian knocked on the door after just another minute. He also did not wait to be invited inside, choosing to open the door.

The old priest, with hand extended over his wife's bowed head, was praying quietly. Christian stood by the door and watched. He saw the tears on Emalie's cheeks and wanted to interrupt, but seeing the concern on the priest's face, he delayed. Father Elwood finished and lifted Emalie's chin to look at her directly. With a whispered word, he released her and stood.

"Ah, my lord. You are here already."

"I did not want the countess to be disturbed, Father."

Christian walked closer and examined Emalie more closely.

"Sometimes, my lord, tears are good for the soul." The priest gathered up his stole and crucifix and prepared to leave. "My lady, I will keep you in my prayers. Come to Mass as soon as you are able."

Emalie nodded in reply. Christian went to her and sat on the bed. "Are you well?"

"I am tired still, in spite of the hours I slept, my lord. But otherwise I am well."

He lifted her chin as the priest had and used a linen cloth left nearby to dry her tears. "Are you hungry or thirsty?"

"Nay, my lord."

"I have asked that you use my name, Emalie."

"I was not certain of your feelings, my lord."

"Now that I know the truth?"

She looked at him in fear. He had not seen that expression in such a long time and he hated it. Ever so slightly, she moved away from him in the bed. Subtle, but he noticed it nonetheless.

He stood and walked a few paces from her. Turning

to face her, he asked the questions that he had answered in his own mind already in the dark of the night.

"Are we married in truth, Emalie?"

She frowned before answering. "Aye, my lord."

"Is there any reason why we could not marry as the king directed?"

"None to my knowledge."

"And we have consummated our vows?"

The blush that spread upward from the fullness of her breasts onto her neck and then up into her cheeks pleased him somehow. "Many times, Christian."

She chose now to use his name? Memories of those many times flowed over him. She had given herself to him. She was his.

"And did you make any promises to the father of your child?"

Her face lost all its color and her breath hitched as she tried to speak. "What are these questions about, my lord?"

"I simply seek to determine if we are of one mind concerning our vows and our marriage."

A shaky nod was all the response she gave, then she spoke. "I made no promises."

He nodded, satisfied that she told the truth. Her words echoed of Durwyn's in not knowing of any betrothal. If her father had made one, he had done it without her knowledge or his best friend's. Strange that. Durwyn stood as Emalie's godfather and guardian in her father's absence and he felt certain that Gaspar would have told him anything important to his daughter's care. A betrothal was such a thing.

And betrothals were usually witnessed by as many family and friends as the wedding itself, for the Church and the courts had held that the betrothal could be con-

sidered the joining and only a consummation was
needed to seal the contract.

Gaspar discussed all aspects of his estates with
Emalie. Why would he deliberately not speak of something this significant? It made no sense to him. But,
until John took the first step, he was wasting time and
strength worrying over this.

"Why did you need to see your priest?" He was
curious about that. To his knowledge, Emalie saw the
priest only at Mass, and he'd heard comments that she
never sought his advice.

She gazed at him with haunted eyes and the tightness
in his gut told him that he had gone too far. Mayhap
he did really wish to intrude between penitent and con-
fessor. Her hand glided over the bedcovers and when
they reached the edge, her fingers entwined in the bor-
der of the sheets. 'Twas a nervous reaction of hers that
he had seen before.

"I wished it gone."

"It?" He moved closer, for her voice was now a
whisper.

"The child within," she said as she placed her hands
on her rounded belly. "I wished it dead."

"Oh, Emalie," he whispered as he sat next to her.
John's evil was spreading. He did not judge her. He
simply felt her sorrow and pain.

"When I left the hall, I was tormented with fears
over the prince's visit. The thought came to me that if
there was no babe, there would be no threat from him."

She was crying now, tears streaming where he
thought none would be left. He turned and embraced
her as she sobbed. He thought her words were done,
but she forced herself to say them.

"I was on the stairs when I wished, when I prayed,

for the child's death to save me from whatever John plans.''

"Emalie, this is not your fault. Be at peace." He rubbed her back as she cried more.

"Do you not understand, Christian? I prayed for a child's death. An innocent babe. And all so that I would not have to admit to the truth and to my mistakes.''

"You take too much on yourself. You can not be responsible for the destruction that John causes.''

"Another thing you do not understand," she whispered hoarsely. "Because of my weakness, John ravaged another of my people last night. Because I could not protect her, she will…she will…" She cried too hard to speak now. He held her and wished down the wrath of God on the prince. And he felt not a moment's remorse or guilt over the torments he prayed for to befall the evil incarnate that was John Plantagenet.

He did not try to argue with her, for he truly feared for both her and the babe if this continued. Christian waited for her tears to end. He felt her growing still in his arms and soon the sobs had subsided. He believed her almost asleep when she spoke again.

"I did not know until I wished it ill that I wanted the child, Christian. All these months I have tried to ignore it and tried not to accept it, but yesterday, as I lay here bleeding, I knew in my heart and in my soul that I love this child. Regardless of its start or the reason it exists, it is mine. Only mine.''

Her use of the words of claiming that he used so frequently struck something within him. For even as he knew how deeply the words meant to him, he knew it meant the same to her about the child. And he recognized in that moment that any fight for Emalie was also a fight for the child. He could no longer ignore the babe, either, if he planned to oppose John's plan.

Christian leaned forward and let his hand rest on her belly. She did not move away, but he heard her hold her breath. Soon he felt movement under his hand and he sat in amazement as the babe made its presence known to him for the first time. Overwhelmed, he looked at her. A tentative smile lit her face. He bent down and kissed her lips.

"As you are and shall be only mine," he whispered, sealing her and her child's fate with his own.

Chapter Twenty

He only managed to keep word of it from her due to her illness. In being restricted to her bed and then her chamber, Christian controlled her visitors and the news they carried to Emalie. Of course, she did not know that. He would not permit anyone else to invade the solace he'd created for her.

The opening sally came in the form of visitors from the Bishop of Lincoln. An entourage of clerics arrived quietly one night just before the gates were to close. 'Twas only the next morning, after they consulted with Father Elwood, that they relayed their mission to him. A complaint had been registered with the bishop and the ecclesiastical court about the validity of his and Emalie's marriage. No specific details of the case could be shared with him, but these priests were there to ascertain the facts about their union.

Christian almost laughed in their faces, until he realized that this was a matter of life and death. These priests probably had no idea that they were being manipulated by the devil's own and would most likely be horrified to learn the truth. They only carried out the orders given to them by the bishop, who was currently the prince's pawn.

They did however need his permission to question any of his people and he granted it. Better to cooperate at this point and discover John's plan. He arranged to have Luc be his representative to witness all the questioning. If the priests thought this outside the bounds of his rights, they did not protest. He smiled grimly as the priests produced a list of those they would question. He was not surprised.

The only request he refused was theirs to speak to Emalie. He used her recent illness as the excuse, but he would not destroy the sense of security around her that was helping her recuperation. He simply reminded them that as her husband, he spoke for her in all things. They nodded, accepting his rights as a sage practice, for they knew that women lied or did not have the power to think logically as men did. He later thanked God for the self-induced separation in which these priests lived and their lack of exposure to the real world and the women who lived in it.

They questioned servants, soldiers, farmers and villagers—anyone on the list was "invited" to speak with them. Christian did not have them warned in advance and found, as Luc had once told him, they were close-mouthed and protective of their lady. To a one, they praised her goodness and gave no other information to their questioners.

Only once, Luc told him later, did one of the priests become tired of the onslaught of praise and demand an answer to an ignored question. The woman, one of the whores of the village, simply looked at the priests and began to sob. Completely exasperated by this womanly display, the priest ordered her to leave. Tempted to laugh, he remembered his own experiences in dealing with Emalie's people and was grateful that they were on his side this time.

Then, two days and nights after they arrived, they departed.

He did not fool himself into believing this would end it. John was exploring his resistance and would make another offer soon. He was so sure of it that he was at the gate when the next attack came. This one was a frontal assault and not one he could misdirect or assuage with misinformation.

A priest rode with a contingent of soldiers. Once more, they were from the Bishop of Lincoln, but this time they did not ask, they demanded. The papers they carried demanded that he answer the Church's court regarding his unlawful marriage to the Countess of Harbridge. The papers demanded that he present himself to be questioned at the court and, worse yet, that Emalie be brought before the court to answer for her actions.

The words that struck fear in him were the last two sentences written.

The Most Holy Bishop has, in his wisdom, decided that the Lady Emalie Montgomerie, now called Dumont, should surrender herself into the bishop's custody in anticipation of the outcome of these proceedings. Representatives of His Grace and escorts from the Convent of Our Blessed Lady here in Lincoln will present themselves at Greystone in three days' time to carry out this order.

He was sickened at the thought of turning Emalie over into the bishop's custody, for he knew not if this meant she was safe or if she would be accessible to John and William. The order before him gave him no choice.

The messenger handed him a smaller packet before leaving and Christian peeled off the unremarkable wax seal and opened it. John's last best offer. As his stomach churned, he read the note, an invitation to go home, honor intact. John promised to placate Richard with whatever explanation was necessary to make this go smoothly. All Christian had to do was give up all claim to the lands, titles, riches and person of the Countess of Harbridge.

Before he could read the accompanying documents, Luc approached the dais.

"She comes now, my lord."

Christian saw Emalie walking slowly into the hall and toward where he sat. "Take this all away, Luc. She can not know of this yet." He gathered the parchments together, rolled them as necessary and handed everything to Luc.

He stood, reached into his pocket and handed Luc a key. "Put this in Emalie's herbal room. She is not well enough to work there yet. And lock it with this."

Luc efficiently took everything from him and left before Emalie was halfway through the hall. Her progress to him, slowed by well-wishers, was pleasing. Her health was returning and there had been no additional episodes of bleeding or labor pains. He knew that the risk to her, when she discovered what he hid, was great. He needed to find a way to explain the situation to her without alarming her.

"Who were the messages from?" she asked as he helped her up to the table. She sat down and Alyce placed a blanket over her legs.

"Messages?"

"From our chambers I saw the riders enter, but they left too quickly."

Not a moment too soon by his score. He smiled at her, feeling the weight of every lie he spoke. "Nothing to be concerned with, Emalie. Nothing to distract you from your first meal in the hall with us."

She looked around at the table and nodded to each person. He could read the enjoyment on her face and wanted it to last forever. He would give anything to make it so.

At his signal, the servants began serving the meal. All of her favorites had been prepared and the company was lively with talk and teasing and good food and wine. Soon, too soon, he noticed her tiring and suggested she retire. After arguing but with little fight, Luc escorted Emalie to her room. Christian promised to join her soon.

He went to the herbal to study the documents; he needed to see how John's man defended his claim. Risking much, he decided to have Father Elwood examine them for his own assessment. Taking the copies of the betrothal contract and Gaspar's will with him, he sought and found the priest in his room, near the chapel. The minutes of discussion turned into hours and the good father could offer no assistance in disputing William's claim. Christian would have continued, but he realized that Emalie would be waiting for him.

He walked back to the herbal to store the papers. Emalie sat at her table, with John's letter in hand. Opened.

"It would appear that this is not the first offer from John on this matter." Her voice was flat, shocked most likely at the contents of the letter.

"'Tis not. His first *offer* was presented in person during his visit."

"Was it different from this?"

Her quiet demeanor surprised him. She was pale, from the excitement and exercise of the dinner and from this news, but she looked almost calm.

"Emalie, I do not want to upset you with this."

"There is so little time in which to upset me, my lord. The bishop's escort will be here in just three days." She handed him both John's letter and the bishop's decree. "How long have you known?" She stared into the lantern on the table and did not meet his gaze.

"Let us go to our chambers. I would feel better discussing this in that privacy and where you will be more comfortable."

She rose and allowed him to escort her back to their chambers. He brought all the documents. He was not happy that she had discovered it this way, but he would be grateful for her counsel. When they reached it, he closed the door behind them. Then he wasted no time.

"John summoned me even while you lay senseless and ill here the night of his visit. He offered me the chance to take DeSeverin's place in his arrangements to have you and the wealth of Harbridge."

"Have me?" she asked.

"Aye. I would be husband and earl here and manage the estates. You would be wife and countess. John would take whatever wealth he desired and he would have you whenever he desired."

Emalie shuddered so deeply that he ran to her side. He reached for a cup of wine and forced her to sip some.

"Apparently that is his agreement with DeSeverin

and so he believed I would accommodate him in the same way. He must have sensed that I would not, so he offered me an escape.''

"What was that?'' she whispered.

"I could simply leave, take Geoffrey and my men and go back to Poitou and my lands there. He would arrange for the annulment and I would be free of all of this.''

"Annulment? On what grounds would I be given an annulment?'' She looked at the documents on the table.

"DeSeverin has produced a betrothal contract, signed by him and your father.''

She shook her head in denial of his words.

"It was signed last year before his death, Emalie.''

"There was no betrothal, Christian. You must believe me.''

He held up his hand, stopping her from her arguments. ''I believe you, but they have the proof. The contract and a copy of your father's will, both naming one William DeSeverin as your betrothed husband and guardian in the event of your father's death. The courts, both secular and ecclesiastical, put great stock in proof.''

She threw the papers at him. ''They are a waste of costly vellum and not worth the cost of it. These are lies—my father entered into no agreements with William.''

"Emalie, how do you prove lies? You say there was no agreement yet DeSeverin has the contract. You say your father would not give you to him, yet he has the contract and your father's will. Tell me how to fight this. Tell me if I should.''

"Do you mean that you will walk away from this? From me?''

He did not answer her right away. There was a part of him that knew the outcome already and that it would not go in their favor. Did he try to cut his losses, soothe John's outrage and make as good an agreement with the prince as he could on her behalf? Or did he fight all out and lose everything in the end? Did he walk away with his honor now or walk away with nothing in the end?

He dropped the documents back onto the table in front of her. For a few minutes all was quiet. Emalie examined everything in the packet before saying another word.

Christian knew that she must understand the reasons for their marriage before she could understand why he would even consider John's offer. He sat across from her at the table and began.

"I married you as part of an arrangement with the king. My release from prison, my life and Geoffrey's was based on my fulfilling an agreement with the king."

"Prison?" she whispered, her gaze moving over him. Now she could understand the sores and the condition of his body when he had arrived here.

"We had lived through eight, nearly nine, months of constant hunger and filth and rats. Being attacked by other prisoners was commonplace, too. I managed to keep us alive, but it was a close thing. I suspect that Geoffrey was within days of dying and I would not have been long behind him."

"But why, Christian? What crime had you committed?"

"Crime? No crime of our own, but we were paying for our father's treason against the king. In the year before Richard's ransom, my father had gained control of several other estates and then swore allegiance to Richard's enemies. Before the king's release, his chancellor decided to act and he struck with a vengeance. Richard continues to do so even now in his Angevin and Pontevin lands.''

"Had you a part in it? Or Geoffrey?"

"I had taken Geoff and spent most of the year with cousins in Scotland. On our return we discovered our father's fate and our own.''

"He is…'' She could not say the word.

"Hanged. By order of the king's chancellor. Our sentence was to follow him to the hangman's gallows, but I think that the starvation would have killed us first.'' He saw her wince at his words.

"Then one day I was dragged before the king and offered a chance to live and regain my titles, my lands, our lost honor. Although I feared the task, what choice did I have? Any delay would cause Geoff's death. I agreed to carry out whatever task was demanded of me.''

"You did not know? I thought you were surprised by Eleanor's words.''

"I was, but in all candor, I would have begged, stolen or killed if asked. Marriage was a more attractive task.''

"Even to me?'' she asked.

"Even to you. In spite of your animosity toward me and your request for a reprieve, marriage was still preferable to the other things I imagined I'd be asked to do. Emalie, the most important thing to me was to regain the name and honor that my father had lost. I did not hold Richard responsible for his fate. I held my father guilty. And if I did not carry out the king's command, I would be as dishonorable as my father had been.''

''Was there something else you had to do?''

''Richard demanded that I report to him anything that linked his brother to whatever task his mother had in mind for me. I believe he knew John was stirring up trouble and wanted to keep an eye on it.'' Christian stood and walked over to the window, peering out into the darkness.

''Have you told him yet of this?'' She pointed to the pile before her. ''Will he intervene?''

''These sons of Henry go from fighting to loving and back again on the change of the wind. If John is in Richard's good graces, then he will prevail. If he has done something that Richard can not ignore, then he might stand against him. If what John says is true, Richard is beholden to him right now for his recent efforts in Anjou.

''And so,'' he continued, after walking back to his seat at the table, ''if you can not give me some other proof against these claims, I will have no choice but to honor them.''

''You would honor them? You would leave me to them?''

''My own honor would demand it.''

There it was—the worst of it. When he was ignorant of this, he could honor his vows to her. Now that he knew of this prior claim and could not disprove it, he had no right to her. In spite of his desire to fight for her, he had no right or standing to do so.

She gasped and began to shake. He handed her the wine and waited as she fought to control herself.

''When we married and I found out about the pregnancy, I could accept that because I believed that

Eleanor arranged it to cover some ill-planned affair on your part. It is not uncommon to marry and give a bastard a name. I could ignore it—'' he pointed at her belly ''—and still remain married to you. My honor did not suffer since no one knew that I was not the father.''

''Some know.''

''But they would, as you said, carry that secret to their graves.''

She closed her eyes for a moment. Then she looked at him. ''You know John is behind this.'' He nodded. ''You know these are false.'' She held out the betrothal contract and the will.

''So you say.'' He did not mean to insult her. ''And so I believe, but you can not go to these proceedings and blame all on the prince. Without proof of his complicity, it is a crime in and of itself.''

Her gaze moved over everything in the room but avoided him. ''And this is your decision?''

''My God, Emalie! I am torn in two by this.'' He slammed his fists on the table as he stood before her. ''I had just become accustomed to the babe you carry and decided I could live with accepting another man's child as mine.''

''But only if you did not know the father?'' Sarcasm laced her question.

''If the father is gone or has no knowledge. I can not fight for a child against the father who claims it.''

''What do you now? Will you walk away? Will you even speak on my behalf at the proceedings?'' She was losing strength now; he could hear it in her voice. The stress was taking its toll on her, as he knew it would.

''Give me some proof! Give me some evidence to use so that I can.''

"I have none to give you."

"Then tell me your truth, so that I can examine it and…"

"Judge me?"

"Aye, my lady. Because in that court, you will have many judges and every word and gesture and hesitation will be held up to scrutiny by men who know you not. You will be picked apart by strangers before they decide your fate and they may not even allow you to speak. Give me something, Emalie. Please."

"I have nothing for you, Christian. If you…" She choked on her words and did not say more.

"Think on it. There is not much time left."

Looking around the room, he knew he would not stay here this night. Christian walked to the door leading to his chambers and opened it. He had not slept without her for months, but he would not sleep tonight anyway.

Chapter Twenty-One

If you loved me.

Those were the words she almost said to Christian as he begged her for proof against these claims made by John on William's behalf.

If he loved her, he would claim her and fight for her.

If he loved her as she loved him...

She smiled sadly. He did not know of her feelings, for she had never told him. She burdened him with so much already that expressing her love in words was not something she would do.

Love had no place in a modern marriage between a noblewoman and a nobleman. It had taken her a long time and much suffering to learn this simple truth. Her parents were an extraordinary exception and, although happiness could be found, love did not usually exist for a wedded couple.

She looked at the documents on the table one more time. Perhaps she had missed something the first dozen times she'd read them? When morning came, she would seek Father Elwood's counsel over this. He knew Church law; he knew her father.

Morning was a long time from now, but Emalie felt

no need or desire to sleep. Again. She had spent the last night and day within the confines of her chamber, for she had not the strength to face those in the keep or the village. Or him.

She felt like walking. Without waking Alyce, she took her heavy cloak and headed for the battlements at the top of the keep.

Taking deep breaths of the cold wind, she walked to the place she liked and looked over Greystone. Christian was right—winter would come early this year. Already the air was tinged with a frostiness that usually came later than this.

She had one more day here before everything would change. If the courts ruled in William's favor, her marriage to Christian would be set aside and she would find herself married to William. In that instant, she appreciated Christian more than she ever had. She laughed bitterly as she thought of the months she'd spent resisting his efforts in Greystone.

The wind whipped around her and she closed her eyes and let its force move around her. She was still amazed at its power to soothe her frayed nerves in spite of the cold and the strength of it. Pushing her hood back, she let her hair loose in it. Closing her eyes once more, she stood silently and cleared her mind of all thoughts and worries. It would not help her in the long run, but it would bring such relief now.

Only the scraping sound of steps approaching broke into her reverie and she stepped aside to let the guards pass. As she did so, she caught sight of him standing in the opposite corner. He nodded to her as their gazes met, but did not come closer.

Once he had. He had followed her here a few weeks ago and kissed her senseless. When she thought she would swoon, he had wrapped his cloak over hers and plundered her mouth again with his as his hands explored her body. She thought he would take her right up against the wall, but instead they ran down to their chambers and sought pleasure there. Against a wall.

Did he remember it now even as she did? His expression did not change. She reached up and gathered her hair, tucking it inside her hood. Mayhap it was best to leave him and go below? It seemed the right thing to do, so she crossed to the stairway and left him there.

In her room, she thought on his words last night. He asked her for the truth, for her truth. Could she speak it and could he hear it? Would it make any difference at all other than to see disappointment in his eyes? She had seen lust and desire, anger and annoyance, even compassion and caring. Would he consider her dishonored when he heard her story?

She paced for a long time around her chambers as she waited to hear him enter his. Finally, after his hallway door slammed shut, she decided to tell him that which she most sought to hide. Without knocking, she entered his room and waited for him to see her. When he turned and faced her, she spoke.

"I did not intend to disturb your privacy above."

"I know you did not intend to." He smiled at her words and his deliberate misuse of them. "'Twas fine, though, for I had been there before you arrived."

"I did not see you."

"No, you did not, but I saw you."

It struck her then, about why he liked wild winds blowing against him.

His months in prison.

"I understand now, my lord. The need for the wind above. The door always ajar. The way you eat."

He nodded. "Regrettable remnants of my time in prison. I did not think anyone noticed."

"I did, but said nothing. I thought them just Pontevin arrogancies."

He smiled at her insult. "Here, sit." He moved a chair closer to the hearth and helped her to sit. "You must be chilled from the wind."

"I would speak to you of my truth." She started without any preamble or warning, for she could feel her courage dissolving.

He sat on the edge of his bed and watched her. The ease that they had together was gone now. Concern. Compassion. But nothing held them together any longer. The bonds they had built, layer upon layer, testing and strengthening, were gone. If she had tears left, she would have cried.

"My parents had an extraordinary marriage. I'm certain you have heard of it."

He answered with a nod and she continued. "My mother died a few years ago and my father realized that I would be his heir. He trained me in the management and record-keeping and planning for our estates. We worked side by side for the good of our people."

She shifted in the chair, trying to get more comfortable for the telling. "About a year and a half ago, William approached my father about a betrothal, which he promptly and completely refused. My father had it in mind to request a new betrothal from Richard when he was freed. I saw the letter he sent to Longchamp in London about it.

"I do not understand the change in William. The prince was correct in that our families were well acquainted and we had spent much time together as children. But William turned insistent that an arrangement with him was needed. My father refused in spite of his determination to make it so.

"Then Prince John visited Greystone. He had never been here before, at least not to my knowledge. He began to encourage my father to accept William's suit for my hand. But as the prince became adamant, my father became obstinate and refused William admittance to Greystone."

"And John?" he asked quietly from where he sat.

"One does not refuse the prince. John was here almost constantly at that time. Then my father suddenly took ill."

"With what condition?"

"It happened so quickly that I was not certain. We had little time to call the brothers who practice healing from Thornton Abbey. He became ill one night, began having seizures the next day and died the following night."

"And the prince was here while all this happened?"

"Aye. He was very solicitous and helpful. After he left, William would show up, offering his help. I struggled through those months without my father here."

"With estates as large as yours, I am certain that you did," he said. "But you were able to do remarkable things, considering..."

"That I am a woman?"

"Considering that you are young and you were alone."

"Everyone helped me, from the servants to the villagers. Even the stewards on my other properties did not squawk at taking orders from me."

"They knew the alternative, I think."

She nodded. "John's intentions and his recent history of grabbing up land were known to us all. Durwyn, when he could be here, cautioned about being caught up in John's web.''

"Go on," he urged.

"That brings us to this past spring. I had petitioned Richard's chancellor about my wardship and about a possible match, but heard nothing. I assumed that my needs were not important in the grand scheme of running England and the other Plantagenet provinces.''

Emalie stood and stretched; sitting in one place for too long made her back cramp. She went to the table next to the bed and poured them both some wine. Handing him the cup, she paced now as she spoke.

"I sent a note to the queen, asking for guidance, but before she could arrive, it happened. One night, William and John were in my chambers when I arrived there. They bound and gagged Alyce and forced her into a closet to keep her from seeking help."

"Were you hurt?"

She looked at him as she tried to remember the next morn. "No," she said, shaking her head. "I do not remember being hurt. I remember them arguing and William forcing me to drink a goblet of wine. They argued more and then the room began to swirl around me. Someone, William, I think, helped me to the bed and I fell down on it. I remember being dizzy and John came over to me."

She stared at the wall and forced the memories to come. "I can feel his kiss and his hands on me, even as I could no longer stand. Then I remember looking up at them both and they argued again."

"Do you remember what they argued over?"

"Me…something about my resistance. John wanted me to fight him. It made no sense at the time. He was angry at William for putting something in my wine that

made me sleepy." She looked at him as she repeated
the words she heard now in her thoughts. "What use
to me if she lies like a doll and has no life in her? I
had hoped for a show of spirit tonight."

A shiver pulsed through her. Since experiencing the
many different ways of joining and pleasure, she understood what his words had meant.

"There was more yelling and then I felt hands all
over me. Not hurting, just tugging at my laces and my
clothes. Then I remember William's face above me. He
was sweating and moving. He felt heavy and hot
against my skin and I remember the cold sheets below
my legs. And he repeated words over and over to me.
I could not gather my thoughts or move except as he
moved me, but I could hear him."

"What words, Emalie? What did he say?"

"Forgive me."

The room was quiet as they both pondered what she
had shared. She had not remembered William's words
until just then.

"As I said, William was different than before. He
was driven. He was unrelenting in his quest for my
hand, as though John had some power over him. If he
seemed to stumble in his efforts, a word or two from
John pushed him forward."

"Everyone has their price, Emalie. Perhaps John had
discovered William's and paid it?" He paused and then
asked another question. "Did they leave then?"

"I do not know. The next thing I remember is Alyce
shaking me awake and discovering the bloody sheet
beneath me."

He drank all his wine in one gulp and put the cup
down on the table next to his bed. Christian looked

unnerved by her words. She knew that memories of that night haunted her still.

"They stayed away until Eleanor arrived, and then William claimed carnal knowledge of me and offered to wed me."

"He said nothing of the betrothal contract that he presents now?"

"Nothing. He confessed that his desire for me overtook his senses and that he regretted his rash actions and was willing to marry me since I was now dishonored. Eleanor was not impressed and threw them both out while she investigated for herself."

"I feel certain that your people were as close-mouthed about you then as they are now."

She smiled as she thought of the bravery demonstrated on her behalf in the face of John's rage. It was not something pretty to behold then, but now she could appreciate what they had done.

"No one betrayed me. No one could remember seeing or hearing John and William within the keep or in the village the night they claimed to be here. No bloody sheets could be produced. And Eleanor drew the line at having me subjected to a physician's or midwife's exam as John demanded. When I did not cry out about being wronged, there was no way to prove their claim."

Emalie made her way back to the chair and sat down. "Richard was released and came to England briefly before going on to Aquitaine and Anjou. I think Eleanor spoke to him then, for she believed that only a quick marriage could save me and my people, if their plan was to be a success. You arrived here but a few weeks later." She looked up at him and smiled sadly. "You know the rest."

Before he could speak, she added what she had most wanted and most feared telling him. Her lack of disclosure had forced him into the position he was in now and she would not allow him to make this decision without knowing her truth.

"I know that your actions were for other reasons, but I think I began to fall in love with you when you asked me to sit court with you. I knew I was in love with you when you took me to Lemsley for Fayth's wedding and wooed me with your words and touches." She stood and walked to the door that now separated their rooms. "And I will love you always because of the honorable man you are, Christian. No matter what turns our lives take after this day, my heart will be only yours."

She left without another word and her spirit felt lighter somehow for the confession she'd made to him.

Chapter Twenty-Two

He drank himself into a stupor that lasted two days after hearing her truth. He had asked her to speak it, but, fool that he was, he had no idea it would strike so hard at the very core of his soul. And his inability to support her in her time of need ate at his gut. Wine made it all go away.

Now she was gone.

Christian had made her traveling arrangements himself, although she would not know it. He assigned Sir Walter to accompany her to the convent and to stay there until the proceedings began. He gave no promise to attend and the unanswered questions in the man's gaze as he was given his instructions bothered him.

He had no answers for any of them. He drowned any semblance of rational thought until she was gone and then continued drinking to erase the almost unimaginable pain. So torturous was it, he could not even bear to examine the reasons for it too closely. He withdrew into his chambers and let spirits soothe him for now. He did not eat. He did not sleep. Christian simply existed.

Ignoring most of them was easy. Geoffrey's pleas

could be blocked. Fitzhugh's questions were unnecessary, since the man could make his own decisions. Luc was the worst one. He said nothing. He stood in the doorway and stared at him as though he were a stranger. Staying in his room, he avoided the rest of them.

Then, on the third or mayhap fourth morning after her departure, Luc brought word that Emalie had arrived safely and was now within the convent walls. They must have watered the wine they brought him, for questions began to insidiously make their way into his thoughts.

Had the journey been comfortable? Could she tolerate the rolling of the wagon on this trip? Did they treat her with the respect due her position as the Countess of Harbridge or was she treated as all penitent women within their walls? Did they allow her to walk in the wind as she needed to when worrying?

Christian stood in the place where she always looked out over Greystone before he even knew that he had left his chambers. He ignored the winds and the rains that poured over him as he stood by the wall. He turned his face into the worst of it and allowed the forces of nature to rage around him as he raged inside.

He wanted her back. He wanted her as his wife.

He would fight for her.

But could he? Christian lifted his face to the sky and roared out his pain and frustration at not being able to understand the feelings that tormented him. The winds that usually calmed him did not do so this night. Instead, he felt more out of control than ever before.

In that prison cell many months before, he had prayed to the Almighty for an escape. He had begged for any way out of his dishonor. He had pleaded for a

way to save his life and his brother's. And the result
was this bargain with the devil, which now threatened
him and Geoffrey yet more. And now another was involved and in danger of losing life and soul to the evil
that surrounded them.

Still, doubts assailed him in his weakened state,
while the storm pounded him. What kind of man would
claim a woman who was someone else's promised wife
and who carried someone else's child within her?
Where was the honor in that?

A man who loved a woman would.

A man who loved his wife would do anything to
protect her.

A man who loved his wife would go to any efforts
to keep her as his own.

Christian reeled and fell back against the slippery
wall. It was difficult to breathe and even harder to accept what he thought he was discovering. He pushed
his hair out of his face and drew in a ragged breath.

Only mine. He said the words as he claimed her body
and her soul as his own without ever realizing that he
was giving his own in return.

Only mine. He never knew that he was not only
claiming her and marking her as he said the words, he
was pledging himself to her in the same moment.

Only mine. She was and would be again.

In that moment, Christian realized the pain he suffered was not caused by the love he had for Emalie. It
was caused by his refusal to recognize and accept it.
Now, as he accepted the burden this love placed on
him, all was clear.

He would find a way to reclaim her. Or he would
make one. He would try to serve his honor, but Emalie

was the most important person in his life and he would
do whatever it took to bring her home.

The frigid rain penetrated the many layers of clothing he wore and he shivered as the icy cold reached
his skin. He turned to leave, for he had arrangements
to make and plans to discuss. He needed to examine
his enemies' plan and determine his own strategy. He,
too, knew the value of distract, disarm and destroy.
And he would show his enemies, their enemies, that
the Earl of Harbridge would fight for what was his.

With a final battle cry that echoed over the battlements and into the night, Christian felt the exhilaration
of a coming battle.

Not content to wait for the dawn, he summoned servants and Fitzhugh to his chambers and made his
wishes known. Sensing his urgency, they complied
without question, but with many glances shared between them. Dressed once more as earl and knowing
what he wanted, he assembled his most trusted retainers, and Emalie's, in the solar and went to work.

With the clerk intensely copying down his instructions, he prepared many messages to those who he
knew could help their cause. In a few cases, he chose
to give the message directly to one of his men, not
trusting the words to parchment. Servants and soldiers
were dispatched with coin to Lincoln to make ready
accommodations for the earl and his party.

Since possession in some cases guaranteed success,
Christian sought to reinforce the defenses of Greystone
against attack or siege. Calling up more knights from
among his vassals, he informed them of the claims
made against him and the countess and that DeSeverin
would have to take the keep by force if he wanted it.

Le Comte de Langier and Earl of Harbridge would not acquiesce. Buoyed by their support and knowing that John rarely attacked where he could be seen, he readied himself for the bigger battle by studying the documents and learning more about his wife's father and the old earl's precipitous and well-timed death.

A week and a day after Emalie's departure from Greystone, Christian and his party left for Lincoln.

It took less than an hour to reach the convent on the outskirts of Lincoln from the lodgings chosen for him by Walter. Although many settlements of that type were built next to or near the cathedral or church of the town, this one was farther into the countryside. It had many fields and much farmland that provided food for the community and crops for bartering and selling to supply the convent's other needs.

He rode alone, save Luc, who insisted on accompanying him. As Luc said, a lone man attacked in the night would bring no notice and could conveniently, for some, settle the question before the bishop's court. Accepting his friend's wisdom, they rode together.

He was not certain if he would be able to speak to Emalie, but he needed to talk with her before the proceedings began on the morrow. She had the right to know what they were up against. He had spent days discussing and arguing and always searching for something they could use to win. So far, although his intent was strong, their case was not. Even the clerics assigned by the bishop to him for the proceedings could give him no hope since the betrothal contract stood as clear proof.

He also wanted to make certain that Emalie knew of his love for her. The last time they had spoken, he had been shocked by her proclamation and could not think of what to say. Of course, he had not realized the depth of his own feelings then.

'Twas full dark when they arrived and, as expected, the gates were closed against the night and visitors. After much loud knocking and then banging, a man answered their calls through a small window in the gate and firmly told them to return in the morning. Arguing did nothing to convince the gatekeeper to bring the reverend mother forward, so Christian used simple greed to accomplish what words could not. After some coins exchanged hands, with the promise of more to come, the man shuffled off to the main building.

A few minutes later, a group of nuns opened the gates and guided him and Luc inside to the office of the reverend mother. She was an old woman, with hands gnarled by many years of hard work, but her face was lit with the glow of inner kindness. Christian hoped she would allow him to speak to Emalie.

"Sit, my lord," she said as they entered the large room. "I would offer you refreshments, but the hour is late and the kitchens are closed."

He sat before her and Luc stood at his back.

"The countess is…?" He needed to know how she fared here.

"Well, my lord. She was given into our care and we take that assignment by the bishop very seriously. The lady has spent most of her time here resting or in prayer."

"She has been ill," he explained. His words would not come smoothly. Worry over her was wreaking havoc within him and with his intention to be calm.

"Her maid explained the lady's difficulties and our healer has seen to her needs."

"I would see her now, Reverend Mother."

"I fear that all inside these walls have retired for the night." She stood as though to dismiss him. "Come again in the morning and we will talk."

He stood as well, rising to his full height. "I would see her now." Luc whispered words of warning behind him.

"Do you seek to intimidate me, my lord? Here, in God's house?"

"Aye, Reverend Mother. If that's what I must do to see my wife, then so be it."

She smiled at him without guile as though she enjoyed this exchange of threats. "Many others, men both larger and more powerful than you, have challenged me and left without success."

He let out his breath. He would have to take another tack.

"Reverend Mother, please allow me to speak to Emalie."

"Now you try pleading when threats do not work?"

"I will try whatever is necessary to see her," he admitted. "I must speak to her."

"You will see her on the morrow, my lord. Can your words not wait until then?"

"Nay, Reverend Mother. She needs to hear my words this night. She needs to know the mistakes I have made. She needs to know—"

"Of your love?" She smiled as he stared at her. "Aye, my lord, I can hear it in your voice and see it in your eyes." She sat back down behind the table and rang a small bell that rested on the corner of it. The door opened a minute later and a younger nun entered.

"Please tell Lady Emalie that she has another visitor, if she would care to join us here."

"I will go to her, Reverend Mother."

"Nay, my lord. You will stay here. Men are not permitted in our other buildings." She nodded at the other woman, who left without a word.

"Another visitor, Reverend Mother?" Luc asked from behind him.

"Aye, sir knight. The countess would not meet him. Sir William was much put out by her refusal."

He looked at Luc. Both of them were wondering the same thing—what brought William here? What did he want to tell Emalie? He had gathered much information about DeSeverin in the past week and now felt as though he knew his opponent better. Not the one in charge, but more the weapon of those who planned his destruction.

They sat in silence as they waited for Emalie. Looking around the room, Christian's gaze was caught by the many costly books that the reverend mother kept on large shelves.

"The late Earl of Harbridge was most generous to us, my lord. He gifted us with many of the volumes you see there."

"Emalie's father?"

"Aye, my lord. We are nearly neighbors, you know. Part of the convent's lands extend northeast and almost to your lower borders." She paused and looked past him. "Ah, here she is, my lord. My lady, come in."

Christian stood and turned to see her. Standing in the doorway, with her cloak still around her, he could see only her face. Her eyes were haunted once more and he knew he had caused it. He could not break from her gaze, even as the reverend mother left the room. He thought that Luc exchanged greetings with Emalie on his way out, but all he saw, all he heard was her. And then they were alone.

Emalie had thought herself prepared to see him, but she was not. Although he eschewed the wearing of fine garments during their days at Greystone, he was dressed now in every way as the nobleman he was. His finest shirt, his embossed long tunic, his newly tanned leather belt and the thick gold chains he wore around his neck all proclaimed his title and wealth.

At this moment, she did not know which was worse—finding him gone when the proceedings began on the morrow, or his appearance here now to tell of his leaving. When he sent no word to her after they spoke, and when he did not greet the escort sent to bring her here, she knew of his decision. He would leave, return to Poitou and his lands there and avoid this fight.

Her legs weakened and shook. He must have seen her shake, for he held her up and guided her to the chair where he had been sitting. Arranging the long folds of her cloak over her legs, she untied the hood and let it drop to her shoulders.

She could not say a word to him. Where could she begin? *It is so good of you, my lord, to see me on your way home. My lord, how nice of you to tell me of your leaving. Now I will not have to wonder through the night.*

He crouched down next to the chair and waited until she met his gaze. "How do you fare, my lady?" His voice shook as he spoke.

"I am well, my lord. The sisters here take good care of me. I have adequate food and drink, my lodgings are modest but comfortable, and I have the company of kind women." And my heart is broken and my spirit is crushed, she thought.

"The babe within?" He raised his hand as though to touch her belly then drew it back.

"I have had no more bleeding or pains, my lord. Thank you for asking."

If she could get through this polite conversation, she could make it back to her room before the grief of his disavowal hit her. She had tried to prepare for the hurt she knew she would feel, but she was not ready for the all-encompassing despair she felt creeping into her soul.

"Emalie, I have thought on your words since you left." He paused and stood, walking several steps away from her.

She clutched her hands together tightly as she fought to hold on to her control. Hearing his explanation would destroy her, and the urge grew inside to simply flee the room and not hear it. But she was a Montgomerie, born and raised to the duties she carried, and she would not run.

"I told you of my battle to regain my honor."

"I am familiar with the burdens and rewards of honor, my lord. I have grown up with nothing else."

"The true question I faced was what man of honor could claim another man's promised wife and the child she bears. When the haze of too much wine finally cleared, I realized the answer."

"You did, my lord?" She truly needed to leave. She could not bear to have him explain that she was not worth his honor to save. Leaving without any word would have been better than this, she decided.

"Only a man who loves his wife above all, all titles,

all land, all riches, even honor, would do what is necessary to keep her safe and with him.''

Her eyes burned with the tears she fought. She held the sobs within her. It was time to leave. She did not want to hear him deny her in this way. She pushed out of the chair and stumbled toward the door. He reached her just before she could pull it open.

''Emalie, please. You misunderstand my words,'' he said as he pulled her into his embrace. ''I *am* a man who loves his wife above all. I will do whatever I can to keep you with me.''

She stared at him, for she could not believe she had heard his words correctly. He had never spoken of love to her. She knew he did not have those tender feelings for her. But, now, in this holy convent, he declared it to be so.

Emalie began to argue, but he lifted her chin and took her mouth then. Kissing her over and over, he claimed her and pledged his love to her. Still shocked by his declaration, she stumbled and they landed against the door, their mouths still joined.

''My lord?'' Luc's voice came through the closed door. ''I do not think that what you are attempting is appropriate in the house of God.''

''Shut up, Luc,'' Christian growled back. He did stop kissing her and placed her back firmly on her feet. Then he led her to the chair and made her sit in it. He brought a small stool over and placed it next to her so they could talk. Once seated, he clasped his hands around hers and rested them on her lap. She did not want him to ever let go. Blinking through the tears, she tried to focus on his words.

''Although my intention is to fight this, I confess that I have not much to fight with, Emalie. Assumptions, guesses, some bits of information and much uncertainty. At first, I thought to fight his claim that he fathered the babe. Alyce and Walter have sworn you came to me a virgin, but I fear endangering their souls if they swear this under the oath in the bishop's court."

"They would truly do that for me?" She had never wanted to test their loyalty at the cost of their souls and had prayed that it would never come to a public vow.

"They would. They have already privately. But Father Ignatius said that if we disprove the betrothal document, it matters not who fathered the babe."

"How can that be?" If they all knew she was pregnant at the time of her marriage, it could not be Christian's child.

"He said that the only issue is the invalidity of our marriage due to that agreement. That any child born within a valid marriage is considered to be of the husband. The ecclesiastical and secular courts have upheld this time and time again."

Puzzled, she considered his words.

Then the truth hit her. "'Twould not do to look too closely at the chicks in the nest?" she asked. Many children and heirs from noble marriages probably had little to do with the men whose names they bore or whose titles and lands they inherited. 'Twas a sad state of affairs in the land.

"Just so."

Their gazes met and then his moved over her. "You look tired, my lady. I will not trouble you more over this, Emalie. 'Tis clear to me that you need to rest now." He stood and tugged her to her feet. "If you think of any way to attack the document itself, send Alyce with word and I will act on it."

Christian wrapped his arms around her again. This time, they just stayed in that embrace for several moments as the magic of being surrounded by his love pulsed through her. Grasping his cloak, she felt the mail he wore below his tunic. Danger was all around them in this endeavor. She did not want to let him go now that he had come to her and professed his love.

But the sounds outside in the hall meant their time together was over. After the obvious warning sound of scuffling feet, the door opened and the reverend mother entered with Alyce, Luc and Sister Marguerite. Emalie noticed that Luc's expression was one of smug, manly pride, as though he had been proved right. She could only imagine what battles raged between Christian and his friend.

"Come, my lady. The night is already chill and you must reserve your strength for the days ahead. Marguerite, assist the lady back to her chambers."

Before Christian released her, he leaned down close to her ear and whispered words of encouragement.

"I will not surrender you to the darkness, Emalie. Fear not."

She stepped away from him, her heart filled with hope for the first time in a long while. Turning, she smiled at the nun. "My thanks, Reverend Mother, for allowing this visit."

"Your spirit is raised now, your heart is lighter?" the short woman asked in hushed tones.

"Aye," she answered, glancing at her husband.

"Then God's work has been done this night." The nun nodded at both of them.

Christian kissed Emalie's forehead as she passed him and then she allowed Alyce and the sister to guide her back to her room.

"You, too, must do God's work, my lord."

The earl turned to face her after watching the countess leave. "I, Reverend Mother? How can I do that?" She caught a glance of his companion's irreverent expression but knew he asked in earnest.

"Oppose evil in any of its forms. Use all of your gifts, all of your strengths, to fight its control."

He nodded to her, but she knew he was not thinking of her words. He was thinking of the woman he loved and the dangers she faced.

"There is a warrior's prayer that you should remember, my lord. 'O God, you favor the righteous' it begins."

He nodded, acknowledging the prayer that she quoted.

"Pray and remember it during the battle that faces you."

"I will, Reverend Mother."

"Now I must go to pray and you must leave."

The two men bowed to her and left with the gatekeeper as their guide. She made her way to the chapel and walked to the altar, where she knelt on the cold stone steps. Making the sign of the cross, she began to pray.

She knew more about his case before the bishop than she had let him know. She was well aware of the corruption that controlled the man who should be shepherd to his flock. And she knew the identity of the one who corrupted.

Praying to the only one who could save this young couple, she used the prayer she seemed to favor the most lately.

"O God, you favor the righteous man with your grace…"

The reverend mother remained on her knees for several more hours of prayer, for when the devil walked the earth, it was all that God-fearing people could do.

Chapter Twenty-Three

The first day did not go well.

Christian gazed around the large room that was being used for the proceedings. A large number of clergymen observed the hearings, as well as commonfolk who were entertained by the goings-on of the nobility. The only one who should have been there and was not was the lady in question. Her request to be present was refused.

After witnessing a long and private discussion between Prince John and the Bishop of Lincoln, Christian knew that the outcome was already determined. John's departure confirmed it, for if the prince did not feel the need to stay and watch the case, then he knew the result was in hand.

He sat with Father Ignatius and listened as witness after witness proclaimed knowledge of the plan to betroth Emalie to DeSeverin. They spoke of the high regard the late earl had for DeSeverin. Although none of those called were of Greystone, they played their parts good and well and, if he had not known the truth, they would have convinced him.

The bishop and his two highest-ranking clerics heard

the case and nodded as DeSeverin's representative presented their evidence. Examining samples of Gaspar's handwriting, they exclaimed over the exactness of the one on the betrothal agreement and looked upon him with disdain. DeSeverin's copy of the will was greeted with the same acceptance.

Christian's head pounded in helplessness. He had witnesses and documents to testify that no one within the Montgomerie circle of family or friends knew of Gaspar's intention to betroth his daughter to DeSeverin and that no one knew of changes to Gaspar's will. That did not disprove the documents, it simply showed that before they were signed, Gaspar had had no intention to designate DeSeverin as Emalie's guardian and betrothed husband.

Finally the disastrous day was done and he made arrangements to meet with Father Ignatius for further discussions of the plans for presenting their case on the morrow. Luc joined them and they argued for many hours before the parcel arrived.

A package of letters, ones from Gaspar to Longchamp, the Bishop of Ely, concerning a new betrothal arrangement for his daughter. One letter, dated months prior to Gaspar's death, requested such a betrothal. Another letter, signed and dated but a few weeks later, granted permission for a betrothal between the Countess of Harbridge and one *Comte de Langier*. Another sheet outlined the agreement between Gaspar and his own father, Guillaume Dumont, and was sealed with the king's emblem and signature of his chancellor.

Christian smiled grimly as he beheld the documents. Dead men were now signing as freely as the living. Obviously, Richard, or Longchamp, believed that Greystone should not go to John and his cronies and had produced these proofs to combat his claim. Could he use them knowing they were false? Did it matter that they were as false as the others being used to wrongly claim Emalie?

He turned to the priest with his moral dilemma and asked him, without showing him the content of the papers.

"Father, if something is evil or false, can it be used to accomplish good?"

The young priest considered his question before answering. He pulled out some scrolls and examined passages within them and frowned as he seemed to argue the question silently in his thoughts. Ignatius scratched his face and beard and then looked at him and Luc.

"Canon law is quite clear on this, my lord. Evil can not be used even to accomplish good, for its very nature will corrupt all endeavors and all results will be tainted by its connection."

"The ends do not justify the means?" Luc offered.

"Correct, sir. In simpler terms, that is the meaning."

"What is in there, Chris? What is this about?"

Christian handed the papers to the priest and his friend and waited for their reaction. Luc smiled broadly as he peered over Ignatius's shoulder and read the pertinent phrases within the documents. Nodding his head, he cheered.

"Finally! This is exactly what we need. 'Twould have been better if Ely had sent these sooner, but they are welcome at any time, I swear."

"I would like to examine these more closely, my lord, before we present them to the court tomorrow, if you would excuse me."

At his nod, the priest gathered all the documents and took them into the next room with him. When Luc would have spoken, Christian waved him to silence. Once the door between the chambers had shut, he told Luc to keep his voice down.

"What is your problem, Christian? The king's man has given you the proof you need to win this matter. Pray, tell me you do not hesitate to use it?"

"You heard my question of Ignatius. Does the end justify the means?"

"You are saying that those documents are forgeries?"

"As much as the one DeSeverin uses. My father knew nothing of the Montgomeries before his death. Ely never answered Emalie's father in a timely manner with my name. They are all false," he replied.

"Are you saying you will not use them on the morrow?" Luc laughed harshly. "With Emalie's life in danger, you stop to think whether it is right or wrong to use all weapons within your grasp?" Luc glared at him. "Next you will tell me you believe in fighting fair during battle."

He started to say something, but now Luc waved him off. "In a battle to the death, when infidels are crowding in for the kill, you use anything, anything, that you can to survive. You trip them, you throw sand in their eyes or the wine you carry with you, or you cut their hamstrings so they can not stand and fight. The only important thing is to live."

"I am not on Crusade, Luc."

"You may think not, but the infidels here, your enemies, will not stop to measure their means against the Lord's commandments. They will do what must be done to win." Luc walked to the door and faced him before leaving. "I fear that you and your lady will not survive this unless you begin to fight as they do—with every weapon in your reach.''

"Luc," he called out.

"Until the morning, my lord." He heard the words just before the door slammed.

Finally she was given permission to observe the court proceedings. Even though her life hung in the balance, she was not deemed important enough to be present and it took many hours of begging and pleading to accomplish it. With no word from Christian since two nights ago, she had no idea what had occurred the day before or what was to come this day.

She was directed to sit on a chair near the front of the room, away from both of the men who argued over her but near enough to hear and see everything that transpired. Alyce was permitted to stay with her, for the priest who guided her there feared that she would swoon and interrupt the business before the bishop. As soon as she could, she sent Alyce for word about progress so far.

Christian entered with Luc and a priest and walked to the table assigned to him. As he looked around the room, she caught his gaze and smiled. The smile that he answered her with warmed her heart. He headed in her direction, but the stern voice of the bishop rang out.

"My lord, take your place and do not seek to delay these most serious proceedings."

Christian appeared torn for a moment, but the priest's hand on his arm gave him some message. He stopped and nodded to the bishop. "My apologies, my lord bishop. I meant no disrespect to you or the proceedings."

The bishop called out to her. "Heed me well, my lady. Women have no place here. You are here only due to my mercy and kindness. If you choose to disrupt these hearings, I will have you removed."

Emalie nodded in reply, afraid to say even a word.

"Brother Amadeus, please read the record of the proceedings so far."

The cleric stood and unrolled a scroll and began reading the account as recorded by him of all of the witnesses and their testimony. The monotone Latin went on and on and, despite her best efforts, she could not follow it all. She did gain a sense of how badly the day had gone for their case yesterday. When he finished, the bishop whispered to the other two priests with him. At their nods, he spoke.

"That is a true and accurate record of the witnesses and their testimony so far. It shall be marked with my ring and sealed and kept for our deliberations."

The brother did as directed. In a few minutes, he placed the scroll in a basket made for just this and gave it to the bishop. "Now, let us begin. Sir William, did you have anything further to add to your evidence?"

The priest at William's side rose and addressed the bishop. William stared at her. Why had he tried to see her at the convent? What could he have wanted? Emalie broke from his gaze and listened to the priest. From the way he outlined their case so far, she doubted he would have anything else to say. Their evidence was clear and overwhelming with the documents they had presented.

No wonder Christian had not visited her the night before. He could probably not face her with everything going so badly. He was always trying to keep her from upset. From the grim look on his face now, he was deeply and truly worried.

Then, in a matter of moments, the room was in an uproar. Christian began to argue with William.

"You could not get Gaspar's blessing, could you, DeSeverin? So you had him killed," Christian yelled at him.

"You lie. He gave his permission. There is the paper to prove it." William stood to answer Christian's assertion.

"He knew you for the pawn you are and so he was killed and this, this forgery, was produced to back your claim."

"He signed this, my lords. Gaspar Montgomerie—"

"Never signed that while he lived and breathed," Christian answered. "And unless you can explain how a dead man can sign contracts, this is not worth the vellum it is written on."

She smiled even though it was completely inappropriate, for he used her very words to describe the same document. Christian's allegation that William was involved in her father's death shocked her. He might be weak enough to be John's pawn, but she could not see him as a murderer. Her father's death as premeditated did make sense. But it could not have been William.

Christian took some parchments and approached William. Thrusting them in front of him, Christian waited for some reaction. She watched as William's face reddened and flushed. Finally he began accusing Christian of lying and slander and forgery, so many charges that she lost count of them. And with a certain coldly calculated expression, Christian stepped closer to the bishop and called out to him.

"My lord bishop? Although my honor has been insulted by simply conducting these proceedings, I find that I have no avenue of recourse, no method of proving my denial of Sir William's claims, other than by my right to combat."

She began to shake her head. No, he could not do this. He could not. But he did. She tried to stand and go to him, but Alyce grabbed her and held her in the seat.

"I place the decision in God's hands for He favors the righteous with His Grace to defeat their enemies and smite the sinners." Christian called out the opening line of a long-used prayer.

"Do you accept this challenge, Sir William?" the bishop asked solemnly. She prayed that he would refuse, but William nodded his acceptance.

The bishop conferred with the others and confirmed the challenge made. "We do hold as a tenet of our faith that, in a challenge made and accepted to answer a question of faith or honor, God will indeed favor the righteous man and reward him with victory over his enemies. This court declares that all claims made will be proved on the field of battle, at noon, two days hence, in a place to be designated." He looked from one man to the other. "And may God have mercy on your souls."

The clerics and other officials followed the bishop from the room. Soon, only she and Christian and William remained. Although William started to say something to her, he stopped and left the room without ever saying it. Christian ran to her and gathered her in his arms.

"You fool! Why did you do that? You could be killed by him."

He kissed her and laughed, that arrogant Pontevin laugh. "Have you no faith in my abilities? I am known on the Continent for my prowess in battle and in tournaments. Even Eleanor knows of it."

"This is not a tournament. This is a fight to the death."

"Aye, Emalie, I know that. In this I can prevail."

"As you could have here today, my lord." Luc stood at his side. "If you had used all the weapons within your reach."

Emalie looked from one to the other. "What does he mean, Christian? You could have won here in court?"

"With this, my lady. Thoughtfully provided by the king's chancellor." Luc held out the letters to her. Christian looked as if he would argue, but he did not. Emalie read the papers quickly, shaking her head as she did.

"Not a word of this is true." She held the papers out. "My father did not sign this. This betrothal never happened."

"Now you understand my dilemma, Emalie. Do I disprove a forgery with another forgery? Or do I make a challenge which I know I can win? And win on my own terms."

She took his face in her hands and reached up to kiss him lightly on his lips. Her eyes never left him, but she directed her words to Luc.

"He seeks to regain what he never lost among men who know not the meaning of the word, Luc. A man of truest honor among men of dishonor. Not a fair fight, is it?"

"No, my lady. That is what I tried to tell him last night when these papers arrived."

Alyce gained Emalie's attention from the hallway. The nuns were there to take her back to the convent.

"Sir Luc, I beg a favor of you."

"Anything within my power, my lady." Luc added some of his flourish simply to irritate her husband.

"After my husband defeats William and we return to Greystone…" She paused.

"Aye, my lady?"

She gazed directly into her husband's eyes. "Remind me of my anger so that I may kill him myself."

She kissed him hard on his mouth and walked away. So many emotions passed over her. Anger. Fear. Relief. She glanced back just as she passed through the doorway to see his smile.

Love. She loved and was loved.

Chapter Twenty-Four

The next two days went quickly for him and a sense of calm filled him. For the first time in months, he felt as though he were in control. And he felt confident that he would prevail in this battle today.

The first surprise to appear in the tent that was erected near the field of battle for his use was his trunk of armor and his sword. This was surely a favorable sign. Fighting in his own mail and with his sword would give him an advantage over fighting in the borrowed armor he had planned on using.

The second surprise was not so pleasant. He turned to thank Luc for his efforts in retrieving his armor from Greystone and faced John Plantagenet instead.

"My lord," he said as he offered a mediocre bow to the prince.

"Dumont." John dropped the flap of the tent and walked closer to him. "I came to wish you well in the combat."

"Did you, my lord? I would think you would wish me dead."

John laughed. "I do hate to lose a man with your

sense of humor. Actually, yes, your death would assure my plans were successful. As they will be.''

John circled the small tent, examining his armor.

''DeSeverin told me of documents that would give you clear right to Harbridge. Why did you not use them and avoid this?''

''They were forgeries, just as the ones you provided to William.''

''You still believe that honor will prevail here?''

He did not answer.

''Gaspar thought the same thing and, try as I might to convince him to cooperate for the good of all, he refused on his honor. You see where he is now?'' John laughed and the sound of it grated on his nerves. ''Do you know what will defeat you this day, Dumont?''

''I am certain you wish to tell me, my lord.''

''You will defeat yourself this day. For you know in your heart that William fights for his child and because he loves the countess. You will not be able to kill him if you get the chance. You are your own worst enemy.''

Christian fought to remain calm, for he knew this tactic. He must remain focused on his battle and not be distracted by words, no matter how inflammatory they were.

John lifted the flap and stepped under it. ''Mayhap the countess's next whelp will bear his Plantagenet grandfather's russet hair?'' Laughing harshly, he left.

Christian stood in the center of the tent, opening and closing his fists, over and over again. Losing control would end in disaster. He knew that, but it was difficult to separate the words from the feelings.

''He is correct...you are your own worst enemy.'' Luc entered behind him and drew the flap down.

"My thanks for your supportive words." Christian made a rude gesture at Luc who laughed in reply.

"He goes now to visit DeSeverin to stir his resolve, like a puppet master pulling strings."

"There is not much time and we have much to discuss. Here," he said, lifting a gauntlet from the trunk, "help me dress."

"Relegated to the duties of a squire? Will the disrespect never cease?"

The bantering stopped as they both focused on the preparations needed for the combat. Luc helped him slide his mail shirt on over the linen one and then distributed the weight of it over his heavy leather belt. Then he attached the metal segments meant to keep his arms and legs protected. Piece by piece, the armor surrounded him until he was ready for battle.

As Luc handed his helmet to him, Christian could wait no longer. "There is a small casket inside my trunk," he said as he met his friend's gaze. "If need be, you will find my instructions within."

"I will not need instructions, my lord."

"I intend to be here to burn them, but…"

Luc nodded. They both knew what was inside that casket. His will naming Geoffrey his heir to their Pontevin lands and titles. Instructions on his burial. A letter to Emalie.

"He feints to his left and likes to deliver the *coup de Jarnoc* from that side."

Christian nodded. His friend had gathered some extraordinary information about Sir William's fighting habits. DeSeverin liked the French maneuver of cutting his opponent's hamstring.

"Kill him, Chris. Do not play. Do not show him compassion."

"Is it arranged?"

Luc had discovered DeSeverin's other weakness. His young sister had disappeared into John's custody and was undoubtedly the instrument of his downfall. Luc nodded and handed him his sword. Sliding it into its sheath, he waited for Luc's agreement.

"Aye, my lord," Luc forced out. "Our men are on their way even now."

"Regardless of the outcome."

"Do you not see that unless you kill him, nothing will change for her? If William lives, John will simply snatch the girl back and use her and Emalie to continue his control. The raping will go on, of the land and of the innocents. Killing him is the only way. In that, at least you will save the girl and your lady."

Luc pulled on some of the straps, making unneeded adjustments, and then he stepped away to check over the fit. When satisfied that all was well, he looked at Christian.

"Harden your heart, Chris. Stop fighting yourself and fight your real enemy. May the righteous prevail, my lord."

Luc slapped him on the shoulders and left. Ready for battle, he walked from the tent and headed to the strip of land they would use as a battleground. A priest waited to shrive both men. Prepared, body and soul, Christian could not wait for it to begin.

DeSeverin fought like a madman. Christian had read stories of Viking berserkers and this must be what they looked like on the attack. Christian went on the defensive and simply tried to stay upright against this onslaught. Hoping that this initial strength would wane, he met every blow and waited. He could only imagine what John had threatened to make DeSeverin fight so.

On and on it went, for almost an hour. Both helmets were long gone and their shields followed soon. He bled from a slicing blow to his shoulder, but managed to put a massive dent in DeSeverin's chest plate, making it difficult for the man to breathe as heavily as he needed to. He seemed to come back to himself then and Christian felt the battle become more equal. He waited for his opportunity. Working with his sword, he forced DeSeverin to defend his weakened side and exposed his own leg as he circled.

DeSeverin went for it as he expected and Christian knocked him down with a blow to the jaw using the hilt of his sword. He spoke as his opponent rolled to his feet.

"I have your sister."

If his words were heard, DeSeverin gave no sign. They fought on.

He did not know if he said the words to convince himself or to relieve William's burden, but he repeated them.

"I have your sister. She is free of John."

William stumbled then and it gave Christian the perfect opportunity.

Distracted.

He pulled a small dagger from under his chest plate and used it and his sword to send William's sword flying away and into the dirt.

Disarmed.

After a stunned moment, William went running to retrieve it. Christian followed closely behind, waiting for that second of delay as he bent down to grab it.

The blow to his back sent William sprawling on the

ground. Christian walked over and shoved his sword into the exposed neck. Blood spurted from the wound, turning the ground below him into mud.

Destroyed.

Looking down on his enemy, Christian whispered, echoing Luc's words of warning, ''Killing you is the only way to save both of them.''

Dropping his sword next to the body, he turned to the stands where the bishop, the clerics, the prince and others watched the battle. He could barely move, but he forced himself forward. Until the bishop pronounced the words, it was not over.

He tugged off his gauntlets and tucked them under his belt. Wiping the sweat and blood from his face, he searched for Emalie in the stands. He had not let himself see her before or during the combat, for he knew the look of love and fear on her face would be his great weakness. Now he needed to see her.

Luc escorted her toward him and he watched as she approached. Her gaze kept going to the body on the field and he feared she would not forgive him for what he had done. When she would have embraced him, he held her away from the blood and dirt on his armor.

''I want to hear the bishop's pronouncement.''

They walked together to the edge of the field. The bishop stood next to an obviously unhappy prince. When asked what to do with William's body, John shrugged and strode away. He glanced over to Luc and nodded. Understanding his order, Luc went off to make arrangements for the body.

''In the matter of the claim of Sir William DeSeverin to a prior betrothal to the Lady Emalie Montgomerie, this court declares that the claim has been proved false.''

After a pause, the bishop continued. "In the matter of the validity of the marriage of the countess of Harbridge, Lady Emalie Montgomerie, to *le Comte de Langier,* Lord Christian Dumont, and in the matter of his rights to all titles, lands and properties as her lawful husband, this court declares that the marriage is valid and all progeny of that marriage are legitimate, with all rights of inheritance." The bishop and the clerics left the stands quickly.

Christian grunted and Emalie smiled. The clerk of the court informed him that a copy of the court's findings would be sent to him. He felt better having a copy, but prayed that it would never be needed.

The rest of the day was spent in packing and moving the countess to their lodgings. Then Christian finally was granted the pleasure of a steaming bath and a fine meal. Emalie would not leave him for a moment, so he was forced to endure her attentions in the bath and at the meal. When he had put up with the well-wishers for what he deemed an appropriate amount of time, he stood and demanded that they leave. Emalie began to argue, so he kissed her over and over until she was breathless, and then he lifted her in his arms and carried her to the room they would share.

The bed was not as comfortable as the one in her room at home, but it would serve his purposes this night. It would hold them both.

He placed her on her feet and stirred the fire in the hearth. Christian intended to keep her warm with his body, but the room was too cold for even his tastes. Then he turned his attentions to her. As he had done so many times, he unlaced her sleeves and then her tunic. Taking off everything but her shift and her

woolen stockings, he pulled back the covers on the bed
and helped her in.

She frowned at him. "I do not understand."

"Until Enyd tells me there is no problem," he said
as he tore off his clothes as was his practice and
climbed in next to her, "we will not engage in that."

His body told a different tale and it was not long
before she noticed. Truly, all he wanted to do was hold
her. He wanted to learn the feel of her again, for many
weeks had passed since he had touched her like this.
She pressed her back against his body until he wanted
to scream.

"That?"

"We will not join. I do not want to cause you more
injury, Emalie."

"I am well, Christian. Even the healer at the convent
said all was well."

"The healer at the convent was not thinking of you
engaging in sexual practices when she declared you
well." He shifted and turned to his side. "I just want
to hold you, Emalie."

"I am not comfortable this way."

He waited and watched as she pushed the covers
back, pulled her shift over her head and threw it on the
floor. Then she slid back next to him and lay on her
back, exposing all to his gaze. His erection pressed into
her hip and he realized that she was torturing him. He
pulled the covers over them and tried to enjoy the
closeness.

"Did you know that a woman can sheathe a man in
places other than between her thighs?"

He choked at her words. "How do you know such
a thing?"

"Fatin. She said that a woman can use her hands…"

She used her hands around him to demonstrate her newfound knowledge. He could not breathe as she cupped him. He grew harder and thicker in her grasp. Then, as suddenly as she began, she stopped.

"Emalie," he whined. "What do you now?"

"There was another place that interested me, Christian. Fatin said that a woman's mouth can bring pleasure to a man by taking him inside."

She pushed back the covers and studied him. Her gaze was like a caress, sliding over the length of him. She moved her face closer and closer to him. The tension grew and he waited for the touch of her mouth. She teased him unmercifully with the tip of her tongue and her lips until he groaned with his release.

It took him some time to regain his breath from her ministrations. His wife was still an innocent who did not know her own appeal. She would kill him with pleasure if this curiosity continued.

"Christian?" she whispered.

"Aye?"

"Fatin said…"

"I can see that I will need to speak to Fatin about appropriate subjects to be discussed in the solar."

"Did you not enjoy that?"

"Oh yes, Emalie, very much."

"Fatin said that a man can use his mouth…"

He turned and showed her exactly how many ways a man could use his mouth before she could finish the sentence.

She waited for him to wake. They lay like spoons next to each other and she could feel his breathing, deep and steady, against her back. She knew that he would wake and watch her very soon.

"Are you well?" His voice sent shivers through her, and his breath tickled her ear as he spoke so close to it.

"I was thinking about William."

"Not what I would like you to be thinking about while abed with me, but understandable." His understanding was one of the things she loved most about him. "What were you thinking about?"

"What made him follow John? Why would he do it?"

Christian did not answer and she felt as though he was withholding something. She would give him time to tell her in his own way.

"Did you know that William had a sister?"

"Aye. I have not seen her in many years. How did you know?"

"I sent one of my men to find out as much as I could about him before the proceedings. Knowing your enemies is more important than knowing your friends."

"What did you discover? Catherine must be ten-and…"

"She is ten-and-six."

"And?"

"And?" he repeated.

"I can hear you are holding something back from me. Just say it." She wondered if she was wise in asking.

"She has been in John's keeping for over a year."

"Oh, Christian. Is she alive? Is she…?"

"Luc located her and some of my men were able to take her from the place where John had her. She is alive, but not well."

She nodded in silence. It could have been her fate

as well. If Christian had lost this day, she would be wife to William and drawn into John's cruelties without anyone to rescue her.

"What have you done with her?"

"The reverend mother at the Convent of the Blessed Lady has graciously agreed to oversee her care and, hopefully, her recovery. She will keep me informed of her progress."

Emalie turned and faced him now. Tears streamed down her face as she reached out and touched his face. "You are a good man, Christian, and I am blessed to have you as husband."

"'Twas the reverend mother who gave me the idea of challenging him to combat."

"The good sister told you to fight to the death? She did not seem so bloodthirsty to me."

He chuckled at her jest. "She told me that I must fight evil and then said the first line to that warrior's prayer. When I was trying to figure out a way to disprove that betrothal contract, that prayer went through my mind over and over like a chant. Then I realized that combat would make us even, for John could not join us on the field."

"Do you think she did that on purpose?" The sister was an interesting woman.

"Who can know the mind of a woman? Especially a holy one."

She bumped him to let him know she heard the insult he intended.

"I do worry over one thing. Do you hate me for what I did today?"

She wanted to soothe the frown that marred his brow. "How could I? Although I regret that he had to die, I know that you had no choice. And knowing that

William in some way fought for an honorable cause, one that you have championed, lessens my grief.''

He grunted again and they fell silent. This time, unlike the last, it was a companionable one. And safe in his arms, she felt sleep overtake her once more.

Chapter Twenty-Five

Winter's grasp held them tightly and all of Greystone waited. Snow covered the fields near and far and some of the streams turned to ribbons of ice. The season had come early, as the new earl had predicted, but all on Harbridge lands were safe and secure. Preparations would see them through this frigid weather until the earth saw the spring.

Christian wished Emalie could see her lands from the battlements and enjoy the silvery glow to everything that lay covered with snow, but she was too close to birth now and her steps were unsteady. Enyd predicted a babe by Candlemas and with that feast's approach in but two weeks, the people of Greystone waited.

He took advantage of the additional rest periods Enyd suggested for her to handle one task today that he needed to do without her presence or knowledge. Luc followed him as he rode quickly out of the village to the mill. Turning south on the large road, they traveled a few miles toward Lincoln. Watching for the signs, he stopped when he saw a small shrine near the road. A man stood next to it.

Luc dropped back, allowing the two men some privacy. Christian knew that Luc would never speak of this, even to his beloved Fatin. He dismounted and walked to the shrine, the snow crunching beneath his booted feet, and faced the man who used to be William DeSeverin.

"My lord," William said, nodding his head in greeting.

Christian noticed that his voice was still rough from the injury to his neck. The healer said that it might never heal completely. "How does your sister fare this week?"

"There is no change. The reverend mother said that her body is healed, but her mind...she knows me not." William looked away and blinked several times before speaking again. "Well, it will be a long difficult recovery."

"She is in good hands." Christian looked over and noticed the two horses waiting by the road. "You travel now?"

"With Candlemas approaching, I thought it best to leave."

They stared at each other for a moment then looked away.

"I seek a position in the north. I will send you coin when I can to repay you for Catherine's care."

"There is no need. I consider us even in our debts." He wanted no money from this man.

"Would you send word to me when Emalie—"

"No."

"Ah, 'twas more than I could hope." Christian

watched William struggle with words and listened as he spoke. "Does she know what you did?"

"No. She knows only that you fought for an honorable cause, and regrets your death. She told me that she understands that your death, even at my hands, saved her life and Catherine's."

William nodded and turned away. Mounting one horse and taking the reins of the other, he looked at Christian as though waiting for something else.

Christian knew that this was his last chance to ask the question that had tormented him for months, the question that he would never raise again to his wife.

"Was John...? Did he...?" In spite of his intentions and efforts, he could not give voice to the terrifying question that plagued him.

"Nay," DeSeverin answered, shaking his head. "'Twas only me. I am the child's father."

"No longer. Your place in that child's life and any question of paternity ended the moment that William DeSeverin died on the field of honor. They are mine now. And only mine."

Christian knew his words were harsh, but the time for his compassion was over. The worst part was that he feared in his soul that DeSeverin lied out of his sense of guilt. Christian mounted his horse and watched as William moved off down the road without another word. Luc was at his side in a moment.

"'Tis done?"

"Aye, Luc, he leaves now before the babe is born."

"This will be better, Chris. No need to look over your shoulder and see him watching Emalie or the child. I still do not know why you did this. A clean death would have served just as well."

Christian laughed. "I think that you are more barbarian than your infidel wife, my friend. Have you never learned the Christian values of faith, hope and charity?"

He mounted and watched Luc do so. Then he rode home to Emalie, to begin their new life together.

The Earl of Harbridge was going home.

Epilogue

Greystone Castle
Lincolnshire, England
April 1195

The sunlight made her curls appear as if made of spun gold. Her tiny rosebud mouth resembled her mother's, and her delicate features proclaimed her a Montgomerie to one and all. Isabelle, named for his mother, lay sleeping in his arms.

He had fallen in love with her at first sight, just as he knew now he had done with her mother. It took many months and many tribulations for him to admit his love for Emalie, but Christian vowed not to make that mistake with his daughter.

The shadows of the past months were gone and he looked forward to their lives ahead. Emalie assured him the babe would be able to travel by the end of the summer, for he wished to take both of his ladies, as he now called them, back to Poitou and his lands. Their lands.

"You can place her in the cradle, my lord," Emalie said.

"But I can not see her well enough as she sleeps if she lies there." Christian nodded his head at the carved cradle at the foot of the bed.

"She is well, my lord. She grows fat like a suckling pig and more demanding with each passing day."

"Demanding? Like her father?"

His wife did not hesitate to reassure him. "Exactly, my lord. She already has your arrogance."

He laughed as he kissed Isabelle on her head and then gently placed the babe in her bed. The little one shifted around and then nestled down in a comfortable corner. Soon, a soft snoring could be heard.

"Another trait of her father's that she has already learned."

"You would blame me for all?"

"Only the bad things."

He looked across the room where Emalie sat braiding her hair. She always kept it loose for him in the privacy of their chamber, but she needed it arranged when she went about her duties. His hands itched to undo it once again, however he knew Emalie would be annoyed. As if she'd read his mind, she met his gaze in the polished surface of the looking glass and smiled.

"Enyd said that enough time has passed, my lord."

He swallowed and then swallowed again. His body reacted in its own way to her words, pulsing and growing hard in places he could not ignore.

"Tonight then?"

"As you wish, my lord."

Her soft words fooled him not, for she had engaged enthusiastically with him in the ways of pleasure that did not involve that final act. And she had shared his frustration in not being able to take that last step until she was healed of the babe's birth.

He reached her in a few steps and pulled her up into his arms. He needed to kiss her and make promises about the night. But in the end, he could say only the words that repeated and repeated in his mind.

"Only mine, Emalie. You are only mine."

"As you wish, my lord. And you are only mine."

In their passion, they did not wait for the night. They joined right then, with their daughter sleeping unaware in her cradle. Being quiet was a challenge, but they could not resist love's lure.

And in that afternoon of passion and love, they created the son who would become heir to Greystone.

* * * * *

TERRI BRISBIN

When not living the life of a glamorous romance author, Terri Brisbin is a wife to one, mom of three and dental hygienist to hundreds. Born, raised and still living in the southern New Jersey suburbs, Terri is active in several romance writers' organizations including the RWA and NJRW. Terri's love of history, especially Great Britain's, led her to write time-travel romances and historicals set in Scotland and England.

Readers are invited to contact Terri by e-mail at TerriBrisbin@aol.com or by mail at P.O. Box 41, Berlin, NJ 08009-0041. You can visit her Web site at www.terribrisbin.com.

magazine

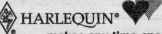
HINTMAG

On the lookout for captivating courtships
set on the American frontier?
Then behold these rollicking romances
from Harlequin Historicals.

On sale January 2003

THE FORBIDDEN BRIDE
by Cheryl Reavis
*Will a well-to-do young woman defy
her father and give her heart to
a wild and daring gold miner?*

HALLIE'S HERO
by Nicole Foster
*A beautiful rancher joins forces
with a gun-toting gambler to save her spread!*

On sale February 2003

THE MIDWIFE'S SECRET
by Kate Bridges
*Can a wary midwife finally find love and acceptance
in the arms of a ruggedly handsome sawmill owner?*

THE LAW AND KATE MALONE
by Charlene Sands
*A stubborn sheriff and a spirited saloon owner
share a stormy reunion!*

Harlequin Historicals®
Historical Romantic Adventure!

COMING NEXT MONTH FROM

HARLEQUIN HISTORICALS®

- **BOUNTY HUNTER'S BRIDE**
  by **Carol Finch,** author of CALL OF THE WHITE WOLF
  In order to gain control over her life, a daring debutante leaves her
  fiancé at the altar and, instead, enters a marriage of convenience
  with a bounty hunter bent on vengeance! But when she does the
  unthinkable and falls in love with her husband, will pride prevent
  her from changing a temporary bargain into a permanent union?
  HH #635 ISBN# 29235-X $5.25 U.S./$6.25 CAN.

- **BADLANDS HEART**
  by **Ruth Langan,** final book in the *Badlands* series
  Kitty Conover knows a thing or two about breaking mustangs,
  but she doesn't know the first thing about love…until Bo Chandler
  comes to town. When another man claims Bo's identity, what will
  Kitty believe—the hard evidence or her heart?
  HH #636 ISBN# 29236-8 $5.25 U.S./$6.25 CAN.

- **NORWYCK'S LADY**
  by **Margo Maguire,** second in the *Widower* series
  After an embittered lord rescues a young noblewoman from
  a shipwreck, he discovers that she's lost her memory. While
  nursing the mysterious beauty back to health, he searches for her
  identity and soon discovers that she's the daughter of his most
  hated enemy.…
  HH #637 ISBN# 29237-6 $5.25 U.S./$6.25 CAN.

- **LORD SEBASTIAN'S WIFE**
  by **Katy Cooper,** author of PRINCE OF HEARTS
  A world-weary nobleman is on the verge of matrimony when the
  past comes back to haunt him. A reckless pledge made years ago will
  now bind him to a desirable, but deceptive woman!
  HH #638 ISBN# 29238-4 $5.25 U.S./$6.25 CAN.

KEEP AN EYE OUT FOR ALL FOUR
OF THESE TERRIFIC NEW TITLES